Heels
He
He

Hollywood High Series

Hollywood High
Get Ready for War
Put Your Diamonds Up
Lights, Love & Lip Gloss

Also by Ni-Ni Simone
The Ni-Ni Girl Chronicles
Shortie Like Mine
If I Was Your Girl
A Girl Like Me
Teenage Love Affair
Upgrade U
No Boyz Allowed
True Story

The Throwback Diaries
Down By Law
Dear Yvette

Also by Amir Abrams
Crazy Love
The Girl of His Dreams
Caught Up
Diva Rules
Chasing Butterflies

Published by Kensington Publishing Corp.

Heels, Heartache & Headlines

Hollywood HIGH

NI-NI SIMONE
AMIR ABRAMS

KENSINGTON PUBLISHING CORP.
www.kensingtonbooks.com

DAFINA BOOKS are published by

Kensington Publishing Corp.
119 West 40th Street
New York, NY 10018

All Kensington titles, imprints, and distributed lines are available at special quantity discounts for bulk purchases for sales promotion, premiums, fund-raising, and educational or institutional use.

Special book excerpts or customized printings can also be created to fit specific needs. For details, write or phone the office of the Kensington Sales Manager: Kensington Publishing Corp., 119 West 40th Street, New York, NY 10018. Attn. Sales Department. Phone: 1-800-221-2647.

ISBN-13: 978-0-7582-8856-1
ISBN-10: 0-7582-8856-5
First Kensington Trade Paperback Printing: March 2017

eISBN-13: 978-0-7582-8857-8
eISBN-10: 0-7582-8857-3
First Kensington Electronic Edition: March 2017

10 9 8 7 6 5 4 3 2 1

Printed in the United States of America

Heels, Heartache & Headlines

1

Spencer

"Spencer, darling..."

Lawdgawd, sweetbabyjeezus... hang me upside down and have your way with me, right now. I beg you, lawdgawd, do me until my eyes cross...

Oooh, I wished I could click my heels three times and blink this trick-momma out of my life. Kitty knew I hated seeing her face on an empty stomach *or* be. Fore. Noon. She knew this the way I knew my way around a boy's man parts. But there she stood, face lightly brushed with whore paint, hand on hip, ringlets of light brown hair cascading over her shoulders, her signature scent—Freak Nasty—wafting around the room, trying to bore holes through me with her piercing, long-lashed hazel eyes.

This two-dollar stamp tramp!

This, this, snot-licking skank!

I couldn't stand her.

Kitty Ellington. Media mogul. Billion-dollar pain in my juicy...

Snap, snap!

"Spencer! Do you hear me talking to you?"

I batted my lashes. Batted them again. "No, lady. I'm ignoring you." I slid my diamond hoops into my ears, fastening them closed. Then fastened my diamond choker around my neck.

"Not today, Spencer, darling. Not. To. Day." She sashayed her ole stank, hooker-looking self over toward me. "I need you to play nice, for once. Do you think you can do that for me, dear? That nutty London Phillips is due back at school this morning, and from what I'm hearing, she's looking more fabulous than ever, but I can only imagine how long that'll last before she's collapsing on bathroom floors and sliding down runways, ready to end it over some boy, again. I want an exclusive on that dizzy little trick before she throws herself over..."

I fastened the clasp to my diamond tennis bracelet. Not. Saying. One. Word. Kitty knew I despised London. I hated her more than I did cheap heels and knockoff handbags. London was low money. Ole tight drawers. Upper East Side trash! She was a sneaky, two-faced liar. She was a schemer. And I wanted to destroy her. Annihilate her. Chase her back to the gutters of New York, where she belonged with the rest of the sewer rats. I wanted to air her filthy Guia La Bruna panties for all to see!

But I was happy she'd gotten her mind right and her life together and stopped dancing with the grim reaper. That horrible suicide attempt of hers made my heart ache. That selfish slore almost robbed me of the chance to do her in. Oh, how the thought of not being able to drag her through the gutters had me depressed for almost two hours, thirty-eight minutes, and forty-three seconds.

But—*me* being my kind, loving self—I marched right

over to her little cottage of a home, barged my way into the makeshift grave site she called a bedroom suite, and nursed her weary soul back to health.

I sure did.

Every. Torturous. Day. I went to her bearing gifts and cards and the latest gossip rags that had her miserable-looking self plastered all over the front pages. I sat with her. Read her nursery rhymes. And filled her muddy little mind with sweet promises on how I was going to ruin her.

But, first, I needed her well. I needed her off of that IV drip—that, that juice in a bag. And I needed her out of those filthy nightgowns. Oh, how I wish you could have seen her sprawled out on her imaginary deathbed—face sunken in, hair all matted, wallowing in her pathetic-ness, starving herself to death, waiting for the grim reaper to snatch her last breath.

Ha! The joke was on her!

The grim reaper was clowning her. He wasn't coming for her. No, hon. Death didn't want her. And the pearly gates to heaven were sealed shut. I told her so. Told her she might as well accept her fate here on earth. I let her know she was an epic fail for trying to hurt herself like that! And I told her I would never step on her neck and crush her windpipe while she was down. Oh no. That wasn't how I did mine. I told Miss Lonely I was there to see her through whatever she was going through. That I didn't ever break bones or throw stones at hookers who were already stretched out on their backs. No. I built them up, *then* tore them down.

I sure did. And in London's time of need, I was the only one there for her. And I'd let it be known that I needed her to fight. I needed her to find her will to live.

I needed her donned in her good heels and good jewels. I needed her back at Hollywood High so I could finally slap her in the face with her tombstone. And drop her dead!

And today was the big day. The welcoming, if you will. I was going to greet London back to school with a smile, then pull her into my loving arms and whisper sweet and low in her big, floppy ear, "Buckle up, *bish*. It's on now."

But I didn't need Kitty standing here telling *me* to play nice. I knew how to play. Getting down and dirty was my favorite game.

"I tell you," Kitty continued, snatching me out of my reverie. "They don't make women like they used to. You little *thots* aren't built like we were back in my day. We knew how to steal a man from his woman, love him down, then take a good heartbreak..."

I rolled my eyes, then tilted my head as I brushed my hair and stared at her through my mirror. "Um, excuse you, ma'am. But...*who* are you?"

She huffed. "Oh, for the love of god, you rotten little demon child. Have you not heard a word I've said?"

"Actually not, lady," I said calmly. "I told you. I'm ignoring you."

She sucked in a breath. "Must we go through this production of crazy every day? I swear, Spencer, sometimes I think you were abducted by aliens, then sent back here just to torment me and get on my damn nerves with your dimwit shenanigans. God, I should have you spayed before you start laying eggs. Spawning another you would be a travesty."

I craned my neck and shot her an icy glare. "Oh, blow it out of your crusty dust pipes, you ole sea horse. Now good day. See yourself out."

Instead of spinning on her heels, she stood there and

laughed. "Oh, Spencer, darling. Just once can't you pretend you have more than air pockets in that pretty little head of yours? Oh, wait." She snapped her fingers. "You were dropped on your head as an infant. Remind me to sue the hospital and file a malpractice suit against that incompetent Doctor Hodgkins for not performing that lobotomy on you, as I requested. I knew someday this would happen."

I sighed. I was really trying to be loving and kind, but this lady was trying to wreck my vibe and snatch me from my happy place.

Kitty and I were like dirty oil and hot butter. One was delicious on a stack of buttermilk pancakes or slathered across a sweet roll. And the other was sludge at the bottom of a murky river. No, no. Sewage, that's what she was.

Kitty and I just weren't a good mix.

She was rancid! A toxic fume!

I was warm, sweet, and buttery.

I forced a smile, but inside my guts clutched and churned. Kitty was more rotten than a skunk bear. Uh, a wolverine for those of you who don't know what I'm talking about. Geesh! Must I spell out everything I say?

Annnyway. Kitty and I were due for another cat brawl. She knew it. And I knew it. And I was itching to pounce on her and give it to her good. Real good. Push it real good!

Oh, how Kitty and I were tearing each other up, like the good ole days when we used to roll around on the floor, kicking, clawing, smacking, and biting each other up when I was eight and nine years old. But Daddy robbed us of that good, old-fashioned beat-down we'd had a few weeks back when he came barging into the kitchen in a pair of overalls and pointy-toed, lizard cowboy boots with a cigar dangling from his lips, shooting up the ceiling with a shotgun.

Hmmph. Kitty and I stood there with plaster raining down on our heads as he started talking crazy out of his mind, calling Kitty some *Cleola Mae*. Poor thing. Bless his heart. Daddy suffers from that old, nasty mind disease Alzheimer's. So he sometimes gets people, places, and things confused.

But for some reason, the look in Daddy's eye that day—when he said Kitty... *my* mother... was some dang *Cleola Mae* from Leflore County, Mississippi. *Wanted for murder.* Made me think his little cluttered mind might not be so jumbled after all. And that perhaps his foolish accusations needed further investigation.

Although Kitty laughed it off, claiming Daddy's alzy-palzy had him delirious, I wasn't completely buying it. Something wasn't right. There was something more going on there. And I was going to get to the bottom of it. Oh yes. Kitty was about to become my next target practice. Real soon.

But for now, I was going to play nice. And toy with her, like I did with all of my prey. Yes, hon. Kitty had it coming, but not yet.

She opened her mouth to speak, but I threw a hand up. "Save it. I'm not in the mood for any of your motherly lies or slutty monologues. So. Don't. Do. Me. Not today, hon."

"Why, you little ungrateful nitwit! Will you for once just shut your flytrap and listen to me. Or would you rather I have you committed? I keep warning you, Spencer. This kind of talk will land you in a padded room strapped to a gurney. Now shut your frothy piehole. I need you—"

I slammed my hairbrush down on my marble vanity, ready to give her the business. "And I *need* you to disappear, lady. I'm here minding my own business, trying to beautify myself for school, and all you want to do is block my dang shine. I swear I don't wanna lay hands on you this morning, Kitty"—I cracked my knuckles, then cracked my neck—"but I will open up the Church of Smack Down and bless you." I raised a hand in the air and waved it. "I will open the gates of hell and slap the fire out of you, you heathen. Then drown you in a bottle of that good communion wine they use to wash away one's sins. Goshdiggitydangit. Now try me. I will slam your casket shut!"

I paused, glaring at her. Then took another deep breath, trying to get my Zen together. "Oooh, you're lucky I'm in a good mood this morning; otherwise I'd do you a favor and give you a face-lift. You know I don't like your negative energy anywhere in my space, you inconsiderate sea gnome. How rude."

She clapped her manicured hands together. "Bravo, my darling. Now do me a favor and save the drama for those little troll dolls you call friends."

I glared at her through the mirror. *This dumbo! Lawdgawd, help me make it to school without clawing her eyes out. Amen!* "I don't have *friends*, hon. I have frenemies. Get it right. Now, how may I help you, ma'am?"

"You insolent little snot," she sneered. "*You* can help *me* by shutting your mouth. Well, dear, that's if you can stay up off your knees long enough to do one thing for me. I know burying your face in some boy's lap is your life's work."

I blinked. Blinked again.

"I swear," she huffed, shaking her head. "You and your whorish ways are an embarrassment. Haven't you learned anything from me? *Always* be a classy lady in the streets and a dirty whore in the sheets, behind closed doors. Not some trampazoid on display in YouTube videos and on Snapchat. As pretty as you are, Spencer darling, you're even more despicable. You're a messy little whore."

Wait.

Did the queen of sleazy call *moi* a whore?

Yes, she did!

Oh, no! Screech! Spin the wheel! Kitty had gone too dang far. Yes, I liked to give a little sloppy toppy—you know, drop down and lick 'em low—in the pool house, on a private jet, and in the girls' lounge at school from time to time. And then there was that one time atop the Swiss Alps when I had the headmaster's son at Le Rosey, the exclusive private school I'd attended—before I got expelled—clawing the rocks and howling like a wolf.

Yessss, honey. It was no secret. I liked a boy with a lot of mayonnaise in his meat basket. There was nothing like the sound of a belt buckle hitting the floor. It was like music to my ears. But Spencer and the word *whore* didn't belong in the same sentence. Ever. Oh no, oh no! That title was reserved for my future ex-bestie.

Rich.

Ugh. God, I loved that girl like I loved panda bears and unicorns. But, once again, she was up to her old tricklicious ways, shacking with some slum dog.

I glanced over at the crystal clock on my stand: 6:38 a.m. Right now she was probably somewhere rolled up in the sheets like some piggy in a corn wrap, slopping up her latest man toy.

Justice Banks.

Mmmph. *Rich.* Don't even get me started on that rotted peach. I'm a changed woman. And I don't like being cruel to hookers, hoes, and strays on Mondays, Wednesdays, and Fridays. So with that being said, I wasn't about to go into any of her deviant trysts. But that poor hyena in a G-string and ballerina flats was allergic to latex. Heeheehee. Trampazoid! Trick!

Rich Montgomery was sly as a fox, but as dirty as a hen. But because she was still my bestie—for now, that was—I wasn't going to pluck her feathers or snap her beak. Or say an unkind word about her behind her back. No. Not today. And definitely not while I had a two-legged dragon to slay.

Well, two dragons, that is. London and Heather. Yes, Heather Cummings. I had a few arrows and poisoned-tipped darts with her name on them also. That Skid Row skeezer. After all I'd done for her—cutting her a check for three million dollars when she was down and out and living in some roach trap; buying her a Lamborghini; *and* sponsoring her trip to Brazil to get that luscious ten-thousand-dollar booty she now sported in all them skimpy little hooker getups—and she'd, once again, turned on me. She practically peeled off her slut-suit and tossed her stained panty liner in my face. Then told me to kiss her fatty. The one *I* financed. So, yes, Heather had it coming too.

But, first, I'd *play* nice. Like I always did.

I blinked Kitty back into view, then glanced over at the clock: 6:52. I was late. Kitty had taken up enough of my precious morning time.

I hopped up from my vanity, quickly slid my feet into a pair of Stuart Weitzmans Guild stilettos, then snatched up my Hermès bag, knocking Kitty out of my way as I raced out of my suite, then down the hall toward the winding staircase.

I had hoes to take down.

I had to get to Hollywood High.

2

London

Now what was it my therapist said I should be working on?

Transference?

No, that wasn't it. I'd been doing that very well. Transferring my emotional reactions toward everyone else onto my therapist. My anger. My rage. My resentments. All tossed into her lap, every session, every chance I got.

Forgiveness? I thought, reaching for a bottle of Kona Nigari Water from the fully stocked marble wet bar as I sat in the backseat of my chauffeur-driven limousine en route to the ultra-exclusive private school I attended.

Hollywood High Academy.

The devil's dirty little playground, where reputation and image was everything. Who you knew and what you owned and where you lived all defined you. And being on top didn't mean a damn thing unless you knew how to stay there.

And right about now, I felt like I'd been tossed into its

bottomless pit, standing knee-deep in hellfire, trying to claw my way up from out of the flames. My reputation of being fine, fly, and eternally fabulous was forlornly being burned to ashes, thanks to the recent filth the gossip rags and those trashy bloggers were spewing about me in the headlines.

LONDON PHILLIPS FALLING DOWN. TEEN MODEL SLICES HER WAY INTO A STRAITJACKET . . .

LONDON PHILLIPS FLIES OVER THE PROVERBIAL CUCKOO'S NEST . . .

LONDON PHILLIPS CRACKS FACE; FALLS FROM GRACE . . .

LONDON PHILLIPS GOES NUTZ . . . !

AMERICA'S NEXT TOP FLOP: LONDON PHILLIPS . . .

I opened the four-hundred-and-two-dollar bottle of desalinated seawater, collected thousands of feet below the ocean's surface off the island of Hawaii, and took a slow, deliberate sip.

Lord God, give me strength . . .

In a teary-eyed haze, I glared at the front page of the latest edition of *Glamdalous,* the magazine for the glamorous and scandalous—staring at the headline burning into my retinas: LOUNGE SINGER AND HEARTTHROB SENSATION JB WOOS HIP-HOP ROYALTY'S DARLING PRINCESS.

Mmmph.

Bastard!

Darling princess my—!

I took another sip of water, then pulled my cell from out of my handbag and sent my therapist, Dr. Ashmina Kickaloo, a quick text. I NEED 2 C U!!! The closer my driver got to campus, the more anxious I was starting to feel.

Yes. Forgiveness. That was it. That's what my two-hundred-and-fifty-dollar-an-hour shrink said I should be working on. To forgive those who'd *effed* me over—*my* words, *not* hers.

Still, the message was clear: Turn the other cheek while the enemy ran off with my fairy tale and lived out my happily-ever-after.

I took a deep breath. Then another. Concentrated on breathing through my nose, taking slow, steady breaths, before I had a full-blown panic attack.

Breathe in.

Breathe out.

I mean, really. Forgiveness? Mmph. That ole powder-puff quack, with her overplucked, painted-in eyebrows, that my parents paid good money for me to see expected me to *forgive* those who'd trespassed against me.

My ex-boyfriend.

Justice!

My ex-friend.

Rich!

That thieving *beeeeeyatch*! What that lecherous, two-faced thot-whore did to me bordered on treason. Stealing my man! So what if she didn't actually *know* Justice Banks had been *mine* because I'd kept our relationship a secret (because my parents would never approve of him)? The fact was, she still spread open her buffalo thighs and let him roam in her swampland. And so what if he dumped me and left me broken-spirited . . . for *her*.

It was bad enough that Rich had flat-out admitted one afternoon over cocktails down at Club Tantrum, during my brief return from Milan a week before Italy's fashion week, that she had slept with Justice.

". . . I gave him a lil taste of goodness, a lil slice of heaven on earth, and he couldn't even handle the heat. Four minutes and twenty-seven seconds of riding cowgirl, his toes curled . . . that boy was dead to the bed! A bore . . . !"

I ended up slinging my apple martini in her face, and she jumped up and snatched her pitcher of beer, tossing suds of beer into my face. Then we started swinging fists at each other, going at it like two street hookers, tearing the club up.

Our so-called friendship ended that night with broken heels, fistfuls of hair, and multiple slaps upside each other's head, before we were both tossed out by the club's security team.

I took another deep breath and glared at the magazine. Although I was slowly getting over the likes of Justice Banks, and finally learning—thanks to my therapist—that having a boyfriend wasn't the cure-all for my insecurities and fears, it still hurt like hell seeing him all cozied up with the enemy. Seeing him all smiles and looking all in love with the likes of Rich Montgomery made my skin crawl.

Screw him! And screw her!

They deserved each other.

I shifted my body in my seat as my driver made his way through Beverly Hills, running a hand through my hair—what was left of it, that is. Thanks to that treacherous Spencer Ellington, I'd been forced to cut my thick, luscious, shoulder-length hair into a funky asymmetrical hairdo after she attacked me with a handful of hair-removal cream.

Spencer had been coming to my home practically every grueling day—while I was confined to my bed on an IV drip, under doctors' orders—toting get-well gifts and fake concern, pretending to be my friend. I'd already been home for almost a week from the hospital in Milan, severely depressed and withering away. I was withdrawn. Wouldn't eat. And had no will to fight.

But that skank had no regard for my misery. She simply

bum-rushed her way into my crumbling world, forcing herself on me.

"... Send in the fat gods! Where is the rest of your body? What are you trying to do now? Slicing your wrists didn't work, so now you want to starve yourself to death...? You want to hang up your big panties, then throw your hands up in defeat! You sore loser...! You quitter...!

"I want you to get it together, London. Get up and fight! I want you back at Hollywood High so I can annihilate you. So whatever demons you got eating up your insides, go get you a flush, a deep cleanse, or whatever, and let it go. Move on... I want you out of this bed, London. And back at school. I mean it. I'll be back tomorrow, and the day after and the day after. So if you want me out of your face, then you had better get your life back. And stop all this tomfoolery! Trying to like you and be nice to you is too much hotdang work..."

Those were Spencer's haunting words to me, several days before she leapt up on my bed and attacked me from out of nowhere, swiping the cream over one of my eyebrows and through my hair, leaving me with one missing eyebrow and clumps of my thick luscious hair falling out around me.

It was awful.

Yeah, Spencer had me looking like Mrs. Potato Head with one missing eyebrow. I had to remove my other eyebrow and draw them in until my own were able to grow back in. What a mess!

I swiped my bangs from my eye, flipping through the magazine. I stopped at a caption: FAST, CHEAP & EASY. TEEN STAR HEATHER CUMMINGS CAUGHT ON TAPE TURNIN' UP! I grunted in disgust. There she was, looking like the poor-trash hooker she was, wearing some god-awful zebra-print body suit and gladiator-type sandals with a bottle of Cirôc turned up to her mouth and what appeared to be a burning blunt in her other hand.

I dared not read what I already knew. Heather was still the junkie she'd always been. Now she'd be able to add *alcoholic* to her dossier, just like her mother, Camille.

Mmmph. Like mother, like daughter, I thought, flipping through the pages again. Heather and her mother were two peas in the same booze-soaked pod.

Drunks.

I kept flipping through the magazine, stopping on page seventeen. I choked back a scream. There were several photos of Rich and Justice holding hands, her gazing up into his eyes, like she was staging for a spot on *The Bachelorette*.

Filthy whore!

I took another deep breath, closing the magazine.

Learning how to pardon the likes of Rich Montgomery was the last thing I needed to do. No, no, what I needed was the freedom to peel that five-foot-six weave-wearing troll doll's edges back and stomp her chestnut-brown face inside out. I clenched my fists. Oh, how I still wanted to rip her scalp off. And fight her to the death. That slore didn't deserve my mercy. No. She deserved her big, brown eyeballs clawed out for what she'd done to me.

I took another deep breath and stared out the limo's tinted window at the crowd of paparazzi lurking, like rabid wolves waiting to claw apart their next roadkill as my driver turned into the entrance to the campus.

My stomach knotted, and I watched with a mixture of disgust and angst as the first few gossip-rag whores noticed my arrival and bolted over, with the others shortly in tow, swarming around the limo, tapping on the windows.

It'd been weeks since my *incident*.

My horrible suicide attempt.

Subconsciously, I rubbed the area of my arm where I'd sliced into my wrist during Fashion Week in Milan, Italy, where I'd been modeling.

Truth was, I was at my lowest, at the darkest point of my life. I thought my whole world revolved around a boy, one who didn't give a goddamn about *me,* a boy who never ever really loved *me*.

Justice.

Yet when he'd dumped me and I'd felt abandoned by him, I felt like my life was over, like I had nothing else to live for. I lived and breathed him. And, sadly, I thought taking my own life was the right thing to do.

It wasn't.

And I felt so stupid for thinking so.

Suicide wasn't the answer.

Living well was the best revenge. And I had to prove to the world—and *myself*—that I was no longer that miserable, sniveling girl strung out on the likes of Justice Banks.

No, I was London Phillips.

A diva.

Born in London. Cultured in Paris. And molded in New York.

I was a trendsetter.

I was a shaker and mover.

Yes, I was perfectly flawed, obnoxiously rich, and fabulously beautiful.

And I wanted that dirty ho brought to *justice*—no pun intended, for what she'd done to me. I glanced at the front cover of the magazine one last time before tossing it to the floor and grinding my heel into it. *He's your headache now, tramp! Good luck and good riddance!*

God had given me a second chance to come back and tell Rich, Spencer, and Heather that they could all kiss my...

"Miss London, you want me to run them down?" the driver asked, his voice booming through the intercom, stealing me from my thoughts.

I blinked the paparazzi back into view.

I swallowed, hard, feeling a kaleidoscope of emotions whirling inside me. I reached for a linen napkin and dabbed it under my eyes. I was torn. Being back in the spotlight and back on campus, having to face that messy whore, Rich, with all of her over-the-top theatrics and loudmouth trash talking, along with the rest of the so-called Pampered Princesses—it all made my stomach burn.

But, then, on the other hand, there was this renewed purpose fluttering inside of me, wanting to get my life back. It was a part of me that was ready to face these Hollywood hoes—head up, back straight, pelvis thrust forward, one diamond-heeled foot in front of the other—and reclaim my rightful spot back on the throne.

I'd been a recluse, holed up in my bedroom suite, for far too long. I'd been avoiding the media long enough, ducking aerial drones and dodging photos. It was time to face the music and dance the dance. Besides, no one ever said it was going to be easy being young, rich, and fabulous.

But someone had to reclaim the crown. So it might as well be *moi*.

"No. Pull over and stop the limo," I said, pulling out my lip gloss, then spackling a coat over my lips. "These bottom feeders will just keep stalking me until I toss them a few crumbs." I tossed my tube of gloss back into my purse, snapping it shut. "It's time to feed the vultures," I said as I slowly pressed the button and let my window down.

As paparazzi called out my name, shouting out questions and flashing their cameras, the only thing I could think of was, *Welcome back to Hollywood High!*

3

Rich

"All hail! Curves have stepped up on the scene. Bidding you a public service announcement," my trumpeter declared, as I clicked my hot pink Louboutins against the red carpet and sauntered past the semicircle of hungry paps. All vying for my attention.

Click!

Flash!

I gave 'em a cat-walk glance and blessed 'em with a full serving of fleek.

A twist to the left.

To the right.

A twirl.

Hands on hips.

Chin up.

Back straight.

Pink-studded Hermès clutch tucked beneath right arm.

Crisp white Gucci shorts framing cocoalicious thighs.

Navy and white striped tank, under the dopest navy blue linen blazer—with the Gucci crest, of course.

And four ropes of soft pink pearls dangling from neck to navel.

Pure hotness.

Straight slayage.

A fly guise that simply stated, "Rich Montgomery is a damn lady. Now get your lil life to-ge-*therrrrrr*."

Click!

Flash!

"Yaaaasss!" I swept my thirty-inch weave from my left shoulder over to my right. Then I braided my fingers together in a prayer position and continued, "I've come before you to correct a trashy *Teen Trend Magazine* travesty."

"And what was that?" Someone from the crowd yelled.

"Okay, so there was a small article written about me *waaaaaay* in the back of the magazine, when Rich Montgomery should *always* be the cover story. And as if that wasn't bad enough"—I pulled the magazine from my clutch and rattled the paper—"the vile reporter had the nerve to mislead these teens and say, 'There were millions of girls striving to be me.' Now, had he stopped there, his ethics wouldn't be in question. But *thennnnn* he played himself." I read on, "And perhaps one day with money and parents who can afford the world, they will be. After all, dreams do come true."

I tossed the magazine at my feet and stepped on it. "Lies, honey. Lies. Gutter-rat trash. How about...umm no."

"Rich! What makes you say that?" Shouted one of the reporters.

"See, here's where he effed up at. There's fantasy and there's reality. Fantasy: Thots having a shot at being like me. Reality: They never will be. I am chocolate diamonds, honey. The goddess of curves. And thanks to my plastic surgeon, I woke up like this!"

Click!

Flash!

"Yaaaaaass! And I stay settin' the bar of beauty and big booty to new heights. Don't let the haters mislead you. After me, there shall never be another me." I looked at the reporters, scanned the admiration in their eyes, and blew them a kiss. "Now, let me announce the details of my upcoming royal and fabu birthday party, because after this I have to go."

"Wait, Rich, may I ask you another question?" An unfamiliar reporter shouted.

I looked over at her. Wrinkled my nose.

Clutching pearls, who is that? I recklessly eyeballed her from her pale peach skin and auburn hair to her ran-over skippies.

Eww.

Clearly she had New York roots. And anyway, I was head of the Monday morning red carpet committee, and she was not on the list of paps I'd called to interview me.

I glanced at my red carpet VP and we had the same confused look. "And who are you?" I turned back to the reporter.

She spat out in one breath, "Kris Stanley from *Page Seven* of L.A. A source close to you called us this morning and told us you were quite a few things. I was hoping to share them with you."

I blinked. Blinked again. Definitely, New York sewage. That East Coast accent poured nastily out of her throat. I popped my cherry red lips. "Proceed, 'cause I don't have all day. *This is a school.* Or did you not graduate? I'm an honors student. A role model. And I need to be on time. Now what is it?" I shook my head. "So gossip greedy and disrespectful."

She smiled. *Phony*. "Thank you, Rich. Well, the source reported that you and London—"

"London! London! Don't tell me, you've fallen off of a unicorn and you can't get up? 'Cause your stupidity level is on an embarrassing ultra high right now, and my time is precious. Er'body knows, you don't *everrrrr* step to me and mention London! That evil hater, who attacked me for no reason. Talks about me like a dog. Pretended to be my friend just so she could be considered important. And to think I used to really love that girl." I sniffed. "We used to be the best of besties! Always at each other's estates. Scratch that; she would be at my estate, and on occasion I'd visit her ranch. Everyone should do a little community service. But you get the point, we chilled together."

"What happened?"

"She turned on me. Turned into a jealous and low-budget slum slut, who tried to play me like Drake and go after every boyfriend I had, especially JB. But her attacking me in Club Tantrum was the final straw. I had to drag her. Bust her in the throat. It was a momentary requirement. And just so you know, I'm not really a fighter, I'm a lady. Which is why, being the good and kindhearted person that I am, when she wrecked her suicide attempt, I went to visit her. Wished her better luck the next time. And do you know what she did?"

I looked over at my red carpet committee and they fed the crowd the answer: "Tossed Rich out and into the street."

"Like. I was. Nothing." I continued. "Check out YouTube,

World Star, and Instagram; there's a video. Trust me. Anything London lying Phillips has to say is fiction. She made it up. Why? Because London's sole mission in life is to ruin me. That's why her suicide attempt was a fake."

"A fake?" The reporter asked in amazement, as if she either didn't hear or didn't believe me.

"Clutching. Pearls! Oh. Em. Gee. Really, lady? Where are you from? The lowest of the Lower East Side, down by the subway or that lil dirty lake? Get it together, honey. You're in L.A. now. And everyone knows that London Phillips's failed drop-dead attempt was all about—" I looked over at my red carpet committee.

"Attention."

"Exactly. Attention. Otherwise, she would've been ghost. Literally. Like, seriously, how hard is it to check out? London Phillips is an Epic. Fail." I blinked and flicked invisible specks of dirt off of my shoulder. "Hopefully that answers your question. And now, my birth—"

"One more thing!" The reporter shouted. "Another source said you were a vengeful, spiteful, nasty ho of a trampazoid, who was addicted to hot wings, blue cheese, and beer. Is any of that true?"

Oh no, she didn't. I clenched my jaw so tight it's a wonder my veneers didn't shatter. I arched my brow with each word. "Spencer. Ellington. That. Ball. Guzzling. Whore. Bucket. Who every time she opens her mouth is either saying something stupid or spitting an STD out. Fire drawls. I'm going to end her life. Tonight."

The reporter spat, "The source was anonymous."

"Lies! No one but Spencer told you that!"

"Why would she say that?"

"Clutching pearls! Er'body knows that Spencer is a bitter trollop, who needs to be effed. Up. She's my ex-ex-ex-ex-ex-best friend from first grade. And all of these years I've always felt sorry for her. Her mother's ashamed of her. Wishes Spencer was more like me and less like Kylie Jenner. And her father is like a hundred and five, and he doesn't even know who she is. Truthfully, somebody should just do Old Yeller a favor: Take him out back and send him back to God. I can't believe that Spencer is ragging on me. After I've been nothing but good to that girl. She's the one who turned on me. Uploaded that video of London's security team tossing me out of the house to *World Star*. How cheap can you play someone? She's lucky I didn't send her to hell that night.

"But I'm a Christian. And I attend the masjid on a regular basis. So my religion saved her. But if she comes for me again, I'ma Crip walk on her and finish her, Watts style. Now try me. And then she called me a ho? I tell you what, I'm not gon' be too many more hoes. This is why I've cut Spencer off and am done with her forever. That part of the Pampered Princesses is no more."

The reporter continued, "The unnamed source also said that you were famous for lying on steel gurneys and counting backwards in Nowhere, Arizona."

"Clutching pearls! Lies! I'm not famous for that. I'm famous for being a socialite. The daughter of hip-hop royalty. Billionaires Richard and Logan Montgomery of Grand Entertainment. Nowhere, Arizona, is a secret! You need to get your thoughts in order."

"One last thing. I promise. Please tell me, was there an incident where you bashed out the windows of JB's car and his neighbor was forced to call the police on you?"

"Slow down, low down. The police were called on Shakeesha Gatling. Not Rich Montgomery. Check your facts.

And if I wasn't a classy lady I would run up on that neighbor and bust her out for lying on me and spreading her fat gums around. Desperate behind. Tryna be a one-hit wonder by making a nine-one-one call on me. I mean, Shakeesha. I promise you, if that neighbor wasn't a walking *My Six Hundred Pound Life*, I'da taken it straight to her temple. But her double chin was too big for me to reach through to her throat."

"So is that a yes?"

"It's a yes for me busting out the windows of JB's car. Hell yeah, I did it. And? So? What? You ain't never been in love? You ain't never been through nothing? 'Cause if you have never bust the windows out of your man's car or karate-kicked him upside his head, then you have never lived."

"Are you two still together?"

"Eww. Ah'cuse you. Stop it right there. Mr. Smoke-filled Lounge and Child-support Courtroom is no longer in my category of boos right now. We're going through a Chris Brown and Karrueche moment. So I'm finished with him. And if he's your source, then you take your lil dirty self back to him, and tell him that I said he got off easy and he needs to be thanking me. Because I could've dripped some scorching Crisco down his ears or set the whole city dump of Manhattan Beach ablaze. Then where would he live? Puhlease, hear me and hear me well," I shielded my eyes, as the wind kicked up and a helicopter flew over my head. Scanning the eyes of all the reporters, I said, "Don't come for me 'cause it's not healthy. And please, before anyone goes there, don't ask me anything about Heather 'cause I don't even know who that skid-row tramp is..."

Oh, hold up. Wait a minute.

My eyes zoomed in across the lawn, over to where

Spencer and London were posted up by London's limo, whispering.

Am I seeing things...?

Oh no!

"Oh hell no!" I yelled as I stormed off center stage, leaving the reporters behind and heading straight for the two strays who were purposely trying to ruin my day!

4

London

"Welcome back, Little Miss Hacksaw Massacre..." That's what that dizzy chick Spencer said when she stalked up to me and wrapped me up in a tight embrace, catching me completely by surprise while making the hairs on the back of my neck rise.

Scheming *bish!*

"Oooh, it's soo good to have you back. I've sharpened my knives, boo. So get ready for the hunger games. I'm gonna slice you down to the white meat, then feed you to your cousins down in the swamplands, slum dog."

And she'd kept a smile on her face the whole time too!

"Now smile for the cameras..."

She struck a pose for the paparazzi zooming in on us with massive telephoto lenses.

"London! Spencer! Over here, lovies! Give us a smile!"

Then there was an explosion of light.

Click-click.

"Watch your face, boo," she'd whispered after the flashes. "I'm coming for it."

Who the heck did that trick think she was, coming at me like *that* first thing in the morning, I thought, as I hurriedly stepped across the glass threshold, walking into a sea of teens lining the marble hallway. My heels hadn't even had the chance to sink down good into the plush red-carpeted walkway before that tramp pounced on me.

And then... and *thennnnn*... that looney bird had the audacity to air-kiss me just as a helicopter swooped over us and a violent gust of wind swept up around me, blowing my hair and lashes every which way.

And, then, to add to what was already starting off to be a miserable damn morning, the headmaster, Mr. Westwick—with his ole messy self, dressed in his three-piece burgundy suit and floral ascot—felt the need to block my path, place a pudgy hand up on his hip, raise his bushy eyebrows, then proceed to shine a large flashlight in my face, momentarily blinding me as he told me he was going to be keeping his one good eye on me.

I blinked.

Then he demanded that I open my purse and empty out its contents for a security search.

Me?

Searched!

Like, like, I was some criminal!

Treating me like I was some common thief!

The nerve of him!

"I'm glad you're back, Miss Fancy Pants," he'd said, all the while rummaging through my handbag with two Hollywood High security officers. "But know this, Little Miss Sunshine, leave the razors at the front door. There will be no slicing *or* dicing of any body parts up in here. Oh, no, young lady. Not here. This academy is a ratchet-free school zone..."

I blinked. Blinked again.

"I beg your—"

"No," he snapped, stamping his Birkenstock-clad foot. "I beg *yours*. You're a disaster waiting to happen, Miss Phillips. A runway misfit. Now, mind your manners while I'm still talking. It's unfortunate what you've been through the last several weeks. And I'm happy to see that you're still among the living. But that'll be no excuse to come back up in here with your hoodlicious shenanigans. So let me be clear. I expect you to follow the Hollywood High Academy protocol or be escorted off the premises in handcuffs or wrapped in a straitjacket. The choice is yours."

He shut off his flashlight, then twirled it like a baton.

I batted my lashes several times.

"Now proceed to your locker expeditiously, or be fined."

I frowned. "Or be *fined?* Fined for what?"

"For blocking my hallway. For trying to hurt yourself. For being an epic fail! Take your pick."

"You know what," I huffed, stomping off. "I can't with you. Not today, Mister Westwick. Not today."

"And you can't with me any other day, either, Miss Prissy," he yelled out. "You don't want it with me."

I couldn't get to the girls' lounge fast enough, all the while feeling as if all eyes were on me.

Watching me.

Judging me.

Snickering at me.

Pointing accusing fingers at me.

Ugh! I can't stand that man!

I shook my head, bringing myself to the present moment—me in the bathroom, feeling myself slowly becoming undone.

Ugh. Maybe I'm not ready to be back yet, I thought as I stared at myself in the wall mirror in the girls' lounge, pulling out my iPhone and quickly texting my therapist—again. SOS!!! SOS!!! THIS IS AN EMERGENCY. REPEAT. THIS IS AN EMERGENCY!!!! I DON'T THINK I CAN DO THIS!

I took three deep breaths. *Screw Spencer! And screw that Mr. Westwick! All they want to do is get me riled up and see me get derailed. They want to see me fly over the proverbial cuckoo's nest.* Well, guess what? I'll be damned if I give them the satisfaction of seeing me unravel.

Not today.

I took three deep breaths, then texted my therapist *again,* for the twentieth time in the last thirty-seven minutes. WHERE R U?!?!

I tossed my phone back inside my bag, then stood at the mirror and fixed my face and hair. *That whore tried it,* I thought as I applied a fresh coat of shimmering cherry lip gloss over my lips. *Trying to rattle my nerves. Tramp, please. And Rich. Mmmph. That bloated cockroach! Standing up there at that podium like she was in the middle of an identity crisis, looking like a fake Pocahontas meets East India. Wrapped in all that silk like the ugly moth she is.*

I gave myself one last glance in the mirror, tossing my cosmetic case back in my bag, then quickly gathered my belongings and rushed off to the last stall to relieve myself.

I locked the stall door, then pulled my buzzing phone out of my bag and stared at it. I had three text messages from my therapist.

Finally!

The messages read:

TAKE DEEP BREATHS, LONDON. REMEMBER OUR RELAXATION EXERCISES!

FACE YOUR DEMONS HEAD ON.

I CAN SEE YOU @ 4 TODAY.

I typed, NOOOOOOO! I'LL SEE U @ 3! Then sent it. And just as I was about to ease up off the toilet, I heard the bathroom door swing open and the clicking of heels against the tiled floor. Two sets of heels!

"I'm warning you, Spencer. Don't. Do. Me."

A gasp caught in the back of my throat. *Oh, no! It's Rich and Spencer!* My stomach clutched. *I thought I locked that door too!* Instantly, my mind reeled back to the horrible day Spencer kicked open the bathroom stall and snapped pictures of me on the toilet. "Say cheese, you gutter rat! You ole funky turd mama!"

She literally had me trapped in a stall while on the toilet with my silk essentials wrapped around my ankles, threatening my life and threatening to sell the photos of me using the bathroom to the tabloids.

I shuddered, shaking the horrid thought loose. I was still traumatized by the whole sordid ordeal. Spencer was a nutty *biotch!*

"*Whaaaat?*" I heard her screech. "Don't do *you?* Girlie, bye . . . ! Get your life! The question is, who hasn't done *you,* Miss Easy Lay! Don't have me claw your goshdang eyeballs out, trampette. My name isn't Go Both Ways. You better google me, man eater. I don't lick 'em down low. And I don't go deep-sea diving. If it can't touch my esophagus I don't want it. So don't ever disrespect me like that."

I frowned. *Ugh! What a nasty jizz licker!*

"Ewww!" I heard Rich squeal. *"Esophagus?"*

"Yes, hunni, yes! Finger-licking good, boo."

"Clutching pearls! Spencer, you are some kinda nasty. You take freaky to new heights! You need to brush your tongue and get your mind right! Keep sloshing boy juice around in your mouth if you want, and you're gonna end up catching kidney stones. I heard there's no cure for that mess."

I blinked. Kidney stones? Really?

Mirror, mirror on the wall... who's the dumbest ho of them all?

Drum roll, please...

Rich Montgomery!

I heard Spencer giggle. "Oooh, Rich, you're so smart. I see why you pay for your grades, boo. You have the IQ of a light switch."

"Trick, don't do me. And don't change the subject, either. So what if I didn't get an A in human astrology? I know all I need to know about the body. Now, back to you. Why were you all grins 'n' giggles with the enemy? You know I don't do that two-faced *bish*."

My heart skipped a beat.

"And you know I don't go dumpster-diving with the trash. So stop hallucinating."

"Lies! I saw you hug that runway catastrophe..."

"Heeheehee. That catwalk klutz."

"Yes! That fifty-foot humpback!"

"Yes! Yes! Miss Do or Die Low Rider!"

I cringed.

"Yes, hunni, yes! Miss Thirsty for Someone Else's Man!"

I could hear Spencer cracking up. "Bwahahahaha. That orangutan on stilts."

"Exactly! So if you want me to keep you on as one of my so-called, make-believe BFFs, Spencer, then you need to tell me. Right. *Now*. What you were doing down at the other end of the red carpet with that big-foot slutasaurus when you were supposed to be standing in back of *me* up at the podium as I served the world my press conference.

You knew this was a big day for me. You're so damn insensitive and thoughtless, Spencer." I heard a foot stamp. "You don't give a damn about no one but yourself. Why I continue to put up with your disrespect is—"

"*Whaaat?* Hold up. Wait a minute. Let me stick my switchblade up in it. Don't you stomp your little piggy-hoof at me. I don't answer to *you,* boo. And I don't have to tell you a goshdang-diggity-dang thing, little Miss Muppet. Who the heck died and left you the roll call queen. I don't check in with you, girlie, especially when I see you smutting it up with Heather, the junkyard junkie."

"*Ex*-junkyard junkie. Get it right. Heather's cleaned herself up. She's not the same skittles popping crack whore she used to be."

I heard Spencer snort. "Lies. That tramp is about as clean as the gutters she crawled up out of. Skid row trash!"

"Ohmygod, Spencer! Clutching pearls! You're so judgmental. And this is *exactly* why no one likes you. People change. But you wouldn't know anything about that since you're still the same ole hating, man-sharing tramp."

"Oh, *please!* Says the girl who slept with the substitute teacher..."

I blinked. *Ohmygod! She did what? Who? When? Keep talking, Spencer. Keep right on running your jaws.*

"Ooh, *bish!* Shut your gutter trap, you messy heifer. How was I supposed to know that fine Mexican was a teacher?"

"Well, if you went to class and paid attention, you would have known. And he's Puerto Rican."

"Yes, god. Hunni! And hot like Tabasco sauce. He had me ready to lick the guacamole bowl and cross the borders of Tijuana! And you know I don't do Latin America like that. I'm a Cali girl. Crenshaw, baby! Bang-bang! But that's beside the point, Spencer. The point is, people change. And Heather's changed."

"Girlie, bye. The only thing Heather's probably changed is her panty liner. And even that's questionable. That street-walker hasn't changed a dang thing else, *except* who she's grabbing her ankles for."

"*Whaaat?* Clutching pearls! Oh, no. Oh, no. Let me stop you right there. Jealousy is so not cute on you, Spencer. Why are *you* all up in Heather's hot pocket? Who Heather is doing booty shots for is none of your business. She's my good, good friend now. And you will *not* defame her good name in front of me. Oh no, oh no. Not over here you won't."

"Lick cow turds, girlie. Heather's a traitorous tricka-zoid," Spencer spat. "And when she turns on *you* and stabs *you* in the face, back, and chest, don't you dare come crawling back to me. Because if you do, I'm going to step on your neck and watch you bleed out."

I heard someone suck their teeth. Then heard Rich say, "Bye, Felicia, bye. You're so overdramatic. That's what you get for tryna buy your friends. You're pathetic. Nobody told you to go out and buy that girl a brand-new Lamborghini—one she turned around and sold for some tricked-out hooptie. And no one told *you* to spend thousands of dollars for her to get that new bouncing booty she so graciously tells you to kiss every chance she gets. And you damn sure had no business writing *her* a check for three million dollars, when *you* know that money could have easily gone to *my* foundation."

"And what charity is that, Rich? The Reformed Hoes Alliance?"

"No. The Make A Bish Wish She Was Me Foundation. I'm making dreams come true, while keeping hope alive."

"Hahahaha. Hilarious. From the looks of it, the only thing you've been *keeping* open are your legs."

"See. And *that's* exactly why you don't have any friends, Spencer, because you're messy and selfish. S-e-l-f-s-i-s-h..."

I blinked. *Ohmygod, the Dimwit Blonde award goes to... once again, Rich!*

"Rich, shut your dang flytrap before I stuff it with Gorilla Glue. I'm two seconds from going into my trick bag on you. And the correct spelling is s-e-l-f-i-s-h! Get your dictionary skills up before you try me this early in the morning."

In my mind's eye, I imagined Spencer pulling out a can of Mace and scorching Rich's eye sockets out. *Would serve her right!*

"Ugh. See. There you go. Tryna do me. I don't know what kinda games you're playing, Spencer, but you had better respect my gangster. I swear. You are so incompetent. And disloyal! A disgrace! I tell you. You lollipop hoes ain't loyal. And I've been nothing but good to you."

"And I've been good to *you.* And I've kept every dirty, little secret of yours."

"Lies! The only thing you've ever *kept* are your knees on the floor and your mouth pressed into some boy's crotch. Like I've said, you've been nothing but judgmental. And I'm sick of it! Just when I halfway start to like you, you show me what kinda trick you really are."

I heard something slam down on the marble vanity.

"*Judgmental?* Girlie, bye! You're the one with all the dirty tricks. If I were *judging* you, nutbush, I'd be coming at that kangaroo pouch you're *trying* to hide. How many baby kangaroos are you hopping around with this time, Rich, huh? And I'd be talking about you keying up Thug Daddy's car, and smashing his windows out, like the ratchet trash you are. But. Not. A. Word. Mammals going wild is none of my business."

My stomach heaved as I absorbed the weight of what Spencer was implying. *Is Rich pregnant? Oh, God, with Justice's baby?*

"*Mitch!* Get yo' life! Don't. Do. Me. You must really want me to boom-bop-drop these fists on you. First of all, me keying up my man's car was done out of love. But you wouldn't know anything about loving a man—a *real* man, that is—because you're too stuck on little boys barking and stomping the yard in purple long johns and gold combat boots. It takes a real woman to smash out her man's windows, then love him down right. So stay out of *me* and *my* man's damn business!

"Second of all, I'm on my period. So there goes your pregnancy theory. Now stay the hell out of my honey well. And *if* you're trying to say I'm fat, you've failed terribly, sweetie. You wish you could be me. *Thick*labulous. Yesss, hunni. Thick and fabulous combined into one sweet, juicy package."

"Ohhhhh, so that's what they're calling it these days, *thick*. *Mmmph*. Real classic."

"Oooh, the hate is real. *Annny*who, trampalina. Back to *you*. You need to let me know *why* I should consider keeping you around all of my fabulousness after the trickery you pulled outside because I will not tolerate fickle hoes in my inner circle. And, once again, *you* have proven you are not to be trusted."

I heard Spencer laugh. "Woo-ooh! Tick, tock, tickety-tick-tock! Ring the alarm! Send in the clowns! You're a real sideshow, girlie. A dirty, low-down skank-a-dank, no-panty-wearing, man-eating whore! But I'm not judging you. But like I *saaaaaid* before. What I *was* or *wasn't* doing with that bubblehead London outside is none of your gosh-dang beeswax!"

"*Mmmph*. And you call my new good, good friend Heather a traitor. But, trick, you better be grateful that I continue to worship in the Church of Stay Fly and Be A Lady At All Times, and that I don't ever believe in throwing the first punch; otherwise I would straight get it crunked up in here. Take it right to your face..."

I glanced at my timepiece. I'd had enough of this! It was clear these slutty kooks had no intentions of leaving up out of here anytime soon. And there were only eleven minutes left until the homeroom bell rang. I had to get out of this bathroom stall. Fast.

I quietly shimmied my Strumpet & Pink–laced goodies up over my hips, then eased down my skirt. I flushed the toilet, took a deep breath, then unlocked the stall door.

It was time to step into the light *and*—as my therapist would say—face these demons in heels head on.

5

Heather

Just above the level of public stall toilet shit. Those words flooded my thoughts as I pressed my forehead against the helicopter's thick glass, looking down at the sprawling Hollywood High grounds. I scanned the heads of the reporters, semicircling Rich and her red carpet committee . . . and for a moment, a split second in time, I wished I knew what it was like to be her. A real Montgomery. The apple of our father's eye. Instead of his abortion nightmare come to life.

But.

I was nothing.

I wasn't WuWu.

I wasn't Luda Tutor.

I wasn't a Pampered Princess.

I wasn't straight.

Gay.

Black.

White.

I looked Mexican. With bronze-colored skin and thick, sandy brown coils.

But I wasn't Mexican.

I was a mutt. White mother. Black father.

And I didn't have any friends.

And I didn't have any money. Not any real money.

All I had was my mother, Camille, whose pale-peach-colored face and icy-blue eyes stayed on the grind of ruining my life.

And today was no different.

Eight a.m. I'd stood looking in my ensuite's mirrored wall, wanting desperately to stop my sinking thoughts that told me:

You ain't good enough.

You ain't gon' ever be good enough.

And you need a pinch of Black Beauty so you can feel like something.

But I didn't want Black Beauty. I just wanted to get into the groove of admiring my hot and fire-red leopard catsuit and my custom-made fox stole—with diamonds in the eyes and pink-painted claws on the feet. And just when I'd finally stopped telling myself that I wasn't shit, but instead was *the shit*, in stepped Camille. Mudding up my freakin' moment.

I lifted my lavender-colored eyes—contacts, of course—and stared at her reflection. Her shoulder was pressed into the doorway as she swirled her daily breakfast of scotch with a splash of Sprite.

A Virginia Slim dangled from the corner of her thin cherry lips, and her sheer white gown hung loosely on her reedy and shapeless frame. She wore open-toe mink and matted slippers that showcased her long, thin toes, which she stretched out and moved like an accordion playing the same beat. Over. And over. Again.

Ugg!

"Dear God, no." Camille smacked her lips and huffed, "Baby Jesus. Buddha on high. Heather Suzanne."

I hated when she called me that.

"I think we've got a problem." She took a pull of her cigarette and blew an O of smoke into the air.

I sucked my teeth and dug around in my makeup bag for mascara. Found it.

"Did you hear me, Heather Suzanne?"

I huffed and zigzagged Maybelline across an eyelid. "What's the problem?"

"Problem number one is that smug look on your face."

"Fall back. Last I checked, I didn't ask you for a facial analysis." I zigzagged the other eyelid.

"Just who are you talking to?"

I looked directly into the mirror, gave her reflection a piercing look, and my eyes clearly said, *'I'm talking to yo' behind.'* But I didn't let that come out of my mouth. Instead, I shrugged, then reached for my purple lip gloss and said, "Umm... Let me think here... I would be talking to... you." I popped and smudged my lips together for an even glossy coating.

"You must want me to slap your face!"

"Are you really trying to get into the ring with me today? Really? You really wanna reenact Hollywood WWE? 'Cause we can."

Camille placed her drink on the shelf next to her. "You better watch your tone, young lady. Because I know you remember when I dragged you outside and blackened you up real good. Now do you want me to bull's-eye your face again? The last time you got off easy and only landed in a hospital bed." She stepped out of her slippers, gathered the hem of her nightgown to the right and tied it into a knot. "But this time, I'm telling you now, my plan will be to make your lungs collapse and stomp the life out of you. So please inform me of how you wish to handle this, little girl. I've got my lawyer on standby. And believe me, if I have to go to jail, the charge will be murder. You will have your RIP card today. 'Cause I will drag you straight to the gates of hell. Have your fake rump, silicone tits, and face on fire forever!"

For a moment, I considered raising up, but then I decided not to buck. Besides, Camille was crazy, and she roamed the Earth looking for reasons to lose it. She was a blackballed Oscar-winning actress who couldn't get a job if she paid to be on set. Nobody in Hollywood would touch her.

For one: She was a wayward drunk.

And for two: She'd made one too many rounds through Tinsel Town's hoe stroll, pissed off the wrong men—including my father—that she liked to pretend didn't exist, and now she was a worn-out Marilyn Monroe. Minus the bed, the pills, and the grim reaper.

And here I was, stuck with this demon loin. And to think I've tried everything to get rid of her.

Threw all of her booze over the balcony and tried to toss her out behind it, but she snuck me. Dragged me. And I ended up in the hospital, near death.

When she had us homeless and laid up in Sleazy Eight, two seconds from being ladies of the night, I tried moving out and leaving her there. But I was a minor, and I needed her.

I even drugged her. Dumped molly, Xanax, Valium, and a few other pills in her drink. But. It didn't work. All she did was wake up in the back of a paddy wagon—long story—screaming and needing her stomach pumped. Then caught an attitude. And had me sentenced to probation until the age of eighteen.

Thank God for Spencer and Kitty, though. They paid off the judge in money and coochie butter, so my probation was reduced and only lasted for six months.

Now don't get me wrong—I love my mother. I just can't stand her.

I took a deep breath and grimaced. "What. Do. You. Want. Camille? It's too early in the morning for you to call yourself serving me. As a matter of fact, why don't you go and serve yourself a new drink. Or better yet, serve yourself an AA meeting."

Camille walked over to my medicine cabinet, reached for the bottle of Tylenol, and popped two in her mouth, chasing them with a swig of scotch. "Let me just calm my nerves. 'Cause either you're confused, think you have arrived, or both." She paused. Took a long toke of her cigarette and blew another O of smoke into the air.

Flicking her cigarette ashes to the floor, she continued. "But, as your mother, I think you should know... How do I say this..." She snapped her fingers. "You, my dear, are just above the level of public stall. Toilet. Shit."

My eyes popped open, and my throat felt like it had been sliced. Camille was always saying something that felt like death.

She carried on, not caring that I'd turned beet red. "Yeah, yeah, you were on prime-time TV. And WuWu was everywhere. But things are different now. Back then your piss was innocent, but now it's burning holes in cups. Sending the teenage drug-use statistics to new heights. Which is why the only role you're being offered is ratchet reality TV. Kitty litter style. Straight bottom of the trash barrel!"

"You've got hella nerve, Camille! And since that trash is paying your bills, then what does that make you?"

"That makes me the garbage woman 'cause I'm taking the trash out and struggling to clean it up. You are a disgrace. Here I am, an Oscar-winning actress." She pushed her right shoulder forward and cat-walked across the bathroom floor. "Yet my offspring is a low-self-esteem attention whore."

I blinked. Not once but three times.

She carried on, flinging her arms in the air, like she was sharpening her acting skills. "You're out running the streets of L.A. looking for acceptance, when you need to be honing in on your talent. But instead you wanna be friends with Rich, that chocolate pig. And if you're not fantasizing about being a Montgomery, you're hanging out until four in the morning down in K-Town somewhere, twerking on a bar top with that lady boy, Coco Ming. Or picking out boxing shorts with that auntie-uncle Nikki. Or wasting your life away with one of your other Skittle party friends whose idea of fun is to overdose on their grannie's heart medicine!"

"What are you talking about?! Coco is my friend. He's not some lady boy. He's gay. And Nikki is my friend. She's not an auntie-uncle. She's a pretty girl, and she's really nice! So don't you dare call her that!"

"I will call rainbow thongs whatever I like! You think I don't see the way you two look at each other? Huh? I swear if you mess around and get freaked out I will commit you. You're already a junkie, and now you wanna be fruity?! Pick a struggle, Heather Suzanne! Pick. A. Frickin'. Struggle!"

"You need to get yourself a life and stay out of my business!"

"You are my business! And you owe me! I'm your mother, and you know I haven't worked in years. We're all we have. And you need to get these bills paid up in here. I will not live like the hired help. Now what you better do is get your little mind together. You've got a fake behind and fake tits, but you are still Hollywood garbage. And you need to change that. Stop trying to be a Montgomery because you will never be."

Amazing. She won't admit that Richard Montgomery is my father, but she'll tell me to stop trying to be a Montgomery. Blank. Stare.

She carried on, "You need to be Heather Cummings. A reality star with a number one iTunes hit. Get back in the studio and make another track. Turn up the heat on this reality show thing. I don't care if you have to walk down Rodeo Drive naked. Do. Something. And do it big! 'Cause it's time for me to get the respect I deserve."

I rolled my eyes to the top of my head, put my left eyebrow ring in, tightened the small ring in my nose, turned around, and headed for my bedroom.

Camille followed me, and as I reached for the keys to my hot pink '57 Chevy and grabbed my plush leopard clutch, she screamed, "Oh no! Hell no!" She snatched the keys out of my hand. "You will not be going to school in that hunk of junk. You will be arriving to Hollywood High in style."

"Style? I'm always in style. Thank you very much."

"Look, you will not be rolling up in that pink slop bucket. I have written a check from your bank account and chartered you a helicopter."

A what? What did she say? "You did what? Run that past me again. And who paid for this?"

"You paid for it."

"I'm not riding in a helicopter. You can forget it. And you better get my money back! You don't—"

"Oh, you will ride in that helicopter and you will ride in it today." A familiar voice sliced across my words. I turned around toward the doorway, and there stood the devil. Spencer's mother. In red bottoms and a navy blue power suit. "Kitty . . . what are you doing here?"

"I've been here this whole time, and so have the cameras." She pointed to the cameraman behind her. "We've finally gotten some footage we can use to kick this reality show up a notch. I refuse to let you drag my money through the mud another day. It's time for you to get on board. Now, gather your things." She snapped her fingers. "Because you will be flying to school today. The press is already on the grounds. And I need you, you need you, and God knows your mother needs you, to own the spotlight. Because if you don't, I will fire you, and I will shut your whole world down. Your mother will end up on welfare, and by the time I'm done with you, you'll be at the post office shuffling mail around with the rest of the civil service fishbowl of misfits. Now come along . . ."

"Miss Cummings, we're here," the pilot said, his voice bringing me out of my thoughts. I looked out of the window and noticed how the blades had tossed up thousands of dollars' worth of weaves. Rich's hair stood straight up on her head, and her pearls were wrapped around her neck like a noose. Even Spencer and London looked disheveled by the helicopter's wind.

Actually, I had everyone's attention. All eyes were on me like they were supposed to be. So why was I nervous? Scared? Hesitant?

You need some.

No I don't.

Yes you do.

Just a pinch.

I sighed.

Maybe just a little to knock off the edge.

I eased a hand into my clutch and carefully unfolded the foil in my bag. I looked over at the pilot, and he was too busy shutting down the helicopter's gears to notice me.

Quickly, I dipped a long tip of my stiletto nail into the foil, pulled out a pinch of Black Beauty, eased it to my nose, and snorted it in. A few seconds later, a burning, yet calming wave came over me.

You got this.

You that chick.

Own it.

Work it.

Zone it.

Boom!

I sniffed, clearing my nostrils. Then I took the pilot's hand, smiled, and stepped out of the helicopter, "Showtime!"

6

Rich

"Mirror, mirror on my locker's wall, who's the flyest bish of 'em all?"

I blinked.

Smiled.

Flipped my weave, admired my marble brown eyes, and after snapping a quick selfie, I said, "Why you are, Rich. You're the flyest bish of 'em all. And that's why these silly thots stay hatin'."

Snap. Snap. I popped my fingers.

Bam! I clapped my hands.

Yaaaaasss, honey, yaaaaasss!

Spencer and London tried it.

They.

Tried.

It.

And I know Spencer heard me calling her when she and London were all huddled up and whispering like besties. She ignored me, though. Never even turned around and looked my way.

Don't get it twisted: I'm not sweatin' it. I'm not even mad. 'Cause one thing is for certain and two things for sure: It's only a matter of time before those two skanks get to yanking each other's tracks out.

And where will I be?

Posted up. Looking cute. And recording it. Making sure every social networking site has a front row seat at the Pampered Princesses' newest bitch-slappin' hoedown.

Mph, sometimes, you gotta give a funny-actin' trollop just what she wants: embarrassment. And since Spencer wanna switch teams on me—on me!—well, then, she shall see what happens when friends become enemies.

That wanna-be trap queen!

Heifer!

Sleaze!

I can't believe Spencer would betray me. That chick has absolutely no loyalty. And that's why my new gospel is: Everyone from Day One ain't A-1.

Period.

Besides, I don't have time for little-girl games.

I'm a grown, sixteen-year-old woman. Soon to be seventeen. And if Spencer keeps it up, she will not be invited to my birthday party! She wanna be all up in that black widow London's face. Really? Oh, okay.

Know what, let me breathe.

Relax.

Otherwise, I'ma end up sluggin' me a slut today.

I took a deep breath and pushed it out.

Dear Black Jesus, please send me a sign. I need something, to calm me down so I can think clearly and come up with a hellafied way for these tricks to pay... WHAM!

I jumped as the locker next to me slammed shut.

I peeked around to see what kind of beast was trying to tear up the place.

I frowned. Heather? Eww. Really? This raggedy bird. Why is her locker next to mine? When did this happen? This is not cardboard box row. I will be going to Westwick today…

Wait.

Hold it.

I paused, and a smile lit up my face.

Heather had TV cameras filming her at her locker. I forgot she had a new reality show.

Hmmm…

And every reality star has a best friend.

And nothing pisses off the old bestie like a new bestie.

Hmmm…

And since Heather and Spencer no longer rock out…

And since Spencer tried to play me out…

And since Spencer hates Heather—at least right now she does—I know exactly how I could serve my sweet revenge.

Yaaaaaaaasssss, baby. Yaaaaaaaasssss!

Let the games begin.

I was cheesing all over the place. My eyes danced in delight, and my smile was a mile wide.

I looked up the hallway, and I swear the God of Get That Hoe Back For Being The World's Stankest Friend must love me again, 'cause Spencer was coming this way.

I quickly shut my locker, leaned against it, and looked Heather directly in the face. "Hey, girl. I see you." I snapped my fingers in a Z-motion. "That's a cute costume you got on."

Heather looked at me like I was crazy, then twisted her lips and gave me her back to kiss as she walked away.

Oh hell no. She needed to be punched in the face.

I tossed a quick eye over at Spencer and flipped her the bird for even looking my way. She flipped her hair and continued down the hall. Whatever. Now back to Heather. I can't believe she walked away from me... and on TV.

Remember, you're on a mission, my guardian angel whispered.

So I rushed over to Heather and draped my arm over her shoulder. "Heather, girlfriend. Did you hear me speak to you when we were over at the lockers?"

Heather took a step forward, causing my arm to fall off of her shoulder. "I heard you. Now watch my fatty shake as I walk away."

Oh no, she didn't leave me in the middle of the floor with the cameras zooming in on my face! Deep breath. Don't lay her to rest, yet.

I almost tripped over my feet to catch up to her. "Eww, girl." I fanned my face. "I'm tryna be nice and peaceful witchu now, but you tryna bring out the Watts in me. Whatchu mean you heard me? Whatchu can't speak, homie? Crack crippled your mouth?"

Heather arched one brow. "Excuse you." She paused. "First off, I'm not your homie, and I'm not your girl. And second of all, yeah, I heard you speaking, but I ignored you. Which I'm trying to do now."

I wonder if I have that box cutter in my bag. I cleared my throat. "What's the problem? You don't know how to act when someone's being nice to you? Like really? Word. Can't nobody say hi to you?"

"And why would you want to speak to me? You don't do me, and I definitely don't do you. Or did you forget that the last time I saw you, you tried to bully me, I had to cuss you out in the cafeteria, and my whole crew was about to body slam you."

"Body slam! I wish a tramp would try it! 'Cause I will," I paused.

Tsk, tsk, Rich. Stay focused. My guardian angel stepped in.

I cleared my throat. I needed to stay on track. "Oh, Heather, honestly, I don't remember that ever happening." I sniffed and dapped at the corners of my eyes. "I've been, umm"—I bit the corner of my lip and forced my voice to quiver—"I've been diagnosed with selective amnesia."

Why is this trick giving me a blank stare?

I continued, "So let's just let bygones be bygones and move on. Life is too short to hold on to something so petty. Agreed?"

She didn't respond; she simply blinked.

I carried on, "Now look, girl. I'ma need the four-one-one on how you got your money up and was able to afford that helicopter. I hope Spencer didn't give it to you because if she did, girrrrrrrrl! Prepare to be talked about like a dog, honey. 'Cause she straight puppy clowned you and told all yo' lil business when you sold that car she gave you. Don't do it, Heather. Don't."

"I have my own money, thank you."

Chile, cheese. Boo, please. Low-income housing is written all over you. "Of course you have some coins. But anyway, I was just saying the helicopter was dope. And you are so rude, Heather. You didn't even introduce me." I looked into the camera and said, "I'm Rich Montgomery, dahlins. Heather's new bestie, baby!" Then I looked back at Heather. "I just took your show to a whole other level. Now, you wanna eat lunch together? I'll have the chef prepare sushi. You wanna have some drinks after school? Beer is on me. And no is not an option. Plus, I need something to take my mind off of JB."

"I don't know about that, Rich..." Heather said, as Spencer walked by again, giving me the evil eye.

Yaaaaaaaasssss, bish, eat it!

I smiled, and as Heather continued to talk, I pretended to listen. I knew she was giving me some excuse about having somewhere else to go after school or something like that. Truthfully, I didn't care what she said. I was more concerned with Spencer turning beet red.

Mission accomplished.

I smiled as I zoned back into Heather and realized that she was serving me.

"Now bye, Felicia." Heather said, swerving her neck and flicking her fingers at me and leaving my face cracked on the floor.

7

Spencer

"Oh no, you two-faced, backstabbing slut," Rich sneered as she looked up from her platter of crab cakes and garlic/cheese grits and noticed London at our table.

We were having lunch in the Déjeuner Café, where the juniors ate their meals. And it was where the Pampered Princesses—well, what was left of us—held court. Perched high up on our pedestals at the table of all tables, one fit only for Hollywood High royalty. The one positioned right in the center of the room for all to see.

And, no, no, I wasn't even about to say anything messy because I was loving and kind, at least six days a week.

But...

Rich was busy chasing kinky romps and making eggplant stew with her thug daddy. Mmmph. And I know that ole chocolate hood daddy laid hands across her face last night, especially since she went street-whore-ratchet and clawed his car up. She thinks I didn't see that little bruise on the side of her precious face this morning when we were in the bathroom. But Mother saw it. Mother sees *every*thing. I didn't say a word, though. Nope. Not one blubbering word.

No, no, no.

My cute lips were sealed.

Mmmph.

For now.

Then London, bless her little stank raggedy soul, that walking cuckoo clock was busy chasing crazy. And I had nothing more to say on that.

Heather was too busy bouncing her Brazilian-bought booty, chasing rainbow flags and skittles—tricking up her coins on Korean knockoffs and cheesy animal coats, like this morning dropping down from the sky wearing some nasty wolf up over her shoulders, like it's her best friend.

That ole wolf walker! She's lucky I didn't call the SPCA on her.

And, me... well, heehee, I was chasing the next scandalous takedown.

I didn't know who should be first to get dropped.

London or Heather?

That was the question.

Ooh, there was a time when being one of the Pampered Princesses meant you had arrived at the *queen*dom of fabulousness. It meant you had climbed the mountaintop and dropped skunk bombs on the peasy heads of everyone else below you. You'd dug your stilettos into the sand and drawn a deep line that separated you from the riffraff.

But these days so much had changed, thanks to Rich scrounging around in the gutters—like I told her not to—taking in strays, like London and Heather. I knew London was rancid roadkill the first time I laid eyes on her East Side trashy self.

And, Heather... well, that junkyard trash was on her way to becoming the next front-page tragedy with all of her trickery.

Mmmph.

I could claw Rich's dang tonsils out for not listening to Momma. And now look at us. In constant shambles. The Pampered Princesses' popularity stock was way down in the poop chute. And I was sick and goshdang tired of being knee-deep in turd soup!

Something had to give. And fast.

But first...

Rich pointed her fork at London, then at the chair in front of her. "Don't even *think* about sitting down over here, Benedict Betty, until you apologize to me."

London frowned. "You don't own me. I'll sit where I damn well please." She pulled out a chair and sat. "And what do I need to apologize to *you* for?"

"What do you need to apologize to me for?" Rich shrieked, repeating London's words. "Umm, let's see, boo-boo. How about for having me waste all of my love and energy on some two-faced leech like you, for one. For trying to breathe the same air as me, for two. And for being the hateful, jealous trick you are, for three. I gave up good karma messing with you, London. And all you did was turn around and backstab me."

I tooted my lips, shifting back in my seat and crossing my legs.

Do Momma proud, Rich, I thought, folding my arms over my chest.

"*Mmmph*," I grunted. "She shanked you real good. Gutted you all up in your jelly fat, then licked the blade clean."

"Ewww! Clutching pearls!" Rich snapped. "Get your

nasty mind out of the gutter, Spencer. The only one licking blades clean is you. Ugh! Gross!" She glared back over at London. "Now back to you, tramp. You ran out the bathroom this morning before I could get you together. And you're lucky I'm sitting here feeling sorry for you, London. Otherwise, I'd hop up and peel your face off. But it's Monday, and I'm taking a day off from beating tricks and hoes down today. But don't test me. Now, like I said, *you* owe *me* an apology."

I tilted my head and stared at London. But Trixie pretended to not see me eyeing her down as she kept her stare locked on Rich.

Oooh, I wanted to hop up and smack Big Foot four ways into silly for trying to ignore me. Skank-a-dank!

London huffed. "Fine, Rich. You want an apology? Then so be it. I apologize for whatever you think I might have done to you. But being jealous of *you* is not what I am."

Rich slammed her fork down. "Tramp, lies! Look at me. Look at you. And look"—Rich twirled her left hand up in the air, flaunting her ring—"at the ring finger, boo. Bam! You see the bling? You see the sparkle? Got your eyes blinded by envy because I got the man *and* the ring. And what did you get, boo-boo? Dumped by Dr. Corny. And weeks laid up in a bed with an IV drip."

Yessss! Yessss, goshdangit! Go for the jugular, Richie Pooh!

"Anderson didn't *dump* me, for your information," London hissed, defensively. "We both just decided to take a break and give each other some space. Not that it's any of your business. Or that I owe *you* any explanations."

I giggled. "Oh, is that what they're calling it these days, taking a break? From what, London? Sharing beauty tips?

Exchanging panty and bra sets? Or taking a break from your little cover-up? You and I know your little love affair with Anderson Ford was a sham."

"Spencer," London sneered, "I don't know what you're trying to imply, but—"

"No, girlie, I'm not *trying* to imply anything. I just said it. Anderson Ford likes fishnets and garters, not girls."

"*Whaaaaaat?*" Rich squealed. "Clutching pearls! Clutching pearls! Say it ain't so, Heather. Doctor Corny is a..."

I nodded my head. "Yes, honey. He is."

Rich clutched her chest. "Dead to the bed! Flat-lined!"

"*Shut your trap!*" London snapped, shooting an icy glare at me. "Just shut your filthy, jizz-guzzling mouth. You don't know anything about Anderson, or about what he and I shared."

I smiled. Tilted my head. It was so, sooo good to have London back. "Oooh, give it to me, Big Face. Give it to me real good and juicy. Let me see you twerk with it. Yes. Yes. Leap little froggy, leap."

She flicked a dismissive wave at me. "Whatever, Spencer. Like I said, Anderson and I are taking a break from each other."

Rich twisted her lips. "Uh-huh. Yeah, okay. And you just *thought* my boo Justice would want *you*, which is why you tried to toss hate all up on me when you came at me down at Club Tantrum—don't even think I've forgotten about that, either, trick. Telling me he was no good. *After* you were the one trying to force him on *me* in the first damn place. Then when I finally give him a lil taste of this sweet honey, you get all Olivia Pope on me, wanting to be the next gladiator. Girl, bye. You couldn't even be happy for me when I announced my engagement to him."

London gave Rich an incredulous look. "Are you kidding me? You insidious *bish!* You waltzed up in my room throwing me shade, wearing *my* engagement ring."

"Whore, lies! See, there you go. Still being your delusional self. Still showing just how desperate you are. What do you want, London? For me to show you how to take a permanent dirt nap? Justice told me you'd say anything to try to break us up. Like he'd ever buy you a ring." Rich laughed. "Girl, bye."

"Can we say, med check," I said, joining in on Rich's laughter.

"Whatever, Rich. And screw you, Spencer. Believe what you want. I have no reason to lie to you. If Justice is whom you want to be with, then be with him. That boy is nothing to me, anymore."

Rich tossed her head back and let out a loud laugh, then stopped. "Lies. He was never anything to you in the first place."

"He is everything to me. And you are nothing to him, up here lying," I smirked. "Oooh, somebody's got a dirty little secret. Do tell, London. Heehee."

London rolled her eyes at me, then eyed Rich. "Rich, think whatever you want. It's obvious you think you've won the door prize, so have at it. If you think Justice is ever going to be capable of loving you, good luck with that. All you are is a meal ticket and an easy lay."

"Boo, trick, booooo!" Rich clapped her hands, emphasizing each word. "Here you go with your desperate behind. Tryna come in on my shimmy-shimmy boo-boo love." She rolled her eyes in disgust, flopping down in her seat. "Instead of tryna kill yourself, you should have tried to kill your hatred. That's what you should have done. So save your wasted breath, skank. Coming up in here with your nastiness on an all-time high."

London huffed. "Girl, get over it. You've been nasty toward me from the moment I left for Milan up until the time I returned."

Rich sneered. "*Mmmph*. And we all see how that turned out for you. With you bleeding out, flat on your face."

I blinked. Rich could be so, so callous and condescending. She was insensitive and heartless. Ooooh, and I loved it!

But this wasn't the time for that. The bobcat needed to reel this field mouse in. Toy with it. Box it in. Then go in for the kill. Not chase it, *her,* away.

Peter Peter Pumpkin Eater. I swear. Rich never stayed on script.

"Oh no, ohhh, noo," I said, shaking my head. "Play nice, Rich."

"She doesn't have to *play* nice," London retorted, twisting her shiny, painted lips, "or do nothing else except be the nasty trick she is. If she wants to keep throwing shade, let her. I don't need to be friends with her. And I'm definitely not gonna kiss her behind."

"And I'm not kissing *yours*," Rich snapped back. "But I don't go that way, anyway. So keep your sexuality right on over there, and go find some other nasty trick to kiss crack with, because you'll *never* get your mouth, lips, or anything else on my sweet and juicy."

"You know what, screw this." London stood. "I'm out."

"Lonnnnndon," I cooed, twisting a lock of hair around my finger. "Don't be messy, Pumpkin Head. Look around you, girlie." I waved an arm around the café. "Where do you think you're going? There's nowhere for you to hide. So sit. Down."

"Spencer, *eff*. You." She flipped me the finger. "I've just about had it with you."

I clapped. "Oooh, yes, yes, yes, Amazon.com. Do me, baby! Wet my liner, girlie! Ding dong, the witch is dead." I shook my curls. "Push it real good. Give it to me dirty, boo. Give. It. To. Me. Real. Good."

She huffed. "Oh, shut up, Spencer. You dimwit."

I smirked. "Uh-huh, says the girl who lost her secret thug boo to a man addict. And her phony-baloney cover-up is now off pretending with some other model, who'll probably end up the next runway catastrophe once she finds out what he really wants to be."

She started gathering her things. "Whatever, Spencer. Think what you want! I don't need to sit where I'm not wanted. Good day, hoes."

Rich slammed her hand down on the table. "*Whaaaat?!* Clutching pearls! That's so typical, London. Go run like the coward you are!"

"*Coward? Bish,* the only coward in the room is *you*." London jabbed a finger in Rich's direction. "You're nothing but a loudmouthed, evil-spirited bully. And I don't have to put up with it. And I don't have to put up with *you*. You don't ever want to be friends, fine. But you will *not* talk to me like I'm trash, whore."

Oooh, nookie nookie chocolate chip cookie. This was starting to get real juicy. Almost as juicy as my... oops. Never mind.

Heehee.

Annnnyway...

These two hookahs had already gone at it in the bathroom the moment London slithered herself out from the back stall this morning, surprising Rich and me.

Eavesdropping on grown folks.

Stall-stalking us.

And now they were back at it again. I already had the front row seat. All I needed was a bag of Twizzlers and a cold Sprite.

Rich flicked a gaze over at me. "Spencer, you see this? This whore wants to run off instead of taking her lickings like a woman. Who does that?"

"Low Money does that," I said, giggling. "Broke Back London."

"Oh no," London sneered, shouldering her bag. "Both of you trifling hot pockets are not worth my time. I'm—"

Rich hopped up from her seat. "I should bash you in your face with my clutch!"

"Now, now, Rich," I said, grabbing her by the arm and pulling her back down in her seat. "All eyes are on us." I narrowed my eyes over at London as Rich took her seat, then said, "London, sit your ole ugly self back down, girlie. Or would you like me to remove your eyeballs, instead of another coat of hair. And, Rich, stop scaring her." I started stroking her weave, petting her like the wild beast she was.

She eyed London. "Why are you so two-faced, London, huh? Why can't you accept you can never be me?"

"No, no, Rich. Down, girl. Down. Let me muzzle you real quick."

Rich started growling and showing her fangs. All she needed was frothy foam around her mouth to be the rabid beast she was. "Grrrrrrrrrrr. I should tear her head off."

I chanted, "Who let the dogs out! Woof, woof, woof. Woof!" I reached into my oversize bag and pulled out my tambourine. I started click-clacking as Rich hopped up from her seat, shook her round hips, then dropped down and did the tootsie-roll.

I barked and chanted. "Yasssss! Yassss! Woof! Woof! Yassss! Yasssss! Woof! Woof!"

Rich howled and twerked. She moved her hips from side to side, snaked down to the floor. She growled and cootie-popped it. She bounced her tail and gritted her teeth.

Then... just like that, as if it'd been synchronized, we abruptly stopped, then sat back down and crossed our legs as if we'd rehearsed the little routine.

Rich patted her weave. And I popped my lips.

I glanced over at Rich. "Ooh wolf dog, you showed out."

"*Whaaat?!*" Rich shrieked, eyes stretching wide. "Clutching pearls! *Wolf dog?* Whore! How dare you disrespect me! Try to play me! I'm no wolf dog! You know I'm well groomed and classy. I'm a poodle! Don't do me!"

Blank stare.

London snickered, shaking her head.

Rich was such a bubblehead.

"Now, back to getting you together," Rich said, eyeing London. "But you know what. I'm going to let you speak, Spencer. Because I don't have no toleration for this ho right here."

London blinked. "Wait one minute. Can't either of you *get* me together. You better get *yourselves* together. Tricking and sucking every Tom, Dick, and Joey; you two despicable tramps deserve each other."

"*Whaaat?!*" Rich snapped. "Clutching pearls! I don't do that! The only one hose slurping"—Rich flicked a finger over at me—"is this Super Slurper here. She's the one doing nasty tongue tricks to boys living in cardboard boxes. Not me!"

I eased my hand down in my handbag, then whipped

out a rhinestone-studded flyswatter, slapping it across the table.

"Oh no, oh no! Rich, I will slap your mouth up, girlie. Don't try me. I haven't seen Joey in years. Now give me a reason to swat them big fluffy lips up. I'll beat 'em up and make 'em puff like two milk biscuits!" I slapped the table with the swatter. "And you know I'll do it."

"Annnywaaaaaay," Rich said, pointing a finger at London. "You need to get your life together. Your thoughts together. Your face together. I made you, ***bish***! Before you came to Hollywood High you were nobody. You didn't know anyone, and wasn't anyone checking for you, boo-boo. *I* made you. I put you on the map, hooker. And you gonna toss me out on the lawn like I'm nothing? Attack me when I did nothing but come to your deathbed and show you my love and concern, and . . . my new diamond ring. But even half dead you were on a full tank of haterade. Had the whole world laughing at me."

"You wait one minute. I didn't have the world laughing at you. Your good girlfriend, Spencer, the dog walker, is the one who took the video of you, then leaked it."

Rich slammed her hand down on the table. "And that's beside the point. Don't you go blaming my good-good friend, you troll doll. This is my sister."

London grunted. "*Mmmph*. From what they're saying in the gutters, I've heard you have a ton of sisters."

I giggled.

"Whaaaat?! Lies! Lies! And more lies . . . !"

Then, as if on cue, the sound of trumpets blared, causing the whole café to fall silent.

"Hear ye, hear ye. Everybody make a way, make a way . . . make room. Heather C's coming through . . ."

Rich and I craned our necks to see what all the commotion was about. Even London looked.

I blinked.

What the heebie-jeebies . . . ?

It was Coco Ming wearing a sequined rainbow blazer with long tails. He wore a pair of red leggings with a pair of wing-tipped, lime green gaiters. A strand of black pearls dangled from his skinny rooster neck.

He and Heather waltzed into the café arm in arm, looking like they both fell off Mars, then into the lap of the Queen of Zamunda from that real old dusty movie *Coming to America*.

We watched in shock.

And horror.

Mouths dropped open as the two of them sauntered over to our table, pulled out chairs, then sat, crossing their legs.

"Yassss, tricks, yassss!" Heather snapped her fingers. "Pick your faces up."

Coco Ming leaned forward, popped his glossy, red-painted hooker lips, then said, "Guess who's back, *beeey-otches* . . ."

8

Heather

I could see her.

She sat in the back of the outdoor ice cream café El Amor in downtown L.A. Her beautiful chestnut-colored skin glistened in the afternoon sun. Her blond-streaked hair was flawless: an asymmetrical bob. Dipped to the left, the right side shaved, and the back faded...

But she couldn't see me.

I was a mess.

My red leopard catsuit looked stupid. And this fox stole was dumb. I'd been dressed like this all day, and by the time she'd texted me to come and chill with her, I had no time to change.

And now I couldn't catch my breath. I was so scared I'd be late meeting her that I ran from my car, across the parking lot, and then I stopped—a few steps from where she sat—and leaned against the back of a palm tree.

Breathe in.

Breathe out.

Suck in your stomach.

Wait.

I need to take out my compact.

I quickly pulled it from my purse and looked in the mirror.

I need gloss.

I rummaged through my purse.

Ugggggggggggg!

Nothing.

Okay. Okay.

Chill.

I peeked at her from around the tree.

Her smile was the prettiest I'd ever seen.

I wonder, is she thinking about me?

Would you knock it off!

Stop being so dumb, desperate, and thirsty!

You are so ridiculous and confused!

I shook sweat from my clammy hands and did my best to kill my thoughts.

Get it together.

You got this.

"Hey, Nikki! What's good, boo?!" I walked over to the small square table where she sat.

Relax. That was a little too hyped.

"Hey, girl!" She stood up and kissed me on the right cheek. Then the left. I *sooo* wanted to kiss her back, but I couldn't. My nerves wouldn't let me.

Nikki grinned. "Girl, I was just getting ready to text you. What took you so long?"

We sat down, and before I could respond, the roller-skating waitress sped over. "Happy days are here again!" The waitress smiled and slightly tugged at the ends of her pink-and-white-striped bow tie. "Welcome to El Amor café, where your ice cream dreams come true! Can I take your ice cream order, or do you need a few minutes?"

I was desperate for the super-deluxe, blond-brownie sundae with extra whipped cream, but I didn't want Nikki to think I was greedy, so I said, "I'll have a Diet Coke."

"A Diet Coke!" Nikki giggled, her dimples sinking into her cheeks. "That's like ordering a salad at a chicken palace. Honey, please. You must have a chocolate-dipped cone or something." She paused. Looked me over.

I felt like shrinking under the table.

I knew I shouldn't have ordered a Diet Coke.

Nikki glanced at the waitress. "Can you give us a moment?"

The waitress smiled and sped away.

Nikki placed her hand over mine. "Heather, is everything okay? If you don't like ice cream, we can leave. Or if something else is bothering you, we can talk about it."

"No. No." I flipped my hair over my shoulder and batted my lashes. "I'm fine. It's just that I need to watch my—"

"Please don't say you have to watch your weight...or your figure."

"Well, I do."

Her eyes popped open in surprise. "Please, you look fab! That body is killing it!"

I did everything I could to keep from blushing. "I'm not short and cute like you. I can't afford to gain a pound. You see how big my behind is?" *And yeah, I ordered it triple sumptuous silicone hotness, but so what? I had to say something. And besides, she didn't know that.*

She flicked her wrist and said, "Girl, bye. Do you know how many people would pay to have a behind like that?"

Of course I know.

I fought off a smile as she carried on, "I tell you what, I'll order my favorite sundae and we can split it. How's that?"

"Sounds like a plan."

Nikki looked over at the waitress and motioned for her to return to the table. "We'll have a super-deluxe, blond-brownie sundae."

Oh my God! I can't believe we have the same favorite sundae! "With extra whipped cream." I added.

"Coming right up." The waitress said.

Nikki laughed. "I thought you wanted a Diet Coke." She winked and stroked my cheek, and an awkward moment of silence slipped in between us. "I'm just teasing you." She stroked my cheek again, and more weird and quiet moments crept in.

"So tell me," Nikki said, excited, "how have you been? Wait. Hold up, you have to fill me in on how your day was at school? Did you serve them chicks?"

"I did it on 'em!" I slapped her a high five. "What! Yes! Slayed 'em! Laid 'em dead in the hills." I snapped my fingers. "Especially since I arrived in a helicopter."

"A what? A who?"

"You heard me. A helicopter."

The waitress quietly set our sundae on the table and handed us each a spoon.

"I'm sure if you google me I'm the hot topic on all the blogs!" I bragged.

"That is waaaaay over the top," Nikki said, shaking her head and dipping her spoon into her side of the sundae. "Who told you to ride in a helicopter? Your mother? Or your publicist? 'Cause that doesn't even sound like you."

"Doesn't sound like me... and why not?" I scooped up a spoonful of ice cream.

"'Cause, you're much more chilled than that. You're not extra like those other chicks."

"Meaning what?"

"Meaning, one of the other Pampered Princesses, now they would charter a helicopter just to get to school."

I laughed. "Yeah. They would. But they didn't. And the helicopter ride was cool. But wait, you should've seen Rich's face."

"I know it hit the floor."

"Straight cracked on the concrete. That attention whore was all up in my grill." I swirled my spoon into the whipped cream. "She came over to me and invited me for drinks."

"Rich?"

"Yes, Rich."

"Wait. I'm confused. I thought you two couldn't stand each other." Nikki took another spoonful of the sundae. "I thought you said Spencer was the decent one. When did you and Rich become friends?" She took another spoonful of ice cream.

"Spencer's okay, but she's two-faced. Always up in my business. And me and Rich, friends? Never. Eww."

"So then..." Nikki shook her head. "Never mind."

"What? Say it."

"No. I don't want you to think I'm being shady or anything."

"You? Shady? Never."

"Okay. No tea. No shade. But. I just don't get this whole Pampered Princess thing."

"What don't you get about it?"

"Why are you four always together? You don't really like each other. It's like you're the best of frenemies. 'Cause you can't stand to be around each other, and at the same time you can't get enough of one another."

"True. But I've known these chicks forever. And in the socialite world, it's about who you're connected to."

"So you have to be fake is what you're saying?"

"You're calling me fake?" My heart dropped into my stomach.

"I would never call you fake. There is nothing fake about you. You're kind, funny, sweet, pretty..." Her eyes locked into mine. "And I like you."

I sank my eyes into the sundae, quickly picked up a spoonful, and then said, "If I could, I would dump them tricks. But it's complicated. Besides it's fun making diss records about 'em." I looked back into her face. "And I like you too."

Nikki cracked up. "My boo's hit is number one on iTunes."

Her boo? I did all I could to kill the blush I felt creeping up. "Yeah, baby, baby!" I hit her with my best Biggie Smalls voice.

We slapped another high five. "Bam!" we said simultaneously and then burst into more giggles.

"Seriously though," I said. "You're right, None of us are friends...on most days..."

"On most days?"

"I mean, with Spencer I do go out of my way to talk to her at least twice a year. Her birthday and maybe Christmas."

Nikki snickered. "What about that girl London? What's up with her? She was all over the blogs and gossip mags when she tried to kill herself. Now that was sad. I couldn't believe it."

An unexpected vision of the time when I took one too many pills on purpose, only to wake up in the hospital getting my stomach pumped, danced before me. I swallowed. Blinked the vision away. "I feel sorry for London.

When you're going through a tough time like that, you usually just want someone to understand you. Talk to you. Love you."

She nodded, her eyes looking as if she understood. "You're right. You have to be feeling really depressed to see death as the only way out."

"Yeah, you feel depressed. Dumb. Rejected. Worthless. Like you're nothing. But I think London's getting better because she was in school today."

"Oh really? That's great. Did you talk to her?"

I frowned. "Absolutely not. Ever. I don't do London. I said I felt sorry for her. Understood what she may have been going through. I didn't say I liked her. I didn't say she was nice. That chick is a miserable, depressed, phony *beyotch* with mad issues. Ain't nobody got time for that? At least I don't."

"So what do you have time for?"

I swallowed. Shrugged. And took a chance. "You. I have time for you. Getting to know you."

She blushed. "Is that so? And what kind of time is that?"

"Time to be friends. And chill. Like we are now."

Nikki stared at me, and I could see that a million thoughts were going through her mind.

Scared that she thought I was fruity or, worse, stupid, I changed the subject and said, "You know, I'm still doing a reality show."

She blinked, and her eyes grew wide with surprise. "No, I didn't know that! That's wonderful!"

I gave her a quick and phony smile. "I guess."

She looked taken aback. "What? You're not happy about it?"

"Not really. Honestly, I just want my WuWu show back, or I'd like to star in another sitcom. Reality TV is so . . . so . . .

musty. And cheap and nasty. It's like performing on a cruise ship or the Vegas strip—where the has-beens go to die."

"You're not a has-been."

"I know."

"So then why do it?"

I sighed, "I didn't have a choice. Camille is broke and pathetic. My manager, Kitty, is a dog. I needed the money, and I needed to keep my face on TV."

"Have you ever thought about doing something other than TV? What about college?"

"College? Me? No ma'am," I chuckled. "No shade. I mean, that's cool for you. You wanna be a veterinarian and everything, that's wonderful. You were raised like that. But me, Hollywood is in my DNA."

"True. Your mother is a wonderful actress."

A washed-up actress turned drunk. "You're being way too kind. Especially after the way she treated you when you were at my house."

"It's okay. She just didn't understand us."

Us? There's an us?

Nikki continued, "Now, Heather, what does your father do? I've never heard you talk about him. Is he around?"

For a moment, I felt like Nikki had drop-kicked me in the throat, and I couldn't say a word.

I should tell her.

I scanned her eyes.

No. I don't know her like that.

Yes. I do.

She's cool.

But can she be trusted? Like, really, really trusted?

"Wassup?" Nikki asked, giving me a confused look. "Why are you looking at me like that?"

"I want to tell you something, but I'm not sure if I should."

She glanced around the room. "You can tell me anything. That's what friends are for. To confide in each other."

True. Tell her. I took a deep breath. "You really wanna know about my father?"

"Yeah. Tell me."

"He's Richard Montgomery."

Her mouth dropped. Then there was a long pause. She gasped. "Wait. Shut. Up. As in Richard Montgomery, my parents' neighbor, or as in Richard Montgomery MC Wickedness?"

"As in Grand Entertainment." I said.

She slapped a hand over her mouth. "As in Rich Montgomery's father."

"As in ding-ding-ding!" I said in my Maury Povich voice. "Richard Montgomery aka MC Wickedness. He. Is. The. Father."

Nikki gasped. "Shut. The. Front. Freakin'. Door! You and Rich are sisters?"

"Half sisters." I corrected her in a hushed tone.

"Wow. I'm speechless."

"Good. Because you can't say a word."

"I would never. So now it makes sense. This is why you put up with Rich?"

"No. Truthfully, I just found out. My mother finally admitted it, and all the other times she just brushed it off. And honestly, all of this makes me just not like Rich even more."

"Why?"

He already has a daughter. I swallowed. "Because she's our father's daughter... and I'm not."

Nikki looked taken aback. "Huh? And what does that mean?"

"Means, Rich is his baby. The one he wanted. Me? I'm his abortion nightmare in the flesh."

"Don't say that. Who told you that?"

"My mother."

"Heather." She reached for my hand. "Rich is not the only daughter he has. You are his daughter too, and you deserve to have a father."

He never wanted you. Camille's voice sliced into my thoughts.

I sighed. "All that sounds good, but he knows I exist. And he's never wanted me. Has never gone out of his way to get in touch with me. Meet me. Or anything." My eyes welled with tears.

What are you crying for? Camille's voice edged its way into my thoughts again. *Just suck it up and deal with the fact that you don't exist for him.*

Nikki reached over and dabbed at the wet corners of my eyes with the pads of her thumbs. "You shouldn't be this upset. You owe it to yourself to meet him."

"And how will I do that?"

"Just show up at his doorstep. Go and see him. Every girl wants to know her daddy."

He's not interested in you. Never has been, never will be. He has a family. And yeah, you may have his DNA, but he will never be your daddy. "Nikki, I know you mean well, but that's a terrible idea."

She carried on, "You're a Montgomery too."

You are a Cummings.

Nikki continued, "And most of the time, people are different once they find out you're family. He just might welcome you with open arms. Besides, you've never done anything to him. And Rich might not be that bad." She paused. "And yeah, she's a liar,"

"Check."

"She's scheming."

"All the time. Check. Check."

"Can't be trusted."

"Check. Check. Check."

"And she dates my boy Knox. Dogged 'im. Dragged him through filth. Lied about having a miscarriage and had his mind all messed up. Treating him like he's stupid. But whatever."

"So are you saying thots need relatives too?"

"Exactly. And from what you just told me, that is your sister."

"So, bottom line, what are you saying?"

"You give the Montgomerys a chance. There are always two sides to every story, and you owe it to yourself to know both."

I slowly shook my head. "I don't know. Sounds good, but my mother already warned me to leave it alone."

"Heather, trust me on this. I have a friend who just met her dad a few years back."

"Really? And what happened?"

"He loved her from the first time he met her. They are super close now, and she says she couldn't imagine her life without him. That's why I'm saying you should give it a try."

Maybe I should.

Maybe you should keep it movin'.

I want to know him.

He never wanted you. He has a daughter.

I'm his daughter too.

I shrugged. "Maybe you're right. I mean the first time I

confronted Camille about him, she dropped her drink and it crashed to the floor. I should've known then that everything after that was a lie. She can't think without a drink."

Nikki chuckled. "Heather, be nice. That's your mother."

"That's not my fault. If you knew Camille, you'd know that she never wastes liquor. She will Maxwell House a liquor bottle down to the last drop and then lick around the top in case she missed any."

Nikki cracked up. "You so wrong for that! Stop it."

"I'm so serious."

Nikki laughed so hard that tears shimmered in her eyes. A few seconds later, she looked down at her phone. "Girl, where has the time gone? I need to get back to San Diego. I have a class in the morning, and it's getting late."

She stood up and placed money on the table to pay the bill and the tip.

I stood as well and gathered my things.

As we walked to the car, we linked arms and walked shoulder to shoulder. "You know I've really enjoyed you." I said, really, really meaning it.

"Me too. I had a great time, honeybun." She giggled, squeezing my hand. "We should chill more often."

The butterflies in my stomach caused me to hesitate. "I was thinking we should too."

We stopped at her car. Nikki hugged me and kissed me on the cheek. "Call me in two hours. I should be in my dorm." Our eyes locked and lingered into each other's glare, until I broke the stare and looked away.

"Okay, Heather. Talk to you in a minute!"

I watched her as she slid into her car and started the engine, and a few seconds later she disappeared into the distance.

9

Rich

Dear Diary,

My thugged-out boo-love was everything sweetness was made of.

Almond Joy in the morning.

A Sugar Daddy at night.

Our love was hella right. Tight. And with us being engaged, it was for life.

There was only one problem: Some raggedy ho named Nya kept blowing up his phone. And how did I know it was that particular ho? 'Cause every time she called, her name and contact pic popped up on the screen.

Now, I'ma woman about mine. At all times.

And no, I'm not insecure or unsure.

But Justice *is a* man.

A fine one. Who eats groceries and has a third loving leg.

Therefore, I have to watch these dry mouth-thirsty skeezers, be on my wifey grind at all times, and let 'em know that that tall glass of swagged-out Yoohoo they sweatin' is what? Mine.

Damn. Real.

Anywho, back to how my night popped off. So, after our third round of sweet heat, Justice went to shower. And I swear the Gods of I-got-your-back-homie had to be looking out for me because Justice did what? Left his phone on the nightstand.

Ding!

Yaaaaas, honey, and a few seconds into me attempting to break the code, the phone did what? Rang!

Ding! Ding!

And whose face lit up the screen?

Nya.

Ding! Ding! Ding!

I clucked my tongue as I boldly answered the phone. "Yeah, umm hmm. Hello, Nya."

She hesitated. Clearly, I caught the tramp off guard. "Umm, hi. May I speak with Justice, please?"

I could tell by the sound of her shaky voice that this was a wrinkled ho. At least forty years old. All I could do was shake my head. 'Cause God knows them cougars be outta control. "Negative. How about no, you cannot. How about you need to tell me why you're on my man's phone? And how about this: You better answer my question without saying something slick. Otherwise, I will get up out this bed, the same bed that me and my man been laid up in all morning, come to your crib, and bust yo' ass. And I double dare you to say I won't." I paused, giving this tramp a chance to be daring and pop off. She didn't. So I continued, "Now why are you on my man's phone?"

Queen Wrinkled cleared her throat. "Let me try this again. May I speak with Justice, please?"

"Let me try this again. What part of him being cuffed

don't you get? What? You don't speaka English, trick? You need me to translate I will whup yo' azz over my man? Okay, here goes: I willo tappa-yo' arsio over my man. Got it, ho?"

"Rich," I looked up. It was Justice, standing in the bathroom doorway, wrapped in a towel, with fresh beads of water cascading over his shoulders and down his six-pack. He ice grilled me as he snapped, "Who is that and what is you doing on my phone?!"

I sucked my teeth and arched a brow. "You don't come at me like that! What, you in love with this ho? This yo' bish or something?"

"Yo, you outta control. Now gimme my damn phone!" He mushed me in the head and attempted to snatch it from me, but I refused to loosen my grip. I held the phone to my breasts with one hand and pushed him in the chest with the other. "Oh, you wanna mush me over some ho on your phone! I gathered the sheet and jumped to the floor. "Who is Nya, Justice? Huh? Who is this bish?"

His eyes popped open wide. "Nya? That's Nya on the phone!" The whites of his eyes turned to fire, and his jaw clenched. He mushed me again, and as I took my free hand and swung, he caught my fist and twisted my arm around my back. "Ahh!" I screamed. "Let me go!" His grip tightened. "You're hurting me!"

"Give. Me. My. Phone."

I dropped it, then kicked that ish across the room. "There you go!"

He pushed me, and I tripped face-first onto the bed. Immediately, I hopped up and rushed over to Justice, who was now holding his phone to his ear saying, "Nya, this Justice. Sorry about that. Wassup?"

"Oh, you just gon' apologize and play me by talking to this trap like it's nothing?" I reached for the phone but failed to snatch it out of his hand.

He palmed my entire face, gripped it, and shoved me back to the bed. "Yo, Nya. I'm sorry. Yo, no. Come on. I would love to open up at your club!"

Club?

"I swear, if you give me a chance, I won't bring no drama there." He paused. "I know you didn't appreciate it, and I apologize. But I didn't know she was going to do that. Can you think about it and get back to me?" He shook his head. "A'ight, yo. I ain't gon' sweat you. Thank you anyway." Click.

Now I was speechless and felt like garbage.

"Umm, Justice, baby—"

"Yo," He gripped me by the neck. "You gotta go!"

I could barely breathe, and the sheet I had wrapped around me was now dangling and twisting around my feet. "Stop!" I screamed. "I don't have any clothes on! Stop it!"

Justice didn't say a word as he continued to drag me toward the front door.

"Let me go! I don't have on any clothes."

Silence.

I did everything I could to pound his arm and loosen his grip on me. I failed, and before I could catch my breath or think of what to do next, Justice pushed me out the door, dropped a hard and swift kick on the side of my thigh, and slammed his door.

For a moment I wondered was I in the Twilight Zone? Or was I dreaming?

I kept banging, and banging, and banging on his door. "Justice, I'm sorry. Please, open up, I don't have on any clothes! Justice, please!"

"You two are at it again!" Justice's neighbor cracked her front door and spat into the hallway.

"You're minding my business again! You better shut that door, lady, before I run up in your mouth!"

She gasped. "I'm going to call the cops on you!" She slammed her door shut.

"Call 'em! I ain't scared!" I returned to pounding on Justice's door. "Justice! Please!"

Silence.

Nothing.

All I could hear coming from Justice's apartment was the echo of the TV. And there I stood, wrapped in a sheet, all of my things in Justice's place, and he was ignoring me.

My heart dropped to my feet, and an invisible kick rammed into my gut. I leaned against the wall and slid to the floor, and just when I swore I could cry forever, blaring police sirens were in the distance.

The neighbor! The police!

I gathered the sheet and practically flew to my car. Thank God, I had a keyless entry and a fingerprint starter; otherwise, tomorrow's headline would be RICH MONTGOMERY ARRESTED AT HER BOYFRIEND'S HOUSE, WRAPPED IN A SHEET.

I hurried out of the parking space, and as the police were racing in, I was zooming out, leaving Manhattan Beach behind me.

10

Rich

It's been three days. Seven hours. And too many slow freakin' minutes to count that I've been without my man. And I want him back.

Not now.

But right now.

I just can't take it any longer.

All I do is eat.

Sleep.

And think of ways to get my wifey status back.

I promise you, if I don't recuff my chocolate boo-thang soon, I'ma go crazy. And me going crazy is not the hot headline I need. Rich Montgomery goes loony. Psst, please. Not. I'm already dealing with some mysterious slum-slut who videoed Justice tossing me out of his apartment, wrapped up in a sheet, lookin' all ratchet-Greek.

I swear, these fools cannot let you live! All up in my privacy.

Got me all up in the blogs, with snot and tears covering

my face. That ain't hot. Had my tracks all showing. My edges all thick and bushy.

And because of that I'm now sitting here with my party planner, Natasha, and my mother, the groupie-excon turned Queen Mother Earth, and they are both looking at me all crazy. I tell you what, though, they not gon' throw too many more eye daggers, 'cause in ten point five seconds I'ma pop off. And it ain't gon' be pretty.

Snap. Snap. Boom!

"Rich," my mother ice grilled me. "Are you going to answer Natasha's question or not?"

I blinked. "Huh? What? What question?" I rolled my eyes over at Natasha, and she shot me a fake smile. Then I looked back over to Logan, who frowned in disgust. Her beady eyes dropped from my face to my stomach and back again. She did this three times before Natasha said, "I was asking were the colors still gold and white."

"No." My mother butted in. "Something tells me we'll be doing baby blue."

Natasha looked confused, and a feeling of just put your head between your legs and die washed over me. "Look, are we done here? 'Cause I gotta go." I looked at my watch. One p.m. Justice should be home by now. "I got somewhere to go. And for your information, the colors are not baby blue. They are still gold and white. Thank you." I picked up my Louis V and shoved the shoulder strap up my arm.

"Rich." My mother said sternly. "You better not move one inch."

I sucked my teeth, but judging by the look on Logan's face, she was prepared to drop-kick me at any moment, so I just stood there, leaning from one leg to the other.

"Natasha," I said. "You should have enough to finalize the party plans. The invites should be scrolls and delivered by way of a trumpeter."

"Okay, Rich." Natasha gathered her things. "Sounds like a plan."

"Thank you," my mother said to Natasha, but never taking her eyes off of me.

A few minutes after Natasha left, Logan started her BS and had the nerve to ask me, "How many months? And don't lie."

I blinked. Blinked again. Then cleared my throat. "You trippin'. How many months for what? Christmas?" I said sarcastically, "'Cause I don't know what you're talking about."

"Are you looking for me to bust you in the throat? Or beat you down like a woman in the street?"

I sucked my teeth. "Oh, here we go."

She stood up and walked over to me. She stepped out of her six-inch heels, and her nose was now pressed into my forehead. "You stay testing me."

"And you stay tryna fight me." I took a step back.

"Fight you? Little girl, please. I don't fight you, I eff you up 'cause you deserve it. Now I'ma ask you again—"

"I'm not pregnant. And you need to stop worrying about me and worry about your son over in England gettin' his swervin' swirl on with half of the French population."

My mother blinked her eyes like I'd just said something dumb. Ain't nothing dumb about me. Everybody knows people from England are French.

She gripped my cheeks. "How many months?!"

Silence.

"I tell you what, before I stomp two lives outta you, I'ma

give you a minute to think on the truth. But the next time I ask you how many months—which will be very soon—you better have a straight answer for me, or I'ma drag you by your tracks until you tell me the truth. And you know I will. All I know is that I'm not taking care of no babies, and you have already exceeded your abortion limit times two!"

I started to cuss this chick slam the freak out, for coming at me all crazy, but her ringing cell phone saved her life.

Logan loved to play Billy Bad Ass, but I kept my cool as she wildly loosened her grip on my face, stepped back into her heels, and answered her phone. "Yes," she said before leaving me standing there, "I'm on my way."

I watched her walk out of the room, and the moment she disappeared from my sight, I grabbed my car keys and jetted down the stairs and out the servants' entrance.

11

Spencer

Daddy knew I was watching him. He heard me knock on his door. Heard me walk in, then slam the door shut behind me. Heard me call out to him. Yet he defiantly stood there with his back to me—peering out the window—passing gas and digging and scratching his butt. Oooh, what a barbarian! This old hunched-back man was a dirty ole pig, clawing at his hind parts as if he were searching for some hidden treat.

Ugh.

He stood guard at the huge floor-to-ceiling window as if he were waiting for someone or something to come barreling through his suite's door to save him. From what, I wasn't so sure—maybe from himself, maybe from Kitty-Kitty-the-cat's-meow. Oh sure, Kitty avoided Daddy at all costs. I was certain she was afraid she might trigger some long-lost memory he kept tucked away in the corners of his little dusty, cluttered mind if she were around him. Of course she denied it. She brushed it off with a flick of the hand, claiming to despise the sight of him. Claiming she loathed the smell of him. Trying to make me *think* I was going cuckoo-cray-cray.

Mmmph.

There was nothing Looney Tune foolish about me. I was as sane and lucid as could be. The only kook-a-dook in this equation was Kitty Ellington. And that lady tramp was a goshdiggitydang heathenish liar! And I smelled her fear like I smelled the stench of a skunk.

It was rotten, just like she was.

And I was determined to get to the bottom of her funky ways if it was the last thing I did, even if it burned out my nose hairs and killed me in the process.

Daddy was the key to all her dirty little secrets.

I knew he was.

I felt it in the swell of my boobs and the arch in my back. 'Cause my back was arching, my hips just right, my boobs were shaking to the left and to the right.

Yesssss, yesss, goshdangit! I did that. Oops. I almost got swept up into the moment. All I needed were a set of pom-poms, and one of those cute little tennis skirts to turn this mother-suckey-suckey out.

Heeheehee.

I swung open the door to Daddy's suite and slammed it shut again.

He finally felt gracious enough to turn to me. Slowly. He sniffed his fingers. Then stared at me, hard.

Oh, two can play these games, I thought, folding my arms.

I tilted my head and stared back.

He squinted his eyes.

I squinted mine.

Then he asked, "Why am I here? Is it for ransom?"

"*Ransom?* Daddy, no. No one is holding you for ransom. This is your home."

He scowled. "My home is in the wild. Not here in this, this fortress. I'm king of the jungle."

"Well, sorry to inform you, your majesty. But there is no jungle. And, here, you're just *Daddy*."

He narrowed his eyes. "Then where are my children?"

I blinked. Ohfortheloveofpigfeetjuice! *Here we go with this again.*

I sighed. "Daddy, you only have one child. *Me*."

"Oh, I see. Then why am I being held hostage?"

"You're not a hostage," I said in the most sweetest, calmest voice I could muster. But inside I was churning. My guts were bubbling with agitation. My patience for daddy was wearing thinner than his hairline. But I was determined to stay loving and kind.

I glared at his shiny forehead, talking myself out of snatching the fresh-cut lilies from out of their crystal vase and, and, and—

"I demand my release. This instant." He jabbed a finger toward me. "You don't know who you're dealing with, you thief. I'll have you hung from a tree and tarred and feathered."

I took a deep breath. Forced my eyeballs from swirling around in their sockets. It was seven in the morning, and Daddy was trying my nerves already. I wasn't in the mood for any of his shenanigans. Not. To. Day.

I had to get to school.

I took another deep breath. Then the theme song for *Mission Impossible* started playing in my head. I pulled my Chanels down over my eyes and shimmied across the room in step to its beat. All I needed was some six-inch gladiator sandals and a black trench coat.

"No one gives a damn I'm missing, anyway," he said, sounding defeated, plunking down in one of the leather wingback chairs.

"Well, I do," I said gently. "But it's a good thing you're not missing. Then I'd have to go looking for you. I'd hunt you down real good too."

He grunted. "Yeah. That's right. Hunt me down like a wild boar. Then cage me in, before roasting me on an open fire."

I sat in the other chair beside his. I reached for his hand. "Oh, Daddy, stop. No one's going to roast you. Or cage you in." I crossed my legs, then patted his warm, frail hand. "Now, I might put a cute little studded collar around your neck and leash you to keep you from wandering off."

He squinted. Studied my face. Then asked, "Who are you again?"

I sighed. This was what I had to go through, moments when Daddy didn't remember my name or know who I was to him.

I fought the urge to dig my nails into his flesh. This wasn't his fault. I had to keep reminding myself of that to keep myself centered and on task. I had to remind myself *why* I was in here this morning.

"Da—um..." I caught myself from calling him *Daddy*. "You don't know who I am? Look closer." He leaned in closer, his nose barely touching mine. I could smell his morning breath.

It stunk.

Hot and funky.

After several moments of me holding my breath as he

stared me in the face, the *Mission Impossible* theme song started playing in my head again.

"Tell me your name," he demanded.

"Your mission, should you choose to accept it..."

Yes, yes! I accept! Bring it on, goshdiggitydangit!

I leaned over and kissed Daddy on the cheek, then stage-whispered. "It's me. Cleola Mae."

12

London

I was over him. I knew I was. But for some reason, my mind still reeled back to him.

The ghost of my past.

Justice Banks.

My first love.

The first boy I'd ever kissed. Really kissed. With an open mouth and lots of tongue.

The first boy I gave my mind, body, and soul to.

I was fourteen.

Young.

Dumb.

And blinded by fairy tales.

And make-believe happily-ever-after.

I was so swept up in the fantasy that he and I were connected forever that I gave up every part of me for him. Not because he asked me to or expected me to, but because I needed that boy like I needed air.

He'd quickly become my guilty pleasure. My dangerous

addiction wrapped in chocolate ropes of muscle and sweet warm kisses. He'd become essential to my living.

Had become my... *every*thing.

The air I breathed.

My heartbeat.

My total existence.

Everything I was, everything I ever thought I'd be, was because of him.

Justice, Justice, Justice...

My nightmare.

My worst mistake realized.

I would defy my own parents. Go against everything I was taught. Sneak off to be with him every chance I got. Knowing my parents would never approve of him. Never.

Because he was from the projects.

Because he was ghetto.

Because he was a hoodlum.

Still, my heart wanted what it wanted.

And it wanted Justice.

Wanted his warm touch.

Wanted his watermelon kisses.

Wanted his heated passion.

Whenever he wasn't around, every nerve in my body ached for him. I needed to hear his voice. Needed to feel his touch. Needed him in the softest places reserved only for him.

I'd given that boy the key to every part of me.

And what did he do with it?

He'd twisted and turned and yanked me apart.

Tore my heart out. Then stomped all over it.

Justice had taken my love for granted.

Mistreated me.

Disrespected me.

He didn't ever love me.

How could he?

All he ever did was love me down in the sheets, then leave behind his imprint and a bunch of empty promises. All he ever did was leave me in a state of panic. Kept me somewhere crouched down on the floor crying and wringing my hands every time he broke up with me. All he did was keep me crazed and desperate and chained to pain, snotty-nosed and boo-hooing every time he refused to return any of my calls. All he did was have me begging and crying and pleading for him to answer his phone, for him to take me back, to give me another chance after chance after chance to do better, to love him more. To prove to him that I was all he needed.

But I wasn't.

"Stupid-azz trick! You're pathetic..."

"If you was a dude, I'd break ya jaw...for bein' so effen stupid..."

"...If I woulda knew how silly you was, I woulda never effed with you from the rip..."

"You make me sick, yo. Wit' ya ugly self. You insecure. Fat, nasty..."

I'd always been a cameraman's dream, but Justice had said many times I was ugly. That four-letter word *ugly* slashed into my psyche and had me believing him. That I was ugly. That I wasn't worth a camera's flashbulbs.

"...Look at you, six-foot-tall, giraffe-neck self. Big-foot Amazon. Don't nobody want you. I was the best thing you'll ever have..."

"Stop it!" I hissed, holding my hands up over my ears. "Just shut up! Get out of my head!"

I shot up in bed—the same bed I'd laid up in so many days and nights with Justice, reaching over and clicking on the light on my nightstand. I pulled my knees up to my chest and wrapped my arms around them, rocking. Allowing my tears to fall unchecked.

"London Elona Phillips, will you marry me?"

"I can't wait to spend my life with you... you're so beautiful. Ain't nobody ever gonna love you like me. You're all mine, London..."

Oh God! What a crock of lies!

How could I have been so blind?

Justice had had me stuck on stupid. Had me so caught up in the thrill of doing something I knew I shouldn't have been doing, all for the sake of experiencing that same exact rush I'd felt the very first time I'd done it.

That boy had me playing Russian roulette with my life *and* my inheritance. Because had my mother ever caught us together, she would have certainly snatched my trust fund away from me, banishing me to a life of soup kitchens, flea markets, and sidewalk shoe sales.

I'd thought I'd been the perfect girlfriend. But apparently not perfect enough. Aside from not hooking him up with Rich, like I was supposed to, I'd done everything else right. I let him sex me down whenever he wanted it. I'd drop whatever I was doing to be with him whenever he'd be kind enough to make time for me. I didn't stress him. Didn't question him. Didn't smother him—well, tried not to. Still, I gave him his space. Let him do him. But, obviously, that still wasn't enough.

Silly of me.

I reached up and swiped tears from my face. Justice had been cancerous. A user. And, finally—thanks to him breaking up with me, I'd learned to cut him out of my life. He'd given me no choice when he'd chosen Rich over *me*. Still, the scars were fresh. The pain was real. He had hurt me. Cut me deep.

But I was healing. And therapy was really helping me see the light. And, *yes*, I was over the likes of Justice Banks. But what I wasn't over was my so-called friendship with Rich. I thought I was. But seeing her at school confirmed what I'd been trying to ignore.

I missed her.

I missed our banter.

Missed our sisterly fights.

We were frenemies, for a lack of a better word to describe our love-hate relationship. And I was torn and confused, and one big ball of contradictions. I liked and loathed her at the same time. I admired and despised her equally.

True, she made me sick. But I was sicker without her than I was around her.

True, I wanted to smack the crap out of her, but I wanted to hug her too.

True, Rich Montgomery was toxic and poisonous, but she was also a good-time party girl and lots of fun.

And she was right.

I *did* owe her an apology.

For not being a good friend to her, for going behind her back and telling her ex-boyfriend Knox (the boyfriend I didn't know she even had because she'd been sleeping with other boys and had been calling another boy, Corey—a senator's son, from Hollywood High—*her* boyfriend) that she'd had an abortion, not a miscarriage, like she'd lied and told him she'd had.

I'd done it to break them up.

Her obsession with Knox had become an unexpected

obstacle in a much bigger plan, to get her to fall for Justice. First, I had to introduce her to him. But before I could make that happen, I needed to put a wedge between her and Knox.

I needed her single and vulnerable.

And ready to fall into Justice's waiting arms.

But then Justice turned on me. Said I wasn't moving fast enough. That he was sick of waiting for me to make moves for him. That he was taking matters into his own hands, which is what he'd done when he went behind my back and called her.

So how could I be mad at her for falling head over heels for Justice when she'd had no clue about me being with him or the fact that she was only going to be used for his own personal gain?

In honesty, I couldn't hold her whorish ways against her. She was what she was. So it was only a matter of time before she spread open her thighs and welcomed Justice into her mantrap.

Still, I owed her the truth. That Justice and I had been boyfriend and girlfriend since I was fourteen. That we'd been scheming, plotting, planning from the moment he and I started going together to get him his very own record deal. That the plan was for me to introduce them; he'd pretend to like her, then they'd start kicking it, then eventually dating.

I knew Rich was a whore—and so did all the teen tabloids. Knew she was hot and easy for fine, rugged boys.

Justice was just that.

And he could sing. Really sing.

So his dream to become a famous singer to secure our future so that we could be together became my dream too. I wanted what he wanted. To see his name plastered all over billboards and his face on the cover of every magazine, from *Rolling Stone* to *Vibe*.

The plan was foolproof. Or at least I thought it would be.

But then things unexpectedly changed.

I changed.

I'd had a change of heart.

I'd tried to back out of the plan. Tried to get him to reconsider, maybe go independent. But he wasn't trying to hear it.

"Yo, you must be on crack! Talkin' about some independent. I haven't been puttin' in all this time with you to be hustlin' out of the trunk of my whip. I coulda stayed in New York for that..."

Needless to say, that had turned into another one of Justice's nasty tirades, with him belittling me, all because I was having second thoughts. He just didn't get it. I hadn't planned on liking the boom-bop-crunk-it-up drama queen known as Rich. Hadn't planned on getting close to her. Hadn't planned on halfway loving her like a stepsister.

Yes, she was a loudmouth. Yes, she was a bully. Yes, she was hateful. Yes, she was a scandalous ho-bag. But, still, she'd been the closest thing to a friend out here. She'd shown me around California. And we'd had some fun times together. She was Tinseltown royalty and had gotten me into all the hot spots without a second glance.

No, she wasn't a loyal friend. Heck, the girl probably couldn't spell *friend*. But she'd still been a half of one, nonetheless.

However, what I hadn't planned on was Justice really playing *me* for her. Or for him to sleep with her slutty butt, even though it was supposed to be just an act, while he was *still* with me. Nor had I planned on him really wanting to be with her.

No, no, no.

I hadn't planned on that.

So, sadly, everything had backfired in my face.

I'd lost my dignity.

Lost my self-esteem.

Lost my will to live.

And lost Justice to a whore.

But losing him to her sadly forced me to see the truth about him.

That he was never any good for me.

That he was trouble.

That he never, ever deserved me.

Although I was convinced that Rich and Justice deserved each other, she still had the right to know the truth.

I glanced over at the pile of gossip magazines that sat at the side of my bed. Rich's face smirked over at me from one of the covers. I closed my eyes and wished she'd wake up in the morning and be cursed with crow's feet, then reached over and swiped the pile of trashy publications to the floor.

I settled back into bed, clicking off my lamp.

Yes. Tomorrow the truth would clear the air between Rich and me.

And set me free.

13

Rich

"Yo, for real, yo?" Justice said, as he leaned against the door frame, with one bushy eyebrow arched and the other dipped low. He pointed behind him to his apartment. "Didn't I just put you outta here the other day, yo? And you think you just gon' show up to my spot like it's all good? Oh hell naw."

My heart thundered, and the Goddess of Eff-Him-Girl told me to gather my cuteness and my pride and leave his busted behind right here.

But I didn't.

Instead, I stretched my hand toward his face and tried to rub his beard, something he usually loved for me to do. But not today. Today he pushed my hand away. "You buggin'."

"Don't be like that, JB. You my baby-boo. My honeydew. My destiny. My pop-pop-get-it-get-it-daddy. And I'm here 'cause I know you miss me, and I miss you too. So let's make it do what it do and be boos again."

His brown gaze told me he was unimpressed, and his

lips confirmed it. "Word is bond, yo. Here's what you gon do: Step." He flicked his fingers and practically mushed me in the head. "You don't come up over here without calling. Unannounced. Runnin' up to my crib like somebody stole yo' phone and yo' bike."

I was trying to be patient and play nice, but I could feel my attitude about to shift, which meant Justice was on his way to being cussed out. I sighed, "Justice, you know how many times I've been here and not called you, and you let me in? Don't front. Now I'm trying to be nice to you, come inside, and turn you out. You trying my patience, though."

He shook his head. "Your mouth never stops, yo. For real you need to be slapped in it and be made to eat the cake, Anna-Mae."

I started to roll my eyes, but instead I bit the inside of my jaw and remained silent. Not because I didn't have anything to say but because I was not in the mood to be tearing it up outside his front door. I could take it to his head in private. This way we could passionately make up, like we always did.

"Justice—"

"I'm serious, yo. Step. Then when you get to wherever you goin', call me back and ask for permission to come over here."

"You buggin'."

"Bye, Felicia."

Wham!

He slammed the door in my face and left me standing there, looking mortified and feeling stupid. I couldn't believe he just played me like that! It's okay, though. It's cool. 'Cause I'm done here. Finished. Eff him. Eff his mama. And eff the trap house he grew up in!

I stormed to my car, peeled outta the parking lot, and

raced up the highway. If he thought I was about to ask for permission, then he was crazier than I thought. I wish I would call him. Psst, please. Clutching pearls. Rich Montgomery don't do that and don't play that.

I turned the radio up and did everything I could to block out thoughts of Justice and jam to Jasmine Sullivan's Reality Show.

Then it hit me. *Call Corey.*

Yes! My ex-boo-thang. He always wanted me, so I knew I could spend some time with him and get Justice off my mind. I dialed his number, and he answered on the first ring, "Whatup?" He whispered.

"Hey, poo!"

"Hey, wassup?" He continued to whisper.

"No. I wanna see you. And why are you whispering?"

"Ohhhh, about that." He hesitated. "I gotta new side chick. I can only handle two chicks at a time. And I can't tell you her name, but I can tell you this: She's a Kardashian. So you already know what's up, I gotta get this sex tape poppin before she move on to the next. So don't sweat it. They don't let the same dude hit it for long. So the side chick spot will be vacant in a minute. A'ight? You good, though?"

Click! I hung up on him. I can't believe he asked me, am I good. Hell no! I need the comfort of a man!

I turned off the highway and into the drive-through of Buffalo Wild Wings. After paying for my order of twenty extra-hot wings, I called Knox.

Brnggg...

"Hello?"

He was my baby-pop even though I hadn't seen or heard from him in months. And things ended real nasty, but still, he could not resist me. "Hey, poo!" I said lovingly.

"Rich?"

"Yeah, Knox. It's me. How are you?"

"This is really you, Rich?"

"Yeah."

"Oh, okay. Just making sure before I hang up on yo' azz." *Click.*

Done! Absolutely finished. I couldn't chill with Corey. Knox turned on me. And after I practically had to bust my mother upside the head, I was not going home.

Call Justice! No!

You know you miss him.

I know this.

Then for once, just swallow your stupid pride and call him.

I pulled in a deep breath, then pushed it out.

Okay. Okay. I'ma call him. But if he talks slick, I'ma cuss him out.

Brngggg... Brngggg... Brngggg...

"Yeah, wassup?" He answered.

I sighed. "Hey, poo."

"What you want?"

I hesitated, and for a moment, I thought about hanging up but quickly changed my mind. "I wanna come see you."

"For what?" He said dryly.

"'Cause you my baby. And I miss you, and miss those lil tongue tricks you do, and the way you make my honey heat. And I know you miss me too."

"Yeah, a'ight, whatever. Your mouth too slick, yo."

"I'm not trying to be slick. I'm trying to make up."

"Well, make up then."

Deep breath in. Deep breath out. "I can show you better than I can tell you. Can I come over?"

"You gon' know how to act? And if you say anything other than yes, I'ma dead this. You a wrap. I'm over this dumbness with you. You know I got mad feelings for you, but I swear, yo. You gon' have me bust you in your mouth."

"Yeah, umm hmm. Yes. I'ma know how to act. I'm not gon' talk slick. I'ma change my ways, poo. I promise. You know it's hard, though. It's hard being me."

"Yeah, a'ight. Whatever, that's what your mouth says."

"Is that a yes? Can I come over?"

"Nah. You on punishment. Hit me up tomorrow."

14

London

The next morning, I spotted Rich at her locker. *Great, she's alone.* The fact that she didn't have her little one-girl hype squad with her was a good thing. Still, I didn't know what to expect. Rich was unpredictable. Erratic. Ratchet. And her *ghetto*-ness had no boundaries. She'd make a scene just for the heck of it.

She lived for the drama.

And the spotlight.

Because she was a self-proclaimed attention whore.

I took a deep breath, relieved that my morning cleanse had rid me of my excruciating bout with gas and bloating, and mustered up my confidence, taking tentative steps toward her, my heels clicking against the polished floor; each determined step causing anxiety to creep up in me.

"Here's my friend's number," I heard in my head, replaying the night I'd handed Rich a shiny business card with Justice's name embossed on it. It was the first part of the master plan. *"Call him."*

What a disaster. *Mmmph.* The best-laid plans of mice and men, I thought, as my mind flashed back to the poem "To a Mouse," which I'd read in my ninth-grade literature class about plans going astray no matter how well thought out they might have been.

Mmmph.

Always expect the unexpected.

"Have you spoken to Justice?"

"Justice? Who's that...? Oh wait. You're talking about that sweet piece of chocolate, that stud daddy, who you acted all stank and overprotective over? The one you wanted to introduce to me?"

"Yeah, him. Justice, who you practically seduced in front of me."

"Girl, bye. He's cute and all. But I'm not checking for him like that. That boy has issues. I don't do issues... why would you try to hook me up with some jerk like that? He doesn't even know how to play the sideline. He's too busy tryna be all front and center. I can't mess with him. He'll ruin my life. And disrupt my get-right with my man. And I can't have that..."

I blinked. Swallowed. Pushed back the memory. Of that day at Club Tantrum. Of that horrid conversation. Of Rich admitting she'd whored herself out to Justice.

The closer I got to Rich's locker, the more anxious I became. I felt myself shrinking in my heels.

Girl, relax. What's the worst that can happen?

We tear up the hallway.

I silently hoped the boom-bop queen remained civil. That she wouldn't become defensive. That her loud mouth wouldn't get too reckless. I didn't want this to turn ugly. But if she pressed it, I'd have no problem banging my fists upside her head. Well, that's if she struck first. I wasn't going to lay hands on her first. Not this time. No. I was going to stay classy and approach her like the lady I was.

But Rich didn't always respond well to niceties. Sometimes you had to step down and meet her where she was. On the street corner, hugging the block like the thugette she was.

I shook my head. No. Negative thoughts wouldn't do. I had to focus. Stick to the plan. Give her the truth. Then go on my merry way, leaving her to marinate in its juices.

I fluffed my hair. Took another deep breath. Then forced a smile. I could do this. I was London Phillips, for God's sake. I'd been pretending all my life.

I cleared my throat. "Um. Rich. Can I have a word with you?"

She knelt down and started rummaging through the bottom of her locker, not once giving me a glance. "Uhhh, no. You may not." She said nastily, stuffing a few colored folders into her oversized bag, then—as if she'd remembered she didn't come to school to learn—she pulled them out of her bag and tossed them back into her locker before standing up.

She pulled out a lighted travel mirror and started gliding a coat of gloss onto her plump lips.

I twisted mine in response and kept from rolling my eyes.

"Listen, Rich," I said, mindful to keep my voice low, my tone even, "I really need to have a word with you."

She grunted. "Then have it. Then be on your way. I don't do you, London. You're a snake. And I have no use for you."

I blew out a breath. "Well, can you at least look at me?"

"No, ma'am. I'm allergic to your big face. And the last

thing I need is my eyes hurting first thing in the morning. You're ugly, London. Zoo ugly. And I will not be blinded by your hideousness. So state your business, then go crawl back in whatever sewer hole you slithered out of."

I blinked. "It's obvious you're looking for a fight. But I'm not—"

"A *fight*?" she snapped, finally eyeing me. "Girl, bye. I'm a lady. I don't fight. I'm saved. Sanctified. And too damn blessed to be fighting nobodies."

I sighed. "Okay, I see you want to sling insults."

"*Insults?* Bye, lady. Not once have I insulted you. I've stood here, letting you blow your dragon breath all up in my space, killing up good oxygen cells. And not once have I mentioned how atrocious you are. Or how pathetic you are, *Lonnndon*."

"Listen. Say whatever you want. I'm coming to you to apologize."

She batted her lashes. Then stepped back. "You're *apologizing* to *moi*? Uh, for what, Lonnnndon? For being ugly? For being two-faced? For being a lying trick?"

She folded her arms and tapped her heeled foot.

"Take your time. I'll wait for the lies. That's all you're good for, L-Boogie. *Lying*."

I cringed. *L-Boogie* was what Justice had once called me in front of her during another one of his unannounced visits to my house. Days had gone by with no word from him. Then, as if on cue, he'd shown up—waltzing into my bedroom, after one of our many quarrels and him being absent for days—just as Spencer was swinging open my suite's door and storming out, causing her to practically knock him over. Rich stood in the middle of my bedroom, meowing and purring at the sight of him. Then she practically pounced on him, throwing herself at him. She'd bounced and shook her D-cups in his face and practically offered to have his baby right there on the spot.

And he'd grinned.

And drooled.

And flirted.

And nearly offered up his bedroom services right there in front of me, as if I wasn't in the room, as if I didn't exist or matter.

Then Rich scribbled her number down on a piece of paper, and . . . and . . . he'd taken it. That was the beginning to my end, the ending to my love story.

And now this . . .

"I'm sorry," I pushed out, hoping like hell my words sounded sincere. I was sorry. Sorry for ever allowing myself to like this girl. Sorry for ever concocting such a ludicrous idea to hook her and Justice up in the first place. How silly of me to think that it would have ever worked the way *I* wanted it to.

Rich narrowed her eyes at me. Tilted her head. "You're sorry for *what,* London? *Sorry* for telling Knox them lies about me . . . ?"

I blinked. This girl was delusional. *They weren't lies. You didn't miscarry. You were up in the hills of Arizona, stretched out and strapped on a table having your insides vacuumed out. You told me this!*

"I told *you* that lie about being in Arizona just to see what you'd do. I don't believe in abortions. I'm team Morning After pill. All day. But, anyway, Spencer was right about you. You're two-faced. She'd told me you'd go running back with that bone between your teeth, like the rabid dog you are. I knew I couldn't trust you."

Then why'd she slap Spencer? She had to have thought Spencer was the one who'd told Knox. Right? I know what

I'd seen. And what I'd heard that day in the hallway when Rich punched a locker. She was livid. Tears had sprung from her eyes as I led her into the girls' lounge. That wasn't acting. There was no pretending. Rich had thought Spencer had betrayed her, as I wanted her to.

And then I egged her on, goaded her into handling Spencer.

"The best way to an enemy is with a smile. Get her away from her purse," I'd told her. *"Pretend to be real nice and sweet, then reel your hand back when she least expects it and slide her face across the floor... leave your business card in her face... you step up to her face. Sling her with words. Then you strike!"*

"It was all Spencer's idea," Rich said, pulling me from my thoughts, "for me to slap her down in class to make you *think* that I believed that *she* was the one who blabbed her knob slobber to Knox. Girl, bye. The joke was on you. You fell for it hook, line, and sinker. You're an epic fail, *Lonnndon*. A total waste!"

I blinked. No. No. That couldn't be. *This girl is crazier than I ever imagined. And I'm the one with the shrink.* My heart started pounding in my chest. I fought to keep from balling my hand into a fist. No, no, no. I wasn't about to let Rich lure me into a catfight. Not today.

She slammed a hand up on her thick hip. "I'm waiting, *Lonnnndon*. What are *you* sorry about? *Sorry* for being born? *Sorry* for taking my kindness and goodness for granted? Sorry for..."

I swallowed. "I'm sorry for not telling you about Justice and me."

She frowned. "Excuuuuuse *you*? Come again. What about *you* and *my* man?"

I swept my eyes around the hallway, hoping no one was

trying to eavesdrop on our conversation. So far, no one seemed interested in what was going on with us, at least not at the moment. "Can we speak in private?" I asked, keeping my voice low.

"No, heifer. We can't. So say what you gotta say, *Lonnndon*, and get up out of my face. Your breath is killing my nostrils."

I pressed on, ignoring her comment about my breath, which I knew was minty fresh. "I'm sorry for trying to hook you up with Justice. I should have told you that we were going together. That we planned—"

"Bwahahahahahaha!" Rich laughed, buckling over and clutching her stomach. "Bwahahahahahahaha! The lies you tell!" She cackled long and hard, catching me totally off guard. "Ohmygod, *Lonnnndon*! Good one! Hahahaha-hahahaha."

She straightened herself. Dabbed tears from her eyes. "Ooh, you really tried it, boo-boo." She shouldered her bag, then pointed a finger at me. "Now let me get you right together, little girl. Trick, you must be really feeling your Wheaties this morning, stepping to me like you holding the number one slot. Get over yourself, *Lonnndon*. Justice would *never* have *you*, tramp. You're not his type."

"Well, I was his type for two years."

She laughed. "Girl, bye. He told me you'd try to say some desperate mess like that. Get ya life, boo. You have issues, *Lonnndon*. Justice told me all about how thirsty you were. Tricking him to come over to your house, then start begging him to do it to your ole nasty butt. Who does that? Begging some boy to smash you out. Ugh. You're sickening, *Lonndon*. Now I see why Doctor Corny dumped you. You're pathetic, girl. Justice told me how he felt sorry for you because you didn't have any friends back in New York.

"All your mother ever did was drag you around to casting calls, filling your big-bubble head up with lies that you'd be the next Tyra Banks. And look at you. The only thing you and Tyra Banks will *ever* have in common is those big-azz foreheads. So get over yourself, *bish*. All you are, all you'll ever be, is a Top Flop. A washed-up, wannabe runway model. Justice saw how lonely and pathetic you were and tried to take you under his wing and be a big brother to you, but all you ever tried to do was get into his boxers. Get it together, *Lonnnndon*. Accept the fact that Justice and I are together. That we're happy. And in love. And we *will* be married. So there is nothing you can say *or* do that is going to come between us. Face it. I got the ring ...*and* the man. And all you have is a miserable life."

I swallowed. Fought back tears. Mortified, I swept a quick glance around to see who'd overheard her outburst.

"Ohmygod!" I hissed. "You're delusional."

"*Trick*, the only one delusional is *you*."

I shook my head as sadness washed over me. Not for me. No, this, this feeling of melancholy was for her. Justice had really brainwashed her, like he'd once done me. "You know what, Rich. I feel sorry for you..."

"No, ho. Feel sorry for yourself. Look at you. You're lonely. Desperate. And effen miserable. You're jealous. Nobody likes you, London."

"Okay, Rich. Whatever you say. You think you've snatched the brass ring—"

"Brass ring?" she snorted, fanning her ring finger in my face. "Trick, this is all platinum and bling, baby. Ain't *nothing* brass about this right here. Get it right."

"Okay, Rich. Have at it then. You think your life is so perfect. Enjoy it while it lasts, sweetie. But know this: That little fairy tale you're holding onto is going to go up in flames real fast. And you're going to soon find out that *your* life isn't all that picture-perfect after all."

"Ha! My life is everything *you* wish you had. I have two happily married parents. And a man"—she ran her manicured hand over her body, then thrust her hips—"who sings me sweet lullabies and knows how to rock my body to sleep."

I felt my knees buckle. *Don't let this girl drag you down, London*. I rolled my eyes. "Yeah, okay. And when everything around you comes crashing down around your cute little pudgy feet, remember this, Rich: You've been warned."

"Warned? *Beeeeyotch*, please!" she snapped, finally slamming her locker shut and raising her voice two decibels higher just as the bell rang. Her outburst caused a few heads to turn in our direction. "You wish you could be me, whore! Well, newsflash, boo-boo: You can never, *ever* be me. While your life is hanging on life support, mine is fabulous! So kiss my plump, juicy azz! Jealous trick!"

She stormed off, her hair bouncing over shoulders and her heels clicking like angry drums as her hips shook down the hall.

I willed my heeled feet to move, but I was stuck. Jaw dropped, the palms of my hands sweating, the balls of my feet cemented to the floor, I stood there in the middle of the hallway—being bumped and shouldered by kids racing by to get to wherever they needed to be—feeling ridiculously embarrassed.

In spite of feeling myself unraveling, I kept my head up and ignored everyone's muttered jeers as I resisted the urge to go on a killing spree and throw sharp elbow jabs in response to being jostled in the hallway.

Relax. Relate. Release.
Breathe in. Breathe out.
Rich might have gotten the last word, that time.
But that *beeeeeeyotch* had it coming.
And the last laugh would definitely be on me.
Trust and believe.

15

Heather

"I need a favor," I said to Coco as we sat in the school's eighteenth-century-inspired library, having our fraps and attending to our business.

And yeah, it was only ten a.m.

And yeah, me and Coco should've been in class.

But so.

Whatever.

I didn't clock into life until at least noon.

And a promise to be Coco's lookout was the *only reason* why I'd dragged myself to Hollywood High this early.

Therefore and forever more, the last place I was about to be was in front of some teacher and her sweatin' me.

Oh no.

Not happenin'.

So what I was gon' do? I was gon' sit right here and chill. Cross my legs, wait for the third-period bell to ring, and help my homie serve the brunch-time stoners some Beauty, LSD, Xanies, molly, K-2/spice, and weed.

Coco cleared his throat and wiped invisible sweat from

his pale yellow brow. "A favor? Is that what you just said to me? Oh no, honey-boo-boop. I don't do favors."

I frowned. "And why not?"

"The last time I promised a favor, I was in K-Town, twerkin' on a bar top, next to a dragged-out Westwick—catch that tea—the bartender whispered something to me. And I said, 'Sure. I got you. Anything you need.' And before I knew it, I was naked, being videoed, and my truffle butter was about to be snatched—"

"Oh my God! Stop right there! I can't breathe!"

A vision of Coco's naked pancake bootie almost killed me. I dry heaved and was seconds away from throwing up in my mouth, while Coco leaned back in his chair, giving me a moment to soak his nasty story in.

This mothersucker had to be high *and* cray-cray.

I squeezed my eyes shut and put my hands up, hoping to rid my mind of the visual bullet that just shot through it. "What the freak kinda story was that?" I popped my eyes open wide. "You see me drinking my frap! You see this! Ugg!"

I sucked my teeth, and Coco looked down at his hot pink nails and picked at a cuticle. "Bish, don't do me." He lifted his head and swung his bangs, and his tiger-eye contacts pierced through me. "You know how I get down. Jesus is real. And thou shalt not be naked on a video is one of the eleven commandments. It's in the book of Thotlations, next to Rich's picture."

Just when I was ready to reach across this table and slap the ish outta Coco for being so gross, I fell out laughing!

The librarian shot me the "shut up" face. And I shot her a face back that clearly said, "Whatever." Then I topped it off with a flick of the wrist, that said, "Girl, bye."

I returned my attention to Coco. His story was entertaining for about two point five minutes, but then it went left, and he was going on and on too freakin' long. Pissin' me off all over again.

Coco carried on, "Did I tell you about this rapper C-Biddy?"

I didn't answer. I just twisted my lips.

Coco never noticed. He batted his lashes and continued, "Well, honey, he must've forgotten I had hair on my chest and thought I was a fish. So I had to tell 'em, don't let this padded bra get you messed up, bruh. You better sit down. And guess what he was mad about?"

I couldn't care less. "What, Coco?" I said with a drag.

"'Cause I didn't wanna be his down-low secret. I told him, 'Either love me up high or don't love me at all. I got standards. And if you wanna get up in my groceries, then you gon' have to respect me...'"

I couldn't believe this.

It never failed.

Ev. Ver. Reeeeeee time I wanted to talk about me, and what I was going through, he *alwaaaaaaaaaays* turnt up and turned it into Coco's drama hour. And he knew the bell would ring in fifteen minutes, and the hallways would be full with weed and pill heads on deck.

He knew this.

Yet.

He always flapped his back-alley, pig-fat-injected lips, moaning about his life and his whacked-out business, until time was up and all I got to say was... well... nothing.

But that was gon' end today.

I cleared my throat, sucked my teeth, and tapped my nails on the table. Coco continued running his mouth, so I did it again. Cleared my throat, loudly. Sucked my teeth. Long and hard. And practically banged a fist into the table.

Coco looked at me like I had lost my mind, but before I could say anything, the scrawny librarian with the bleached-blond hair and the fake orange tan was at our table. She spewed, "Excuse you, but this is a library. Quiet."

"That's what I'm saying." Coco added, giving me fever. "WuWu, how rude. I mean really. You bringing drama to the library? I had no idea you were so hood. What are you over there going through?"

The librarian squinted and shook her finger with every word. "If I have to come to this table again, you two will be paying Mr. Westwick a visit." She grunted and stormed away.

Coco blinked and whispered in disbelief, "That was so low budget of you. You need to change your ways and get that ratchet fish outta you. What you need is a pinch of beauty. I got a lil taste for you on the house. 'Cause you real bugged out right now. And I don't need you servin' my customers all crazy and deranged."

"You know what, Coco, you got hella nerve," I said in a hushed tone. "As much as I do for you, I say the words 'Do me a favor' and you lose it. The only favor I wanted was for you to listen to me without judgment."

Coco yelled in a loud whisper, "I resent that! I never judge! I am live your life and twirl, honey." He snapped his fingers. "And you know this. Don't play me crazy, Daisy."

"Then why didn't you just say yes instead of telling me some nasty story about your truffle butter?!"

"Nasty?" Coco blinked. Blinked again. "I'ma let that go," he said in an exhausted undertone, " 'Cause right now you're acting like you need a hug. So go on, diva. Proceed. Coco is here for you, baby. Coco is here. What's going on? Camille tripping again? Kitty back to making you piss litter style and do things her way?"

"No."

"Don't tell me you're homeless again? You know that

time you was in rehab and I paid y'all rent? Well, Camille never gave me back my money, so I can't do that again. You my girl and all, but I'm done withcho moms. If it's up to me and you need my money, y'all gon' be back on the streets."

I snapped, raising my voice and then quickly lowering it. "My rent is paid up for the year. Thank you."

"Eww, I'm impressed."

"Funny."

"So tell me. Wassup?"

I took a deep breath, looked around the room. The librarian rolled her eyes at me and then returned to looking at her computer screen. I looked up at the clock. I had five minutes left to spit this out.

"What?" Coco said impatiently.

I took another deep breath. *Just say it. Okay... here goes.* "Remember you gave me my welcome home party at Club Noir Kiss?"

"Yeah, girl! Miss Coco did that! That party was the B.O.M.B. It was er'thang. Yaaaaaaas, bish. Yaaaaaaas! I remember it." He vogued in his seat, then stopped abruptly. "What about it?"

"Well... I met this girl."

"So. And?"

"Well... ummm..." I popped my lips. "Okay... umm..."

"You can't be serious."

"Serious about what?"

He leaned into me, struggling to control the low tone of his voice. "What's with all the umms and lip pops? Just spit it out!"

"If you would be quiet, I could finish my sentence."

"I wish you would."

"Look, I met this chick."

"You said that. Now what about her?"

"I, umm, think I kind of like her."

Coco stared at me like I was crazy, then he grabbed his Birkin bag and started packing up his things. "I didn't come here for no foolishness. I came here about my money, and you playin'. So you like her. Big deal. And what does that have to do with me? Unless you're saying you're done with the Coco? What, you don't love the Coco no more? Is that what you're telling me?"

He can't be serious. "You trippin'."

He stamped his heeled foot. "So whatchu sayin', Miss Heather?" He popped his lips and swung his bangs out of his eyes.

"I'm saying, I like her. *Like her, like her*. Like I kind of have a teeny, tiny, little bitty crush on her. Just a small one. I mean, I'm not on it like that, but I'm on it. Get it?"

Coco's jungle eyes drank me in. "Like feeling her? Like taste the rainbow feeling her?"

"Like she's cute and I don't know... it just feels different. And I think she likes me back."

Coco got up from his seat, rushed over to me, and pulled me into his embrace. "Mama is so proud of you. I knew you would cross over to my side of the world. I knew you were about that life. I knew it. Even after you played rodeo, when you were in rehab, with that dried eggplant counselor of yours, I knew you were a pillow princess with boxing shorts beneath your gown. OMG! We can do pride together now! Yaaaaaaasssss, honey, yaaaaaaas!"

"You two will need to leave." The librarian walked over to our table and demanded.

"Would you chill?" I snapped. "There's nobody else in here but me, you, and Coco. So step away from the table before I call Westwick and have him handle you."

"I will not tolerate you speaking to me like this!"

"Good. Don't."

"Listen to the kitties roar." Coco laughed. "Heather, it's almost time for us to take our post. We can walk and talk."

"I suggest you do that." The librarian snapped before returning to her desk.

Coco and I packed up our things and caught the elevator to the seventh floor, where he always took one end of the hallway and I took the other. But for the moment we stood together, leaning against a random locker. I glanced down at my watch. We had five minutes left before the bell went off.

Coco popped his glossy lips and said, "Okay, bish, now tell me how you're about to bust out the closet."

I frowned. Looked him over from his bangs, his gelled back hair, his sunken eyes and thin, Candy-Yum-Yum-covered lips to his lime green Armani suit with no shirt beneath to his seven-inch red bottoms.

Out the closet? Clearly he had the wrong idea about this. I never said I was a fruit loop.

Coco curled his top lip. "Stankeesha, why are you eyeballing me all crazy, like you want some Asian cookie? You know I don't bump pocketbooks. Ain't no way you gon' get in these panties."

I twisted my lips. "Eww. I'm not trying to get in anybody's panties. And out the closet? Slow down. Relax and fall back. I'm never coming out the closet, because there's no closet for me to come out of. I'm not gay."

Coco clutched his chest. Paused. Then said, "Gay? Who said that? I'm not gay either. I just love who I love. I don't do labels. I do freedom." He twirled. "I do let go and live, honey. Now tell me. How did you two bikinis meet?"

"Well... like I said... we met at Club Noir Kiss and, umm..." I hesitated, and for a moment, no words would come out of my mouth. I'd never admitted this to anyone. Any. One. But I needed to get this off of my chest, otherwise I was gon' go crazy. So I took a deep breath and said, "A'ight Coco, here's what happened. And you better not tell nobody."

He zipped an index finger across his lips. "You know I don't spill tea. I take it all in."

"You better," I said and then began to tell my story, "She came up to me and said..."

"Girl, you killed it!"

"Thank you."

"You're welcome. And this dress! You're wearing the hell out of it." Her eyes drank me in, working their way from my hair to my spilling cleavage to the outline of my hips. "Girl, you are beautiful." She said more to herself than to me, as she boldly tucked some of my hair behind my right ear and smoothly slid a single fingertip down my blushing cheek. "Heather, you did your thing out there, for real."

I didn't know what surprised me more: her touching me, her calling me Heather when everyone in the club that night called me Wu-Wu, or that her eyes were drinking me in again.

I didn't know what to say, so I fell back on "Thank you." And by the time my eyes drifted to her thighs, I realized what I was doing, so I quickly snatched my glance away and turned back toward the bar, sipping my drink again.

"Heather, what are you drinking? Let me buy you another one."

I did my best to resist the blush I felt creeping back onto my face. "No. Thank you. But no... I can barely get through this one."

"Okay." She'd smiled, her beautiful teeth gleaming. "I won't hold you." She swept up and twirled the end of a lone curl of her hair before winking and sashaying away.

I refused to let my eyes follow her, and instead, as unwanted butterflies danced in my stomach, I sank my smile into my glass...

Coco dabbed the corners of his eyes and sighed. "How beautiful. Touching. The story of how two carpets came together. No shade. You should write a book. It would be fire. And I got the perfect title: *Carpet Licker*."

See, this is why I didn't want to tell him! "Would you knock it off? For real!" I clenched my jaw and squinted.

"Eww, why are you so touchy? My goodness. This girl must be awfully special."

"She is."

"So then what's your issue?"

"I don't know."

"Oh, you know. You're too busy worried about what other people will say. And what they'll think. Girl, you better getcho life and say effem, honey. Being worried about other people had me trying to commit suicide. Chile, please. Don't worry about these fools out here. Half of them wish they had the balls to swing and to go after what they want. If you wanna swim in the lady pond, then getcha breast stroke on! Do. You. And do it well."

I didn't know what to say to that. I mean... maybe Coco was right. At least it felt like he was right, but still... "What if I'm wrong though and she doesn't like me?"

Brggggggg!!!

Freak! The bell rang, and instantly—as if someone had snapped their fingers and performed a magic trick—the hallway was full and bustling.

"Coco, did you hear me?" I pressed.

"What?" he said, turning toward his post, as the stoners lined the hallway.

"What if she doesn't like me?" I said.

"You said you thought she did."

"I don't know for sure, though."

"Actions speak louder than words."

"I can't tell, though. Coco, I need your help. I need some advice."

He sucked his teeth and pointed to the stoners, who paced aimlessly. "Girl, you cuttin' into my coins." He huffed. "But since you my ride or die, I'ma hit you with some advice real quick. You ready?"

"Yeah."

"You listening?"

"Yeah."

"Here's what you should do." He paused.

My eyes popped out. "What?"

"Tell her how much you really like her, and then ask her does she like you."

16

Spencer

"Girl, can you believe that thirsty trick!" Rich spat, pacing the floor like the wild animal she was. Her eyes were as wide as two flying saucers. "That *bish* stepped to me this morning, trying to set it off. Telling me I'd better watch my back because she was coming for my man..."

Well, he was her *man, first.*

Heeheehee.

Rich was so stupid. Clueless. And *maybe*... if she was a deserving friend, I'd tell her that what London had told her wasn't a lie, that her thug daddy had been poking his pole all up in Low Money's fish factory long before he'd been poking around in hers, that they'd been undercover lover-boos since her days in New York.

Maybe.

How did I know?

Oh, heehee. I told you. Mother Spencer knew all. Besides, that ole make-believe man-child, that, that... ole puff pastry, Anderson Ford—London's pretend *ex*-boyfriend—

had poured me the tea, the juice, and the strawberry marmalade when he'd told me all about that sham of a relationship. How he was London's cover-up, while she played naked twister with her thug love.

I ran my fingertips over the Cartier diamond necklace he'd given me one evening aboard his three-level yacht, *Buff Daddy*.

Ugh.

I was still praying to the love gods for mercy and forgiveness for wasting all of my good seduction juices on that low-down cooter teaser. Two weeks of nothing. Oooh, I get hotter than a batch of fish grease thinking about it. Shame on me!

Spencer, girl, don't do it. Don't paddle yourself back across that muddy river.

Hmmph. Annnnyway, I'd had a poor lapse in judgment and a moment of weakness when I blindly tried to welcome him into my love cave. But, noooooo. Anderson Ford wasn't ready for this sweet pudding. He'd turned me down. Rejected me. Left me standing in my little sheer flyaway soaked in desire. Then he practically tossed me off his yacht the moment Queen Kong called him in distress. Then he'd had the audacity to tell me that the only thing I'd ever be to him was the *sidepiece*. Me. *Moi?*

His dingdang sidepiece! Oh, that boy had the tick-tac-and-the-*toe* all crisscrossed and crazy. I wasn't interested in playing his sidepiece. I wanted to be the main piece. The front piece. And maybe the back piece. But not some dang sidepiece!

But Anderson Ford wasn't interested. Nope. That nasty trash licker had me wasting good panty sets on him. *Hmmph*.

Then realization smacked me upside my pretty head. Anderson was in love with London. That Lorax! I'd seen it in his eyes. Heard it in his voice. The way he'd said her name. The way he'd defended her whenever I called her out of her name. But he couldn't have her, because she didn't want him.

Heehee.

No. Bigfoot was hogtied to that little chocolate thug delight. She was dumbly in love with that ruffian Justice Banks. That, that R & B–crooning panty-hound. And now she didn't even have him. He'd dumped her. Tossed her out like the trash she was.

Heehee.

Then he picked up some new trash. Rich. But whatever! Not my story to tell. Anyway. He'd probably realized that Prudezilla (uhh, London, duh) was really a man in disguise, with her big burly, long-necked self.

And Anderson...well, he was a big ole, three-way trisexual from what Heather claimed. She'd sworn Anderson liked sword fighting with the lady-boys. Although I didn't really subscribe to rumors, especially second-hand mess coming from the mouth of some so-called reformed junkie-whore, what she claimed about ole *Buff Daddy*—whether fact or fiction—explained a lot.

Mmmph.

All that good man meat gone to waste!

It was sinful.

"How dare that crazy whore try to do me!" Rich ranted, pulling me from my horrid thoughts. I blinked her back into view. She was standing in the mirror with a pair of tweezers, plucking something from beneath her chin. Probably strands of hair, I thought to myself. That little piggy had the ability to be a hairy cavewoman if she didn't stay clipped and groomed.

Scandalous.

"She'd better be glad I'm a damn lady. Otherwise I would have busted these fists upside her damn head. Lumped her face up real good! Coming at me with her lies."

I glanced at my timepiece. Then sloooowly rollllllllled my eyes up in my head, twirling my eyeballs around in their sockets. Rich had been flapping her meat lickers for the last ten minutes and thirty-six seconds. Non. Diggity-dang. Stop.

Blah, blah, blah. Yippity-yip-yapping about London the giant panda.

Like I gave a hoot.

London was a nonfactor. And so was this tirade Rich was having. The only thing on my mind was my upcoming night with Midnight, my love-em-up-lick-em-right freak daddy in the sheets. Mister Stomp the Yard, Mister Long-Legged Go Hard For His Purple 'n' Gold, Rufus—

"Speeeeeencer?! Speeeeeeencer?!" Rich snapped, slamming her bag down on the counter and jostling me out of my lusty thoughts.

I allowed my gaze to flutter over to her.

Head tilted, hand on hip, she glared at me. "God! You're so atrocious, Spencer! Can't you stay focused for once in your worthless life? Are you even listening to me? I'm pouring out my troubles to you and all you can do is sit there, all dazed, looking like the little lost space cadet you are. God, Spencer! You're so dang inconsiderate! What's it gonna take for me to get some respect around here, huh, girlie? Do I need to punch your eyes out? Castrate those long lips of yours?"

Lawdgawd! HolyMaryFrancis! This girl was dumber than a bag of doorknockers.

"I'm sick of you, Spencer, ignoring me. I keep trying to be good to you, and all you wanna do is use and abuse me. Well, guess what, girlie?" She dug into her bag and pulled out her pink leather-bound notebook. The one she kept everyone's wrongdoings in. "It stops today. From here on out, I'm doubling your demerits."

She flipped through several pages before pulling out her Tebaldi fountain pen and scribbling in it. "As of this very moment, *Spennnnncerrrrr,* you have managed to rack up two hundred and forty-seven demerits. You only get three hundred before I terminate this so-called friendship of ours because it's obvious you are not worthy of my love and kindness, even though I'm trying very hard to do what's right and stay true to the words in the Bible."

I blinked. Tilted my head. Counted to twenty-five in my head. "And what's that, Rich? Do tell, boo. Tell Momma what the Book of Harlots says. Give me the gospel according to Jezebel."

She gnashed her shiny white fangs and foamed at the mouth.

Mmmph. What a wolf!

"It says, 'Thou shall not ever take friendship for granted,' which is something you continue to do. And I'm sick of it, *Spennnnncerrrr*. Wait..." She narrowed her eyes. "Was Jezebel the one serving the dinner trays at the Last Supper? I can't remember. The last time I went to Mass I think that's what the rabbi said."

Ugh! What a ditzy-dumbo!

"Ooh, yes, yes...get it, girl! I see somebody got an A in Bible study. Let me pull out the collection plate. You've just earned your way through the pearly white gates, boo."

Rich popped her collar. Then started twerking. She turned her back toward the mirror and glanced over her shoulder, sliding a fingernail between her teeth and making her booty cheeks clap. "See, girl, I can't with you. You're about to have me praise dancing up in here." She bent over and grabbed her ankles. "Ooh, I'm starting to feel the Holy Ghost."

Rich could be so, *so*... ghetto-trash. But I couldn't hold that against her. She really couldn't help herself for being who she was. After all, both of her parents were straight from the gutters of the hood.

So it was genetic. To be ghetto. And trashy.

I leaned forward and smacked her on her pound cakes. "Oooh, giddy-up, little pony. Shake it like a salt shaker."

Rich yelped. "Ahh! Clutching pearls! Tramp, you're way out of order!" She straightened herself, slammed her book shut, then eyed me. "You stay doing the most with your freak nasty self. I'm not going to keep being a friend to you, *Spennnnnncerrrr,* if you're going to keep taking me for granted. You had better start showing me some appreciation. And I mean it. Now, back to what I was telling you. Can you believe that whore?"

"What whore, Rich?"

Rich slapped her notebook down on the counter. "Ohmygod, Spencer! Wake up! London, girl! That's the whore I'm talking about. But if you want me to talk about *you* instead, I'd gladly oblige. Now keep trying me."

"Oh, Rich," I calmly said. "Relax your hoofs, girlie. I heard everything you've said, which, if you ask me, is about a bunch of nothing. Why you care what Low Money says? If you think London's a liar, then why are you sweating it?"

"*Sweating it?* Clutching pearls? I'm a lady, tramp. I don't sweat. I perspire. I drink water..."

I rolled my eyes. "And while you're over there perspiring and drinking water, Miss Wet Stains, riddle me this: What if that thug dog you're rolling around on that flea bed with *is* the real liar?" I paused for a beat, blinking my lashes and letting my words float around the bathroom. "I mean. What if he and that East Side gutter rat *did* go together?"

"*Whaaaaat?* Clutching pearls!" Rich pounded her fist on the countertop. "Whore, you're way out of order! You've stooped to an all-time low with that, trick! And that's not saying much since we all *know* how low you and your rusty knees can go. You ole nasty dome licker! Justice is a good man, *Spennnncerrrr!* How dare you try to defame my man's name with slander! He would never sleep with that girl. Or mess with that girl. So you had better watch your mouth before..."

"Rich, drink bleach." I slid my hand down into my purse. "You must want me to snatch your breath, huh?"

"*Whaaaat?*" Rich squeaked, snatching her phone out of her purse. "Oh no, oh no! I will not be a part of your homicide. You will not yellow-tape me. You wanna pull out weapons on me? First you insult my man's integrity. Now you wanna take my life! Girl, you are *waaaay* out of order!"

I rolled my eyes, pulling out an ashtray and my jeweled cigarette case. "Oh, Rich, shut up. If I wanted you dropped and bagged, do you think I'd do it right here in the girls' lounge? Right here on campus, no less? Think, Rich, think. I've watched enough episodes of *How to Get Away with*

Murder to know how to do you, girlie. I'd get you right after you've gotten all tanked up on hot wings and beer. Jeezus. I'd gut you while your belly was full so I could watch your bowels empty out. I know your insides are filthy."

"Oh. Girl, don't scare me like that. Wait. I'll have you know, my insides are springtime fresh. And I just had a colonic two days ago. Don't do me. Now back to your delinquent ways. You're lucky I didn't press DIAL. You know I have SWAT on SPEED DIAL, girl. They would have swooped in and took you down, like the crazed psychopath you are."

I waved her on. "Girlie, bye. I'm no crazier than you are for thinking Mister City Slickster couldn't be up to no good. I don't trust him. And you know I don't like him."

Oh, I know. If I wanted to, I could simply tell Rich what I knew about her boo-thug and London. But what was the fun in that? No. This man eater needed to stumble on that news the hard way.

"That's because you're hateful, Spencer. And you don't want to see me happy."

"No. I don't want to see you get hurt. That boy is no good, Rich."

"He's a man. Don't let me tell you again. And he's good for me, and good to me. And he feels good. And we're in love."

I frowned. "Oh, really? Since when? I thought you didn't—quote, unquote—do love. Ever. Remember?"

She sucked her teeth. "Spencer, this is why I hate you, okay? You can't be trusted with nothing. I tell you something in confidence, then you turn around and throw it up in my face. What a slore! I told you I didn't do love when I was still trying to find myself."

"Oh? And where were you looking, beneath some boy's stained bedsheet? In the backseat of his Maserati?"

"Girl, no. I gave up backseats and other boys' bedsheets a long time ago. And I'll have you know, Tramp, the last time I was on some unknown bedsheets was at the Howard Johnson when Corey called me."

I blinked. "Oh, really? When was that, Rich?"

"Last week. And he said he's sorry about what happened when you were upside down in that ditch."

I rolled my eyes. I was not even about to revisit that despicable day. Corey was the dang reason why my car ended up in the ditch alongside the road in the first dang place. With his six-foot fine self. That no-good pound puppy had told me he was going to dump Rich, so that he and I could continue our little undercover freakfest. Sure, he was Rich's man at the time. But he was my little lickety-lick, creep-creep.

But that was beside the point. The point was, he'd said he was dumping her. But instead, I caught him and her over by the gazebo after school with him dropping his spit and tongue all down in her throat *after* I'd just had him—with his True Religions wrapped around his ankles—in one of the girls' lounges earlier in the day.

Ooooh. Seeing the two of them all lick-em-up lovie-dovey had me on fire. I'd skidded off in my car, sideswiping parked cars, then swerving all over the road until I'd lost control of my Benz. It flipped up in the air, then landed on the roof.

The. End.

Mmmph.

"Justice is all I need to get by, Spencer," Rich carried on, snatching me from the memory of being upside down in the ditch. "You know I tried to shake him once. Okay, twice. Okay, okay... three times. But"—she bounced her shoulders—"my boo knows how to make it rain down on me." She patted her forehead. "He makes me wanna do things I've never done with anyone else. I'm talking chandelier swinging." She shimmied, then did a two-step.

And I felt myself throw up in the back of my mouth a little bit.

Yuck.

"And I'm happy," Rich continued, tossing her hair over her shoulder. "So stay out of grown folks' affairs. And stay the hell out of my life, Spencer. I'm one pen-click away from drawing a line straight through your name on the guest list. I promise you I am."

I grunted, ignoring the last part of what she said. Like I gave a damn about being crossed off her silly party list. That crack-ho must have forgotten who I was. Or she'd known I'd rev my engine and speed roll right through the dang building. Then smash cake in her fluffy face.

Try me.

I rolled my eyes at her. "*Mmmph*. Is that what they're calling keying up cars and smashing out windows these days? *Happy?*"

She waved me on. "Look, Spencer, like I told you before, until you fall in love, don't question what me and my man have. We have that ride or die, dirty-fighting kind of love. We fight hard. And love harder. That's grown folks love, girl. You know nothing about that. Look at my mother and my father. Logan's smashed out her share of car windows and dragged plenty of hoes by their edges over him. And she's still dragging them, Spencer. Because that's what real hoes do. And that's what love makes you do."

Lawdgawd . . . nail me to the cross! This girl was really starting to give me gas. All I could do was clench my booty cheeks and shake my head.

"No, thanks. I'll have a colonic instead." I twisted the

cigarette butt. Then shifted my booty up on the countertop. "Woman to woman, Rich..." She watched as smoke started rising from the electronic tip. "No, shady trees over here, but..." I took a pull from the cigarette, then tooted my lips and blew out invisible smoke. "What do you really know about that boy Justice?"

"Umm, correction, tramp. Justice is a man. All man, I might add. Get it right. Now don't let me tell you again. I'm warning you. Don't have me pull your invitation to my birthday party. And you know I will. Now get your mind right before I get it right for you. Justice is a M-A-N-N. But you wouldn't know about having one of those since you're only interested in playing doctor with little boys running around in purple pajamas. I swear. Midnight is about as goofy as you are, Spencer. But you don't hear me saying anything about his ole skinny, rusty behind, do you? All I ever do is shower you with happiness and good wishes because I know the two of you junkyard freakazoids really deserve each other."

I tilted my head. Narrowed my gaze. Then blew smoke at her. "I know we do. Now back to you. Have you done a background check on him?"

"A background check on who? *Justice?*"

I took a deep breath. Then slowly said, "Yesssss, Rich. *Justice.*"

She frowned. "Girl, no. I don't even know his last name."

Ooh, I was slowly starting to lose my patience with this Paddington Bear. How do you *not* know your own so-called boyfriend's—oops, fiancé's last name?

Alrighty then...

I see this dog isn't tryna hunt. So let me let it lie right where it is. On top of a pile of horse poop!

My work here was done.

I set the cigarette in the ashtray. Slid off the counter, then reached into my purse and pulled out my cosmetic case. I slid a coat of lip gloss over my lips. Then popped my juicy-glossed lips.

Rich eyed me. "Where are you going?"

"To class," I responded, shutting off my cigarette and tossing my ashtray back inside my bag. "You have completely bored me. I'd rather stare at Mister Sanders's trousers sucked up into his man cakes than to listen to you ramble on about nothing."

"*Whaaaaat?* Clutching pearls! *Class?* Ohmygod, *Spennnn-cerrrrr,* you're so damn thoughtless!" She snatched open her journal. "That's it. You're done, *Spennncerrrrrr*. Finished! This is why we can never manage to stay friends longer than"—she glanced at her Platinum Pearl Master—"fourteen minutes and twenty-two-point-four seconds. Then on top of that, you have managed to rack up three-hundred-and-fifty-seven demerits in less than one hour. It's over for you, *Spennnncerrrr*. You've officially been axed!" She made a chopping motion across the palm of her hand. "*Chop!* You're outta here, girlie. This friendship is over!"

I gathered my belongings, and headed for the door. There was nothing more to say. This girl was a lost dang cause. "Good day, ma'am," I tossed over my shoulder as I walked toward the bathroom door.

"You don't tell me good day," Rich snapped, slinging her notebook at me. It flew over my head and hit the door. "You're trying to wish me dead saying some damn good day when the day's not even over. You selfish trick! What you should be saying is good morning. And you better meet me at the Kit-Kat Lounge at four o'clock. And don't be late, whore!"

"Rich, eat my panty liner!" I snapped as I stomped on her notebook and unlocked the door. "And chew it real good." I slung open the door, then slammed it shut behind me as I walked out.

Trick, please.

17

Rich

I'm sorry for trying to hook you up with Justice. I should have told you that we were going together.

Stop it! I slammed my hand on my Ferrari's dashboard, swallowing tears. I was parked in the back of Justice's apartment complex, debating whether or not I should go shut down his spot. But. I wasn't really in the mood for his neighbor to call the cops on me, again...

You think your life is so perfect. Enjoy it while it lasts, sweetie. But know this: That little fairy tale you're holding onto is going to go up in flames, real fast. And you're going to soon find out that your life isn't all that picture-perfect after all.

"Uggggg!" I screamed, my head reeling.

I had to shake these thoughts.

I had to.

Otherwise, I was gon' go into American Lit class, grab London by her infusion weave, and beat. Dat. Azz.

I can't believe she came at me and my man like that! I

should've just taken my box cutter, gave it to her, and told her, "Please finish what you started."

I'm way too kind, though.

Thoughtful.

Generous.

And I'ma lady. So I was trying to be calm, but the sound of London's voice stuck on repeat in my head was sending me straight into whup-a-trick mode.

She tried it, though. Tried to read me for filth. And truthfully, it knocked me off my square, but only for a moment.

Heck, I had to digest how I'd been played for the third time in a week.

First Spencer.

Then London.

And now Justice? Justice, my man. My baby-daddy. My ride or die. My hitter. My flip it up and rub it down-wheel barrel-boo. My chocolate thirst quencher. The one I'd given my all too. My trap-king. How could he lie to me?

And yeah, yeah, yeah, I know I said it was over between us before, but I *reaaaaallllly* meant it now. This time, we were done. For. Everrrrrr!

Finished.

Over. With.

No coming back.

No looking back.

No more Princess Rich and Peasant Justice.

Eff him.

Eff his mama.

And eff the crack house he grew up in.

Sucka!

Bum nucca!

Like he's even all that. Puhlease. Not. London can have him back.

Mmmph! I was doing him an upgrade by being with him. He ain't do nothing for me. Never have and never will.

And yeah, he might be hey-hey-holler-back, daddy pull my hair and let's pop-pop tonight fine. But so what? I can't let him play me.

I can't.

I stared out my car's window and did my all not to let one tear fall. I couldn't believe that Justice and London really had a bromance.

Like stud muffins. Huddled up and cuddled up.

I huffed and flung away a stupid tear that dripped down my face. It's cool, though. Justice may have gotten this off, but believe me, it's more than one way to muzzle a dog.

I pulled out my phone and posted a pic of a burning broken heart on Instagram.

Then I went on Snapchat and posted a video where I simply said, "Single again and keepin' to myself. Who wanna turn up? I'm open and ready."

After that, I took to Twitter and tweeted out, "Nucca's ain't ish. I'm done wit' er'body. Can't nobody say nothin' to me. Eff y'all!"

And lastly, I texted this low-down scum-bucket of a boyfriend and said, "I'm done witchu. Eff you and your whole hood bugger family. You tried to play me for dumb and didn't think I would find out about it. But I did. This is the thirty-fifth time, and you not about to get a thirty-sixth time off. Peace to the Middle East and peace to you too, boo-boo. #mytimeturnuptimeisreal #abouththatsinglelife #hatenuccas #dontcallmeeveragain #Ilovedyou #shedidnt #triedtoplayme #butIainttheone." I pressed SEND.

A few seconds later Justice called me.

I pressed IGNORE.

He called again.

IG. NORE.

He called again.

I smiled at the phone while sending him to voice mail.

He texted me. "Wassup witchu? I know you see me calling you."

I texted back. "It's over."

He replied. "I miss you."

I sucked my teeth and did everything I could not to smile. Apparently, he thought I was playing. "This is not a game. London stepped to me at my locker, saying you used to be her man. You told me you were friends. Why you lie? I hate liars."

"You trippin'. Stop acting crazy. And hit me up when you get outta school, so I can know what time you comin'."

I blinked five times. *Oh no he didn't!* "Bye, boy."

"I know you miss me. 'Cause I miss you."

Ugg! I hated when he did this! Now I was trying my best to stop my heart from skipping beats and my cheeks from blushing.

Godlee, he made me sick. Always doing the most.

He knows I'm trying to break up with him. "I'm not playing with you, Justice."

"I'ma cook some beer-battered and double-fried hot wings. Enough for two."

I sucked my teeth. He killed me with this. Always thinking of sweet and sensitive ways to say he was sorry. But I was not letting him off that easy. "Psst, please. I can't stand hot wings. And anyway, I'm busy."

A few seconds later my phone rang. Justice.

I started to let him go to voice mail again. But I couldn't. So I picked up and said, "Yeah. What?"

"You too busy for me?" He asked, his voice low, almost hushed and sweet ju-ju-bead sexy.

It took me about five point seven seconds to fight and ultimately swallow my smile; then I said, "Yop. You got it. Too busy for your bull. You tried to play me with London, and now you wanna act like it's nothing. I'm done with you, and that includes being done with your nasty chicken too."

He sighed.

"I don't know what you sighing for. You're the one always lyin'!"

"What I gotta lie for, Rich?"

"Da hell?! Whatchu mean whatchu gotta lie for? You lie 'cause you like it. You lie 'cause it taste good to you. 'Cause you like how lies roll around in your mouth. You lie 'cause you a liar and that's what liars do. They lie."

"Oh word?" He said in disbelief.

"Word."

"Yoooo." He paused, and I could imagine him shaking his head. "It's always a problem witchu you, yo. And this is why you gon' always be fat and miserable, 'cause you too busy looking for reasons to trip. And if you keep it up, in a minute I'ma fall back. All the way back."

"Negative. False. Pause. Excuse you, was that a slight read? You're the one who lied to me about your bromance with London. She told me you were a couple. About to get *marrrrrrriiiieeed!* You ain't gotta lie, Justice!"

"You're right, so let me just hit you with the truth: It was a million chicks before you, and the way you actin', it's gon' be a million more when I get rid of you. I don't know who you think I am, but I'm not that punk-ass college boy. I'll break yo' jaw!"

I felt like he'd just drop-kicked me. "Rid of me? Boy, please—"

"You know what, Rich, you're actin' real stupid!"

"Justice—"

"You got me effed up, and if I was sittin' next to you I'd slap the ish outta you for coming outta the side of ya neck—"

"You will never—"

"Never what? Wife you? 'Cause right about now that's what I won't be doing. I don't deal with stupid-actin' broads like you for long. And since you trippin' so hard, maybe I oughta call London and get wit' her, make her my girl, since you don't know how to act right."

Another dropkick dead in the chest, but just as I shook it off, Justice came at me again, "Can't believe you, yo. You let some hatin' azz trick get in between us? Got you comin' at me all crazy! Word? Actin' all bipolar? I tell you what, I'ma give you just what you lookin' for."

"And what does that mean?"

"Means it's time for you to step off."

Click.

I couldn't breathe. And although my heart raced a thousand miles a minute, it was not in my chest. It had dropped to my feet. What just happened? Did Justice just cuss me out and hang up on me? Did he just tell me to step off? Like we're done? Over? Oh hell no. I can't let my man go like that. Why didn't I just be quiet and believe him? I had to get my baby back. I had to.

I practically tripped outta my car and raced through the parking lot. My stomach bubbled, and I felt like I was going to hurl at any moment, I didn't have time to get sick, though. Not right now.

I took the steps two at a time to Justice's apartment and could barely catch my breath by the time I arrived on his floor.

I huffed as I rushed over to the door, and there he was. Justice. Leaning against the door frame, looking at me like I was crazy.

18

Heather

I'd never kissed a girl before.
Ever.

Never even thought about it...

Until now...when I spotted Nikki.

I was at San Diego State, watching her step across the courtyard, single file with her sorors lined up behind her.

She was lookin' all fly: fitted white jeans, lavender tee with white Greek letters spray-painted across it, three strands of white pearls, and purple heels.

My chick stayed on fleek.

Scratch that.

Nikki stayed on fleek.

I smiled at her. She winked. Then she puckered her shiny pink lips and softly blew me a kiss. My heart skipped at least fifty beats and was seconds from diving for my feet.

I closed my eyes and squeezed them so tight that tears slid through the lids.

Stop.

Breathe.

Fireflies erupted in my stomach, causing my cheeks to blush and my face to glow.

Ugg!

Relax.

Coco's voice rang in my head: *"Tell her how much you really like her and then ask her does she like you."*

I opened my eyes, and my gaze landed on Nikki.

God, I wanted to press my full lips against hers... and taste her lip gloss. Drift into the heat of a sweet and sloppy tongue dance. Place my hands on her tiny hips and breathe her in.

Then exhale.

And melt into her embrace...

But.

I knew I couldn't do that.

So.

I played it cool.

"Cheeeeeeeeeewee!" Nikki and her sorors catcalled as they broke out into a fly dance of stomping their feet, clapping their hands, and moving their arms and shoulders, in the same pulse and to the same beat.

A mob of people stood around, their eyes gleaming and glued to the middle of the courtyard, where Nikki and her crew stomped. There were even other sororities and fraternities anxiously waiting their turn to jump in and show off.

Nikki and her sorority chanted:

"ATZ is the best! Yes! We are the best! Yes!
We are blood, sweat, and heels.
Motivated. Educated. Highly rated.
Always imitated. But never duplicated.
ATZ is what all the girls wanna be.
But not everybody can sit with me!
'Cause we are the what?

Yeah! We are the what?

Blood, sweat, and heels..."

The crowd roared, and some of the onlookers even joined in on the chant and the line dance. I could tell Nikki was in her zone. She was sassy, sexy, and serious.

I jumped up and down, and before I could stop myself, I was sounding like Coco, "Yaaaaaas, bish! Yaaaaaaaaas! Werk!"

Nikki looked at me, and I shot her a high five through the air, and she shot me one back.

Everybody cheered and clapped as ATZ finished their dance, and another sorority jumped in, stepped, and chanted, "Don't wanna be no ATZ, just wanna be DCT! Not nine white pearls. But twenty white pearls!"

The whole atmosphere was crazy! And I was lovin' it!

Nikki ran over to me, and we fell into the tightest hug ever. "OMG, honeybunch! I'm *soooooooo* happy you're *hereeeeeeeeeee!*" She squealed.

"Me *tooooooooo! Yoooooooo*, Nik! That was the business." I snapped my fingers. Yasssssss, I loved that. I could do that, boo!"

She smiled, stood back, and looked me over. "You could do what? Show me!"

"You ain't said nothin' but a verb!" I broke out into a solo step dance.

Nikki giggled. "I could use a chick like you on my team."

And what does that mean? That she likes me? My heart rushed through fifty beats, and for a moment I had to force myself to breathe. "Say word." I said.

"Word."

"Okay. Then I'm on your team."

"Seriously? So you changed your mind about college? Would you really consider San Diego State?"

Wait. Pause. She meant the San Diego State team? Not the get with me and be my boo team?

Now I felt stupid.

Maybe she doesn't like me... like that, anyway.

I forced myself to grin. Well, not a full grin, but I managed a half of one. "I sure would," I said.

Nikki's eyes beamed.

I continued, "The next sitcom I star in I'ma make sure the writers step Wu-Wu's game all the way up and send her to college. And if we get clearance, I'd even suggest that she be a part of ATZ. But as far as me coming personally, umm, no. I'ma stay in Silver Screen University. And rock that team."

"Wait, hold up." A medium-brown skinned girl, about five-seven, with sandy brown Bantu knots, cowrie-shell earrings, and the same ATZ uniform that Nikki had on, stepped into our conversation. "I'm *soooo* sorry to interrupt, but is this..."

The girl paused, looked at Nikki, and then looked back at me. "Are you Heather Cummings? As in Wu-Wu Tanner? As in the Pampered Princesses of Hollywood High, as in the BFF of Rich Montgomery—"

Screeeeeeeech! BFF? Whose BFF? I held up my index finger. "Negative. Now bring it back. I'm not Rich Montgomery's anything." I looked over at Nikki. She tried to hold a blank face, but I could almost read her thoughts. "We go to the same school, yes. And on a rare occasion, like February thirty-ninth, we may chill together. But she is not my friend. And yes, I'm Heather Cummings, as in Wu-Wu Tanner."

"I *sooooo* love you!" The girl snatched me into a hug. "You are the bomb!" She draped an arm over my shoulders. "I know you said you don't do Rich. But you two give me life. And you two kind of resemble. You have the same eyes."

I sucked in a nervous breath.

The girl continued, "But Rich is like the blond-black Paris Hilton. Anyway, I'm Khalila." She turned to Nikki and playfully pushed her on the shoulder. "Heifer, *whyyyyyy* didn't you tell me that you chillin' with the stars and Wu-Wu Tanner is your friend?"

"Because Wu-Wu Tanner is not my friend," Nikki said. "Heather Cummings is my friend."

"You know what I mean." Khalila carried on. "So Wu-Wu, I mean, Heather. I know you gotta be hangin' with us today. Right, Nikki?"

Nikki smiled. "I hope so."

Khalila popped her lips. "That means yes. We're having a dorm floor party. And just so you know, the cuties will be in the hiz'zouse!"

"It would be dope if you stayed," Nikki insisted.

"It would be hella dope!" A Latina girl, with bouncy, shoulder-length black curls and pecan-colored skin tossed in. "My name is Jacinda, and I knew who you were the *whooooooole* time. I'm the one who told Kareema, who told Melissa, who told Khalila to ask. I spotted you the moment we got out here. I watched all of the Wu-Wu Tanner shows, but I hate the new Wu-Wu. They need you back. But, anyway, I read on a blog you're doing a reality show. Is that true?"

I smiled. "Yes, it is."

"That is *sooooooo* hot! You need to bring the camera up here so we can show 'em how college girls get down."

I laughed. "Maybe I will."

"So is that a yes?" Nikki pressed. "You're hanging out with me and my girls?"

"I mean, it's no paparazzi or anything," Khalila added.

Jacinda jumped in, "But we know how to party!"

"Then let's get it, boo!" I said.

We made our way across the sprawling and manicured campus to their sorority house; an eight-story, lavender brick building with ATZ spray-painted in white across the entire face.

I couldn't help but feel out of place, as I noticed how Nikki and her crew walked.

No, strolled.

No, sauntered.

Erase all of that.

They strutted.

Chins up.

Backs straight.

Hips to the left, then to the right.

One foot in front of the other.

They had swag. Divalicious swag. About their business swag. And their vibes all screamed, "I'm the ish!"

They were nothing like the Pampered Princesses, who only had camera-balls and gossip-rag esteem.

Nikki's crew were clearly feeling themselves, but not full of themselves.

These chicks put the Pampered Princesses to sleep. They were pretty, brilliant, and straight fly.

Don't get it twisted, the Pampered Princesses were pretty too. Pretty pathetic and pretty pitiful. And yeah, they rocked Gucci. But these heifers right here, ATZ, were straight Gucci.

There was a difference.

We walked into their dorm, where the lobby was packed with people and music echoed down the hall. "This is the party?" I asked Nikki.

"Nope. They're just hanging out." Nikki said, as we all stepped onto the elevator and Khalila pressed the button for the sixth floor.

"*Daaaaaaaaaamn,* kazam!" I said, as the elevator doors opened. "Party ova here!" My eyes wildly scanned the floor. The DJ was next to the elevator on the left, and pumping from his speakers was the dopest trap music. To the right somebody served dollar shots of toasted punch in Styrofoam cups.

And. People. Were. Everywhere! They spilled out of packed dorm rooms. Lined the hallways. Some twerked, danced, popped it. Some just chilled, leaned against the wall, and kicked it. And others simply sipped their drinks and nodded to the music.

I couldn't believe it. I thought college parties like this only existed on TV and in the movies. Not in real life. I always thought that—with the exception of Nikki—college kids were a bunch of misfits. Like Spencer, but sane. I had no idea they were all the way live.

The moment ATZ stepped off the elevator, Khalila walked over to the DJ, grabbed the mic, and announced—like she had nothing else to do or be but a blabbermouth—"This is Heather Cummings, as in Wu-Wu Tanner. As in the hit 'Put Your Diamonds Up'! Let's show her some love!"

Within seconds, the DJ dropped my tune, and everybody danced.

I should've rocked out. It would've been fly had I reached for the mic and said, "Check-one, check two . . ." and spit my rhyme. Tore the frame out the spot. And had this been any other place, or if I'd had a pinch of Beauty, I would've been off the meat rack! Waved my hands in the air, and acted like the only thing that mattered was me.

But I couldn't.

Instead, I was a sober zombie, watching everybody else feel my music.

After the DJ played "Put Your Diamonds Up," he dropped my hit "The Gucci Clique."

I bounced my shoulders a little, but I couldn't get all the way into it. I had too much on my mind.

When my hits were finished, the DJ played more trap music, and people rushed over to me and asked to take ussies, which I couldn't refuse. I was sure they were Instagramming, tweeting, and Facebooking it. I knew by morning the pics would all be featured on a few blogs.

I so wanted to let loose and be free, the way I usually was with Nikki, but I couldn't. All I could think about was peeling outta here, heading home to hide, get high, and tell myself that I was stupid in peace.

And yeah, everybody here seemed cool, so it wasn't them, it was me. I felt like I had *bisexual confusion, spawn of a drunk-coochie and a runaway sperm donor* stamped to my forehead.

"You okay?" Nikki's warm hand reached for mine and squeezed it.

I forced myself to smile. "Psst, please. Girl, yes. Yaaaaasssss, hunni!" I said, way too hyped and clearly extra phony.

Nikki turned and faced me. Her eyes locked into mine. And although we were in the midst of at least a hundred people, I felt like we were the only two standing here. "Wassup? And tell me the truth." She pressed.

"Chill, boo." I rocked my shoulders and popped my fingers. "I'm good. Thinking about getting myself a dollar shot. You want one?"

Nikki's gaze continued to pull me in. She paused, then said, "Let's get outta here for a minute."

"Leave the party?" I frowned. "Relax. I'm okay. Let's stay."

"No." She gently pulled me by the hand.

"Where y'all going?" Khalila, who was hugged up on a cutie, yelled over her shoulder.

"We'll be right back!" Nikki said, as we stepped onto the elevator and she pushed the button for the fourth floor.

19

London

Surprise, surprise... Rich had officially blocked me from her Twitter account like she had already done on Instagram. And I no longer had access to her on Kik Messenger, either.

So what was a girl to do?

Create a fictitious account. And pretend to be a groupie. Yes. I was cyber-stalking her. How else was I supposed to know what was going on with that troll doll? Aside from reading about her on the blogs, I had no other means of staying abreast of her shenanigans since she'd banned me from her life.

And here I offered to extend her an olive branch by going to her like a woman and telling her about Justice and me. I went to that girl with nothing but good intentions. And all she could think to do was lash out at me and call me names.

That whore is vicious.

And hateful!

Dejected, I flopped down in an oversized chair in my

sitting room. I was alone and feeling lonely. Daddy was out, doing God knows what.

And my mother . . . *mmmph*.

Not. A. Word.

Her marriage to Daddy was in shambles. And instead of trying to fix whatever was broken between the two of them, she opted to head back to fricking Milan. *Milan!* Like who does that?

Run off and leave their marriage in disarray?

Jade Phillips does!

But whatever! I wasn't in the mood to think about her, anyway. I never am.

My relationship with her had been, uh . . . strained, for a lack of a better word, ever since everything that happened to me. She still thought I purposefully tried to sabotage my modeling career, just to embarrass her. Like okay. I just woke up one day and had this epiphany to ruin *her* life with a few slices of a blade to my wrists.

God, my mother was so dang self-absorbed.

*Every*thing was about her.

All. The. Time.

What about me?

She'd taken no responsibility for my state of being. Found no wrongdoing on her part, for her browbeating me, pressuring me, strong-arming me into being what she wanted me to be. What she expected me to be.

Perfect.

Well, guess what? London wasn't all that perfect. In fact, I wasn't perfect at all. And neither was she.

Or Rich.

Or Spencer.

Or that horrid Heather.

We were all flawed.

But it seemed like *I* was the only one who knew it. Or admitted it.

But, whatever! I wasn't looking for a pity party. And I definitely wasn't looking for a Hallmark moment. No.

It is what it is.

I knew I'd made some terrible mistakes in my life. Like getting wrapped up in the likes of—

My buzzing cell pulled me from my thoughts.

I reached for it where it lay on the end table, frowning at the screen. *Who's calling me from a restricted number?*

"Hello?"

"Yo, whatda*fuq* is wrong wit' you, yo? Huh?"

Ohmygod!

Justice.

"Whyda*fuq* you tell my girl some BS like that, huh, yo? You straight wildin', yo."

His girl?

The sound of his voice alone caused the hair on the back of my neck to rise. My palms sweated. And I could feel my whole body starting to shake from the inside out.

I hadn't heard from Justice in months. And the last form of communication from him was in the form of a text. No, wait. We'd had one last conversation—after he'd dumped me by way of text—with him mocking and taunting me, then finally making it loud and clear that he was done with me, for good.

"What's up wit' ya peoples?"

"My peoples? My peoples who?"

"Ya girl Rich, who else? Why you so stupid, yo? Ain't nobody else effen wit' you. You was s'posed to be hookin' that up for me 'n' you couldn't even handle that right."

"I tried. But then I had to—"

"Save it, yo. I'm not tryna hear none a ya BS. I don't need no lil silly girl tryna make moves for me. I got this. I already put work in. So go do you."

"What are you saying, Justice? You already hooked up with her? Is that why you haven't had time for me? Is that why you broke up with me? Because you're giving all of your time to Rich?"

"See. That's what I'm talkin' 'bout, lil girl. That dumbness you be on. That silly lil girl jealousy crap you stuck on. I already said it. I'm baggin' that. Move on, yo. It's over. For real, yo. You straight up worthless. I don't know why I ever wasted my time effen wit' you..."

"Yo, you that damn desperate 'n' lonely that you gotta go run ya mouth wit' some BS," he said, his voice slicing into the painful memory.

I felt myself getting sick.

Justice really was toxic. And I saw that now. He was a dog! An abuser! A user!

I almost felt sad for him.

Still...

My heart started aching.

Then I heard Rich's voice, taunting me. *"Is he a user? Or is that he doesn't want* you? *What, are you a reject? You didn't make the cut, is that it? Or am I standing in the way...?"*

I blinked back tears. *Don't you dare drop one tear, London Phillips. Not one! You've spilled more than your share of tears over him and because of him. He's moved on. And so should you. Get your life, girl!*

"Justice," I pushed out, practically squeezing my phone into my hand, trying to mask my mounting angst. "All I did was tell her the truth."

"Bullshit, yo. You know I ain't ever eff wit' ya silly-azz. You crazy, yo. Dumb, trick-azz broad. You need ya effen jaw snapped, yo, for runnin' ya damn mouth. Word is bond, yo. Stay the eff outta me 'n' mines, yo. Real talk."

I blinked.

He was a, a, a... *monster!*

Ohmygod! I couldn't believe him! Couldn't believe he'd deny ever being in a relationship with me. Before I could talk myself out of it, before I could stop the words from stumbling out of my mouth, I asked him what I'd ever done to him for him to turn on me? For him to treat me so nastily?

He snorted. "I'm over you, yo..."

Out of nowhere, my mother's voice started gnawing at me. *"That boy is not to be trusted, London, do you hear me...? He's troubled and from the wrong side of the tracks! I don't want him sniffing around here trying to manipulate his way into your life... he will do nothing but ruin you...!"*

And everything she'd ever said, preached, lectured... was true. Every. Single. Painful. Word.

I swallowed.

Count your blessings!

I took a deep breath. Steadied my racing heart. Then said, "I'm glad you're over me. You and Rich deserve each other, Justice."

"Yeah, we do. So I don't need you tryna eff it up wit' ya BS. So keep my name out'cha mouth, yo; for real for real."

"You don't ever have to worry about me having your name in my mouth, ever again. So now take your own advice, Justice, and do what you told me to do. *Delete* my damn number. Don't call me. Ever. Again."

I ended the call before I could give him a chance to say something else. Before I gave him back power to tear my spirits down. Before I allowed him to drag me right back to that dark place. No. I couldn't let that happen. Not ever.

It wasn't until I tossed the phone over on the table that I noticed my hands were trembling.

Justice Banks wasn't worthy of me.

Sadly . . . he never was.

I covered my face in my hands, and sobbed.

20

Heather

Nikki's dorm room was super adorable. The walls were painted crisp white, and hanging from the open window, which had a view of the courtyard, were windswept sheer white curtains.

Beneath the window was an extra-long twin-size bed. The bed was dressed in a fluffy and snow white comforter, with loads of throw pillows and colorful stuffed animals. There was an all-glass desk on the left side of the bed, with an iMac, a moon lamp, and a stack of books on top of it.

On the walls were posters of Betty Shabazz, Harriet Tubman, Maya Angelou, Zora Neale Hurston, and Alice Walker. There were a few pics of Nikki's nieces and Nikki's parents, and there was also a bookshelf overflowing with black literary classics.

Nikki flopped down on her bed, grabbed a stuffed animal, and crammed it into her lap while I admired her bookshelf.

"Look at all of these books. Wow!" I said.

"I told you I love to read. But I didn't call you down

here to talk about my book collection." She patted the space next to her. "Come over here. We need to talk."

Reluctantly, I did as she asked and sat Indian style next to her. "Talk about what?"

"Wassup? Why did you clam up? You didn't even loosen up when your songs came on."

"I loosened up."

She squinted and twisted her lips. "No, you didn't. I saw it all in your grill, boo."

"Psst, please. I don't know what you're talking about. I was having a ball. You're the one who wanted to leave the party. I wanted to stay."

"Oh really?" She arched her brow. "Is this what we're doing now?"

"Doing what now?"

"Lying to each other."

She can't be serious. "Lying? I haven't lied to you."

"BFFs tell each other everything."

Pause. What? What did she just say? BFF? *BFF?* She had me messed up. I didn't wanna be her *BFF*. Ever. I wanted to be her boo. I just didn't know how to tell her that. But one thing was for sure and two things were for certain, I didn't come down here to be stomped further into the friend zone. We could've stayed at the party for that. "Are you serious right now?" I could feel myself getting ticked. "You called me down here for this?"

She scooted even closer to me. "I called you down here because every time we're together, it's like there's an elephant between us. And we need to talk about it."

My heart revved up and was preparing for flight. Had I been that obvious? "What do elephants, me clamming up, and BFFs have to do with each other? You buggin'."

'I'm not buggin', and you know it." Nikki took her index finger and lifted my chin. "I wanna ask you something, and I want you to tell me the truth."

God, I loved her touching my face. "Always."

"Do you like me?"

I gasped. Damn near choked. *Say what? What did she just ask me?* I swallowed. "Huh? Like you? In what way? How? Like my buddy, friend, pal? Like girls, homies?" I raised a brow. "BFFs?"

"Like boos. Like since the day I met you at Club Noir Kiss I been checkin' for you. And before you even go there, I don't normally check for chicks. But I'm checking for you. And something tells me that the elephant is in the room because you're checking for me too." She paused, as if she were waiting for me to fill in the silence and drop some type of lady-pond-science on her. Not.

I blinked. Blinked again. Maybe I should tell her? No.

Nikki pressed. "Do you like me, Heather?"

My heart was seconds from punching its way out of my chest. "No. Yes. Maybe. Wait." I sipped in a breath and slowly blew it out. "Like you how? In what way? Whatchu mean?"

She looked at me like I had two heads. "I'm not doing this word dance with you. You *know* exactly what I mean."

I paused again. Rubbed my clammy palms on my thighs. "Oh . . . like that. Like you . . . like you? Like rainbow love?" I squinted, then scanned her eyes. "I'm not gay."

"Me either." She looked unmoved. "And that's not answering my question."

Damn, I need some Beauty. Just a lil pinch. Maybe I should go in the bathroom and hit the stash I got in my bag.

No. Don't do that. You got this.

No I don't.

Ugg! I swear, I can't deal, and I need some super-natural Adderall balls to get me through this.

Sweat lined the creases in my forehead, and my stomach felt like I had wild horses stampeding through it.

Breathe.

Relax.

Now say something. "Look, Nikki. I don't need you looking at me like I'm some kind of fruit loop. Not that I have anything against being gay—I mean, my best friend's a queen. But I'm not a king." *I know she thinks I'm stupid.*

"What?" She said, clearly baffled.

"And I'm not transconfused."

"Transwho?"

"I'm just Heather."

"And I'm just Nikki."

Silence.

Inhale.

Exhale.

I continued, "But the truth is..." *Breathe, breathe, relax...*

"Just say it." She pushed.

It's not that easy for me to just say it... because I know feeling like this is wrong. All wrong. But it feels right. "Okay, okay. Look. I can't stop thinking about you." I spat out in one breath. "I even dream about you. I get anxious when you're around. I get nervous. My hands get sticky. My heart races. And I feel like I'm always looking for ways to impress you. And yeah, I've had a boyfriend here and there. And one time I had a counselor. But a girl? Never. But you're different—"

I should just stop right here and leave.

Forget this. Forget her.

I didn't sign up for this.

This is not confessions hour.

This is dumb.

Ridiculous.

I'm not a queer.

And I wish I could just toss these feelings out of my mind and stop 'em from making my heart flutter.

But I can't.

Okay... okay... maybe I should just play this off and act like we're BFFs.

Treat her like she's Spencer.

No. At this moment, I can't stand Spencer.

Coco?

No.

I feel so stupid.

"What are you so scared of?" Nikki asked, interrupting my thoughts. She pressed her forehead against mine and looked into my eyes. "Love is love. A crush is a crush. Makes you human. Nothing more. Nothing less. With me you can just be yourself."

"Really? Just be myself?"

"Just live. Be free. And let's have fun."

"I don't know how to do that. And you already know I can't let something like this out. The blogs and gossip rags will eat me alive. And Camille. Please. She and Kitty will look for some judge to lock me up and throw away the key."

"Heather. Calm down. I'm not trying to be the poster child for rainbow life either."

Silence.

"So in public we hang out and chill like we always do. But when it's just me and you, we go with the flow."

"Go with the flow..." I said more to myself than to her.

"Yeah." She eased her arms around my neck. "So what do you think?" She softly pressed her lips into mine.

I closed my eyes extra tight and said, "I think we should flow..."

And then suddenly, in the blink of an eye, the split second of a beautiful moment, the heavens opened up.

The stars aligned.

Our heated tongues danced.

And finally... I melted.

21

Spencer

"Hey, buttermilk. How's my sweet muffin doing?"

Oh, yabba-dabba doobie-doo. I yawned in Midnight's ear. I liked him. I really, really did. He was smart. And funny. And dark chocolate fine. Rufus Johnson was his real name; he was from Philadelphia. But everyone knew him as Midnight because he was as dark as a summer's night. He attended San Diego State with Rich's ex-boo, Knox—you know, the boy she dragged through the gutters and cheated on, and lied to, every chance she got.

Yeah, him.

He and Midnight were fraternity brothers and roommates. I'd met him while Rich and I were on the run from the po-po after I'd gone upside the head of that ole sheisty street straggler she was so in love with. Justice. Well, I'd *thought* we were on America's top ten wanted list when I'd knocked him out cold. At the sound of sirens, Rich and I scrambled from the ground and fled the scene, leaving her boo for dead.

Anyway. It was an immediate attraction between Midnight and me. We clicked like two light switches the minute I stepped over the threshold of his campus apartment. But—always the lady, never, ever the tramp—I played it real coy. Acted like I really hadn't noticed him the whole three days Rich and I were hiding out in his and Knox's apartment. But I had. Oh, how I was checking him out, his bare-chested self wearing purple and gold long johns.

Midnight was manly and rugged. And, I had to admit, he appreciated all of my good sexual energy. But, goshdangit, he didn't soak my treasure chest. He just lightly moistened it. And this chickie liked her goodies sodden with excitement. But being with Midnight didn't give me waterfalls. No, no, no. Sometimes he gave me tiny puddles, but I was never, ever, drenched in lust when it came to him. I only dribbled, here and there. Midnight just didn't light my campfire, then send it into roaring flames. No, no, no. He just flicked over the blaze, and let my marshmallows scorch around the edges.

Shoot. Most times, this long-legged, lanky, slice of dark chocolate just gave me cramps and bad gas—lots of it, with all his talk of cream sauces and fried, greasy food.

Ooh, lickety-lickety-lick-lick, don't even let me tell a lie because you know that's not in my DNA. No, no, no. But I liked a little kinky-dinky in the boudoir from time to time. But Midnight, God bless his little freaky-deaky soul, always took his lascivious ways to extreme heights, like the time he'd slid fried chicken strips between my toes and then had the audacity to drag a drumstick along the center of the soles of my feet before licking them clean, then eating each chicken strip out from between my toes. Or the time he painted the heels of my feet with barbecue sauce, then sucked them down like he was sucking on two saucy ham hocks.

And I dare not tell you how he loved rolling me over and slathering butter over my fluffy biscuits, then drizzling warm agave syrup over these bouncy cakes before doing all kinds of heavenly tongue tricks. And I won't even talk about the things he did with sliced peaches and Granny Smith apples and succulent strawberries. And the whipped cream! Lawdgodsweetjeezus! All that heavy cream smeared all over me, then lapped off like the hungry dog he was.

Every moment with Midnight was a sticky mess.

"I'm constipated," I stated flatly, flicking imaginary dirt from beneath my fingernails. Lawdjeezus. I desperately needed a deep cleanse after messing with this boy.

He groaned. "Aww, damn, baby. Let Daddy soak you in some prune juice then siphon out them leftovers. I know you good and seasoned."

I frowned. Ooh, this dark chocolate man beast was going to have me lose my religion up in here. Being saved wasn't easy. But no matter the struggle, I had to keep my halo on tight and stay pure and righteous. "First of all," I snapped, tossing my hair as if he could see me through the phone. "I already have a *daddy*. And he's part Indian and part senile. So don't even try to give yourself an upgrade, Midnight. You had better step into the light and see your way over the rainbow. You know I don't play them kind of daddy games with you." I clucked my tongue. "Don't test me my temper."

He moaned. "Awwww, daaaaaayum, pumpkin pie, I love it when you talk dirty. I just wanna roll you in egg batter, sprinkle some cheese over you, then slide you under the broiler and watch you bubble up, baby."

I frowned. I knew I should have never let his belt buckle hit the floor and given him one of my Spencer specials. Now this boy was becoming cuckoo-crazy.

I sighed. I was done. "Second, third, and fourth of all, Midnight," I continued. "This love train we've been riding has gone waaaaaay to the left. It's time to veer off to the side of the tracks and get off. It's been fun, but I'm too young and beautiful and too irresistibly delicious to be tied down to one boy."

"Uh, um, w-what you saying, dumpling?" he asked, sounding taken aback. "Are y-you saying what I think you're saying? You tryna dump a pimp? You tryna abandon all this good lovin' I put on you?"

I rolled my eyes up in my head, fast and hard, almost snapping my sockets loose. Boys and their overly sensitive and enlarged egos! It was draining trying to keep them stroked. My wrists were tired. "No, no. Not dumping you. I still want to be friends. I just don't want to be rolling around in sugar and all them spices with you right now. We need a break."

Silence.

I blinked. "Hello?"

Still. Not. A. Word.

"Midnight? Are you there?"

"Uh, yeah, sweet pea. I'm here. I'm just tryna wrap my lips around what you're dishing. Sounds like you tryna wean a pimp off all that sweet milk. You wanna see daddy go cold turkey, huh?"

I smacked my lips together. "Well, I guess I could be gracious and give you one last teensie-weensie sip of momma's nectar. But you're getting it straight out of a sippy cup."

"Oh word? You gonna ration it out now?"

"It'll be a farewell treat," I said seductively.

I could hear him practically salivating over the phone. "So, let me get this straight, sweet potato. You really wanna dead this? You wanna walk away from all this beef jerky and good gravy I've been putting on you?"

"Yes. But we can still be friends."

"Friends?"

"Yes. Friends."

"Awww, daaaaayum, baby!" He started howling. Then barking. "Aaah-woooooo! Aaaaah-woooooo! *Woof! Woof!*" He started growling. I blinked. Then he started back up with the howling and barking.

"Yes, yes. Who let the dogs out," I sang in my head. I shimmied one shoulder and let myself get caught up in his yowling.

"I could just smear ya face in bacon fat, baby, and lick you clean right now," Midnight said, snatching me from the party going on inside my skull.

"Huh?"

"I'm saying, pop tart, you the best, yo. I been tossing and turning all night and woke up with a bad bout of diarrhea stressing over how I was gonna tell you, baby."

I frowned. "Tell me what, Midnight?"

"About Lil Bit."

I frowned. "Uh, what about that walrus?" Lil Bit, the convict, was Midnight's *ex*. And trying out for a role in *Orange Is the New Black.* Well, not really. But she should have since she seemed to like being in jumpers. This time she was serving a jail sentence for attacking a cashier and manager down at one of the KFCs for giving her all dark meat instead of a bucket of breasts and wings. That cow was merciless when it came to food. But that wasn't the first time she'd had her feet shackled. She'd been in jail for six months prior to that for attacking a cashier at her father's Dairy Queen. That ole humpback whale was rabid. A scavenger.

"C'mon, sweet roll, don't go calling Lil Bit names. She has a big heart."

And a big back. And a big stomach. And a big face. And a big chin.

But who's keeping tally?

I clucked my tongue. "What about her? Did she eat the warden?"

"Nah, baby boo-boo. Lil Bit's coming home on parole."

Parole?

Who in the heck would release her back into the community?

I made a mental note to address the mayor the next time I saw him out with his mistress.

"Parole?" I asked, baffled. "I thought she was going to be away for five years."

"She was. But with good behavior, she got early parole. Cream puff, Lil Bit coming home to daddy. I ain't know how I was gonna tell you. But I'm glad you did it for me. Lil Bit talking like she ready to come home and act right and let me seed 'n' breed."

"Oh, so you want to leave all of this goodness to be with that moose, huh, Midnight?"

"Now hol' up, lamb chop. You broke it off with me, remember?"

I huffed. "Well, of course I did. But that's before I knew *you* wanted to end it with me. So how long have you been seeing that ox behind my back, huh, Midnight?"

"I haven't been to see her, sweet potato. We've only

been writing and talking on the phone. I accept her collect calls."

My nose flared. "Oh, so you've been cheating on me all this time, huh, Midnight? What, you've been writing her dirty letters and talking filthy over the phone to help her get through her lonely nights?"

"Nah, nah, biscuit baby. Nothing like that. We've been taking it slow. Talking about all the new restaurants she wants to try out when she gets out. I told her about the new steak 'n' shrimp basket they have out down at—"

I cut him off. "Save it, Midnight! Go choke on a rib bone! Ooh, you lucky I can't reach through this phone and rip your esophagus out, then split your eyeballs open. You, you low-down, no-good prison husband! You, you hog licker! You couldn't even have the decency to cheat on me with someone out in the free world. No, you had to two-time me with some caged beast."

"Sweet pea—"

"Oh shut up!" I snapped, cutting him off. "When is she getting released back out into the wild, Midnight?"

"Uh, um, see I'm picking her up tomorrow."

I blinked. *"Whaaat?!"* I shrieked. "*Tomorrow*? And when were you going to give me the memo, huh, Midnight? When I walked in on you nibbling on her hoofs? When I caught you massaging her back Jell-O? Oh, you had better hope I don't ever run into you with her. I have a harpoon with her name on it, but I'm going to use it on *you* instead."

"Now, don't be like that, muffin. You real special to me, boo-boo baby. You're like a four piece and a side of mac 'n' cheese and collards with two biscuits. But Lil Bit..." he paused. I thought I heard him sniffle. "Lil Bit's my All You Can Eat platter, baby. She has my heart."

"Boy, bye!"

Click.

I disconnected the call.

How dare that boy want to dump me!

Ha!

Good thing I dumped him first.

22

Rich

"Roll the dice, baby girl! 'Cause I want some customized Jordans!"

I twisted my lips, and my eyes dropped to the pile of money on the floor. A grand. Damn.

I couldn't lose a grand.

Actually it could've been a dollar and I wouldn't wanna lose it. When it came to craps, I was used to beatin' Justice. But obviously the days he spent mad at me he'd been practicing.

I sucked my teeth and said, "Boy, bye. If anything, you about to pay for a pair of heels for me. 'Cause when I sail this dice, I'ma take all ya' lil rent money." I looked up at him, winked, then tossed the dice.

Bam!

Snake eye.

Dead!

Justice cracked up and I almost fainted. Justice collected the pile of money off of the floor and said, "You wanna kiss the ring now, or later?" He slapped me on the behind.

I did my best to play off being a sore loser, so I turned around and wrapped my arms around his waist. "Baby, I let you win."

He chuckled. "Yeah, a'ight." He gently pressed his lips into my forehead…my nose…my lips…my neck. He lifted my shirt about my head and moved on to my navel. Then he stopped. Now that pissed me off. "What the what? Whatchu stop for?"

He smiled. "I won." He unbuckled his pants…

I swear, I loved this man. He was perfect. Everything I needed and more.

And he knew me. Really, really knew me.

And he loved me.

Flaws and all.

We were posted up in his bed. He was asleep, and I lay with my head on his rippled chest, listening to his heartbeat.

After another hour of lying there, Justice stroked my hair and said, "Baby."

"Yeah?"

"You love me?"

I laughed. "Of course."

"You better." He caressed my back. " 'Cause I love you too."

"Awwl, you're so sweet." I kissed his stomach.

He tucked my hair behind my ear. "Babe, when I make it big, we be out this piece, and I'ma get me a fly crib in Holmbly Hills somewhere."

"A'ight now. Snap. Snap. My boo gon' be so hot that people gon' be like Drake who?"

He smiled. "Word. And I know you gon get on the track with me."

"You know this."

"That's wassup." Justice's voice drifted, and I could tell his thoughts had eased into a daydream.

After a few minutes of Justice being lost in his thoughts, I said, "Can I ask you something?"

"Anything."

"How do you feel about babies?"

He frowned. "Babies? Where that question come from?"

I shrugged. "Just asking."

"Nah." He shook his head. "I ain't wit' no babies. I don't even really like kids."

I sucked in a breath, and he hesitated. "Why?" he pressed and sat up in bed. "You tryna tell me something?"

"I was just asking you a question. I mean, we are engaged, and one day we'll have a baby or two . . . I hope."

"Yeah, we're engaged, and I can't wait for the day you become Mrs. Banks. And one day I'll fill you with a lot of babies, just not today."

"Well, when?"

He squinted. "What? You pregnant or something?"

I sucked my teeth. "Did I say that? I was only asking you a simple question. Just like you got dreams, I do too. And one day I want us to have a Justice Jr. and a daughter named Just."

"Yo, you buggin'. I see I'ma have to start wrappin' it up with you. 'Cause you doin' too much."

"Excuse you? And how is that? I'm laying here talking about our future, and now I'm doin' too much? Really? Word?"

Justice shook his head. "There you go, about to start. Take it down and get that base outcha throat. We been doin' good for three days. Don't eff around and get put out. 'Cause I'm not in the mood for your slick mouth, and I damn sure don't wanna hear about no babies. Unless, like I said, you got something you tryna tell me. So I'ma ask you this again: Are you pregnant?"

"No! I'm not!"

"Well, then, don't ask me no more dumb questions! Stop being an idiot, yo!"

Idiot? Oh no he didn't! "I asked you a question and you trippin'. And don't call me an idiot again!"

"Then stop acting like one! You always sayin' something stupid. And the more you talk, the dumber you sound. I see why you failing all your classes. You two steps from special ed."

"I'm not failing all my classes, thank you!"

"Oh, that's right. Your mother pays for your grades."

I felt like he'd slapped me. I told him that in confidence, not for him to throw it up in my face.

He continued, "You don't know how to just chill; you gotta turn up all the time! This is why your mother stays bustin' your behind, and word is bond, if you get to poppin' off up in here today, I'ma press a belt buckle in your back! And that's my word."

"Pause. Negative. I don't know who you think you're talking to. But you won't put your hands or your belt on me! I'm not the one!"

"Shut up!"

"I don't have to shut up! I don't know who you think you talkin' to! London? One of your five other kids' baby mamas?"

Justice's eyes grew bright with surprise.

I continued, "Talking about you don't like kids. I guess not, when you already got fifty you don't take care of! Yeah, nucca. You didn't think I knew that, did you? Well, gut check. And you may as well admit it instead of fixing your big lips to lie."

"Lie? You're the only liar I see. You lied to college boy about that last abortion you had. You lie to ya mom and pops er'day. You lie to the media, pretending to be a Pampered Princess. But you can't lie to me 'cause I know you. You're insecure, fat, and a whore. Easy. You like a stray dog around here. Any nucca that feed you can have you grabbing your ankles."

Whap!

I tossed a slap so hard across Justice's face that it stung my fingertips.

Before I could figure out what to do next, Justice had dragged me out of the bed with one hand and snatched his belt off his dresser with the other.

23

London

Anderson.

God I missed him.

Anderson.

Anderson.

Anderson.

I'd let him slip away.

Pushed him aside.

Rejected him.

And now I missed him. Terribly.

I missed his goofy laugh. Missed his quirkiness. Missed the way he used to look at me whenever he was trying to figure me out.

Oh, God, how I screwed that up.

He'd been my parent-approved boyfriend since I was fourteen. One, we'd been paired because he was from a wealthy family and from good stock, as my mother would say. Two, his mother and my mother were sorority sisters. And, three, he'd make a fine husband one day, as my mother had always insisted.

My mother's voice played in my head.

"Anderson is a good man...You will learn to love him..."

I wiped my tear-streaked face with my hands.

How could I have been so stupid?

I spent all of my time looking for love from Justice when it'd been already staring me in the face all along.

Anderson was the one person who saw me for me.

Flawed.

Yet, he'd accepted me.

Wanted to love me.

And all I ever did was push him away. Treated him coldly. And only wanted to be bothered with him when it was convenient. When I needed to sport myself on his arm for my mother and for appearance's sake.

Anderson knew about Justice and me.

He knew Justice was all I was ever consumed with. And yet he still stood by me and played along, pretending to be my boyfriend, always covering for me whenever I needed him to.

And he was the one who'd comforted me, on many occasions, every time Justice would do or say something to crush my spirit and make me cry.

Yes, he could be a pompous jackass at times. And, yes, he was arrogant and egotistical and...okay, corny. But he was handsome, kind, thoughtful, and highly intelligent. He was everything Justice wasn't.

A gentleman.

And my parents adored him.

Unfortunately, he'd finally had enough of all of my confusion and Justice drama that he told me he wanted nothing else to do with me.

Right after he told me he *loved* me.

That he was *in* love with me.

"I'm done throwing myself at your feet. I'm not going to exert any more of my energy on someone who doesn't want me the way I want them... I'm done being your adviser, your confidante, and the keeper of all your lies and secrets. I'm taking off the superhero cape and moving on. I'm in love with you, London. But I'm not playing this game with you. Delete my number..."

I choked back a sob from the memory.

I have to find a way to get him back.

I was so wrong for treating him the way I did. For taking him for granted. For calling him names and insinuating that he liked boys when, in fact, it was all a misunderstanding. I just thought he did because of something he'd shared with me.

And I didn't think he was really interested in *me*—in *that* way.

Until, until...

The night he'd kissed me.

The night I'd called him at almost four in the morning when I was too distraught to drive home after a night of pacing outside of some lounge after I'd received anonymous text messages that Justice was up in one of the hotel rooms getting filthy with some tramp.

But I didn't catch him in the act. Instead, I'd caught him speeding out of the hotel's parking lot, and I started following behind him, running red lights and swerving down one-way streets just to keep up with him, but when I lost him, I broke down in tears. Became too hysterical to drive.

And called Anderson.

Thirty minutes later, his limo was pulling up behind me. He'd slid into the driver's seat. Wiped my tears with the pads of his thumbs. Stroked my chin. Tucked my hair behind my ear. Then grabbed me by the chin and guided me to him, kissing me. It was a quick peck at first. But then he kissed me again. And it evolved into something more. It'd caught me off guard, but, surprisingly, I hadn't pulled away.

I hadn't resisted.

I'd simply melted into his lips.

Because I liked it.

Maybe because a secret part of me wanted it.

Maybe.

No. If I were perfectly honest, there was no maybe in it.

I wanted it. And I liked it.

Oh, God... Anderson. I miss you so much.

I wiped more tears from my face, then reached for my phone. I scrolled through my contacts, then dialed the number I wanted.

"Anderson Ford here," he said, picking up after four rings.

It was soooo good to hear his voice.

"H-hi, Anderson." My voice cracked.

"Who is this?"

"It's... me," I said meekly. "London."

"*Who?*"

I swallowed. "London." I forced a laugh. "You've forgotten who I am already?"

"Oh, London," he said, dryly. "I didn't recognize the number. I guess that's what happens when you delete numbers from your phone. Out of sight, out of mind. Feel me?"

My stomach lurched.

I held my breath, then meekly said, "I guess I deserved that."

"Yeah, maybe," he said curtly. "But, uh, how can I help you?"

My heart ached as I swallowed back the thick knot slowly coiling around in the back of my throat. "I was thinking about you."

"You were thinking about *me?* Ha! That's a laugh. What for? You've never given me a thought unless it was convenient for you. So, what? Now that that YouTube gangster has dumped you for your little bestie, you're feeling all alone and thought you'd reach out and touch, and I'd take your hand? Is that it?"

"No," I said, my voice barely audible. "I don't care about that. They can have each other."

He laughed. "Yeah, okay. Well, count your blessings. I told you that bum was no good for you, anyway. Told you he had three baby mamas and you *still* wanted to be with trash. You didn't want a good man, London. You wanted some thieving thug-boy."

". . . I'm done trying to be your savior. I'm done playing boyfriend with you. You don't even realize what you have in front of you. You either want a man who is ready to love you and accept you for everything that you are and aren't. Or you want to keep being with some idiot who keeps disrespecting you . . ."

I choked back a sob.

I wanted so badly to tell him that I was ready. Ready for a good man. Ready for *him* to be my man. Ready to be his girl. Ready to be loved by *him*. Ready to give *him* my love. But something deep inside of me wouldn't let me.

My lips quivered.

"I feel so stupid. I should have listened to you."

"Yeah, maybe you should have. And I also told you to delete my number, remember?"

"I know, but. I-I . . ."

"Hey, listen. Let me call you back. I'm in the South of France with my new boo. I'll holla."

My heart sank.

So the rumors were true. He was really seeing that Russian model chick. Ivina Something-or-another. I'd seen her around the fashion circuit. And we'd even paired up during Fashion Week in Milan. She'd moved to Paris when she was seventeen. And was signed to Viva Models. And her face was always plastered on the cover of *Russian Vogue*.

And now she was with Anderson.

Bish!

"Oh, okay. I just wanted to say—"

Click!

My stomach lurched.

I'm sorry…

24

London

"I know who your mistress is..."

Those six words had been haunting me ever since I'd heard them spoken. No matter how hard I tried to shake it, the statement *"I know who your mistress is"* replayed in my head over and over, like some old dirty juke joint song being sung-cried by a love-scorned, jilted lover.

My mother.

I'd pressed my ear closer to the cracked door the night she'd spewed those words out to be sure I'd heard her right. There was no mistaking it. She'd said it. Daddy was cheating on her. *I know who your mistress is.* Those were her words to him, slung out at him like hot grits as they were down in his study, arguing over *me*.

A part of me still blamed *me* for that night.

Maybe they wouldn't have argued if I hadn't unraveled, if I hadn't become undone, if I hadn't let go of the proverbial rope and fallen into a dark, ugly pit.

Maybe.

Daddy had come home from our father-daughter night, mentally spent that night, after he had to literally scoop me up in his arms and carry me out of Nobu—one of my favorite Japanese restaurants in West Hollywood. We'd gone for dinner. But everything around me started to spin out of control. Fast.

Much of the evening had become one big blur. But fragments of that night still floated around in the dark corners of my mind.

That night, I'd felt myself slipping in and out of consciousness, almost like I was having an out-of-body experience. I was there, but I wasn't there. I was fighting to keep it together. I wanted to be there with Daddy. Wanted to be in the moment with him. But my heart wouldn't let me.

A few days prior, Rich and I had had a nasty fistfight at Club Tantrum over *Justice*—well, not really over him, but about him—and I was still sulking over it. I'd confronted her about my suspicions that she and Justice had hooked up. I'd attempted to show her the anonymous photos sent to me via courier, while I was in Europe, of Justice's hand spread over the butt cheeks of some girl with a colorful butterfly tattooed just above her booty crack. The hand was Justice's; that much I was sure of. The tattoo of a small black dagger with blood dripping from its tip on the webbed part between his thumb and forefinger had been the giveaway.

And the *only* girl who I knew with a butterfly over her butt crack was . . . *Rich*.

But that night down at Club Tantrum didn't go as planned. Rich got nasty. Became belligerent. Berated me. And, then, the rest of the night got terribly ugly after I tossed my drink in her face. We tore that lounge up before security tossed us both out.

On top of that, Justice had still been refusing to answer any of my calls. Then he'd blocked my number.

Justice had dumped me. Rich had betrayed me. Anderson had had enough of me and no longer wanted to be bothered with me. And my mother, with her constant micromanaging of my life, had finally gotten the best of me.

She wanted to rearrange me.

In her eyes, from the neck up, I was perfect. *"Face, gorgeous. Neck, fabulous; so graceful and swanlike..."*

But from the neck down, she wanted to have me go under the knife because I wasn't catwalk perfect. My ethnic booty was too much excess baggage for the runway. Or as she'd so lewdly put it while swiping her manicured hand over the curve of my behind, "*There is just* waaaaay *too much of this... if we can just do away with this camel hump...*"

My mother had called my behind a *camel hump!*

She'd said she needed me hanger thin. That she needed to do damage control in order to keep me booked for more shows. For her, my plump rump was a hindrance, a liability to my career on the runway.

And she couldn't have that.

Being a model is what she'd aspired to for me since my birth. Forget what I might have wanted. It didn't matter. My mother had had her own plans for my life already mapped out for me. And there'd be no deviations from it, as far as she was concerned.

So her browbeating and ridicule, coupled with the stress of Justice dumping me, then Anderson giving me an ultimatum—him or Justice—then walking out on me when I couldn't make a choice—it all had taken a disastrous toll on me. All of my lies and loneliness and hurt and secrets had finally ripped me open and spilled out of me right there on that bathroom floor as I cried and cried.

That night, Daddy saved me from myself. And I told him everything. How my mother wanted to drag me to a plastic surgeon to get rid of my breasts and butt. How I'd been sneaking to be with Justice—even though I knew he and my mother forbade it. How Justice was the reason Anderson broke things off with us. How I'd hurt him.

I'd cried and cried. Daddy broke in the door, then carried me out of the restaurant in his arms.

And then, after he had gotten us home and carried me up to my suite and laid me on my bed, he'd gone down and confronted my mother. Till this day, I don't know how long they'd been arguing. But I know that by the time I'd come downstairs to make my way into the kitchen, going by Daddy's study, I'd heard them quarreling like never before.

"You've done nothing but put your modeling career before me, our daughter, and *this marriage!"*

"Oh, don't you dare even go there with me, Turner Phillips! Like you haven't put your law practice before this marriage! I was modeling way before *I met you. You knew it was my life!"*

"And wanting to be a mother *and* wife, *instead of galloping up and down the runways, should have also been your life, Jade! It's what you signed up for when you married me! But it wasn't your life. And now look at us! Look at our daughter! I've always stepped back and let you raise London the way you saw fit, but I see now that that was one of the biggest mistakes I made. I should have been more involved."*

"Yes, Turner, you're right! Maybe you should have

been, instead of running off to your filthy mistress *every chance you got!"*

I blinked, fighting to shake away the memory. Fighting to fast-forward to the present, instead of reliving that horrible night.

"I know who your mistress is..."

Daddy was a cheater.

And now I was in a late-model rental with dark tinted windows—wearing a god-awful synthetic wig and dark shades—crouched down low in the driver's seat, eyeballing his mistress's every move.

So far, it'd been nothing exciting going on. She'd stopped at a high-end boutique on Rodeo Drive. Then, an hour later, she'd stepped out carrying one shopping bag.

Next, she'd made her way to David Yurman, probably to buy herself some cute piece of jewelry to wear in her nakedness the next time she snuck off with Daddy or maybe some other woman's husband.

Rich's face flashed in my head.

I gripped the steering wheel.

That trick was the product of cheaters.

Her mother was a home wrecker, a nasty, cleanup woman.

Her father was a low-down, dirty womanizer, a rolling stone.

And Rich thought her life was so damn fabulous.

Delusional trick!

I eyed Logan Montgomery as she made her way to a bakery. *Whore!* I rolled my eyes as she walked purposefully, tossing her weave over her shoulder, as she made her way back to her Maserati.

Bish.

When she pulled out of the parking lot, I tailed her. I

kept several cars between us, making sure she didn't notice she was being followed. After several minutes of driving, she headed toward Santa Monica Boulevard. She turned left onto Sunset Boulevard. Then made a slight right onto Wilshire Boulevard, eventually making her way onto the interstate.

My parents' voices floated around the interior of the car.

"I want a divorce."

"Fine! Go be with your mistress, Turner...!"

Trying to keep from swerving off the road, I blinked back the onslaught of more tears. I loved my father with all my heart. I swear I did. I loved him more than I loved my mother, because I felt like he understood me more than she did. And he was more forgiving of my shortcomings than she would ever be.

However, lately, sometimes I couldn't bear to look at him. Knowing what I knew. That he was planning to abandon me, leave me stuck with my mother—*alone,* to run off with his whore.

My parents' arguing voices pushed their way into my thoughts again, invading my head, forcing me back.

"You pushed me into someone else's bed when you stopped wanting to handle your wifely duties in and out of our bedroom..."

"Oh, Turner, stop! You were screwing that ghetto tramp long before I stopped letting you crawl up on top of me. So don't you even go there with me! You and I both know the real reason you wanted to relocate here! And it had nothing to do with getting London out of New York or being closer to your firm in Beverly Hills and everything to do with you wanting to be near that gold-digging home wrecker!"

God . . . what did he even see in her?

She was uncultured.

Ghetto.

Lacked sophistication.

She was groupie-trash.

The only thing she had to be good for was her bedroom skills. She had to be turning nasty tricks in the sheets, I'm sure, in order for Daddy to want to walk out on his family.

To want to leave *me;* abandon me!

Sure my mother was a cold-hearted witch.

And she neglected Daddy *and* me.

But that didn't give this trampy slut the right to swoop in and break up our home.

Sure, Daddy and my mother might be in a loveless marriage (I blamed my mother for that), but that didn't give Jezebel the right to snake her way into Daddy's boxers. She had to have taken advantage of him. Used her womanly wiles to break him. Women like her were treacherous, relentless, when they wanted something. They had no shame.

Like mother, like daughter.

They were both harlots. Bottom feeders. They both had thieved their way into the two most important men in my life's lives. Justice and Daddy. Justice, I was over.

Daddy, I was disappointed in.

Rich, I was willing to forgive.

But this harlot, this, this . . . skank, I wanted to see her suffer.

Nasty gutter rat!

She must be lonely and miserable to sleep with someone else's husband.

Well, that's what whores do.

While tailing her, I realized I couldn't hold Rich's whorish ways against her. She was who she was because it's what she was taught. Her mother groomed her to be slutty.

Just like her.

I had to fight the urge to keep from pressing down on the gas and ramming into the back of her car. *You're going to pay for coming in between my family!*

Relax, London. Reel in your emotions.

I took two deep breaths. Then eased my foot up off the accelerator.

An hour later, we were no longer on the I-10 freeway. My knuckles practically turned white as I gripped the steering wheel. We were traveling along the Pacific Coast Highway, into Malibu.

Five minutes later, I eased back and watched as the home wrecker pulled up to a gated entry, rolled her window down, and punched into a keypad. Within seconds, the iron gates slowly opened and she drove through, leaving me staring at the back of her headlights.

Who lives here behind those gates?

I wonder if your husband knows about your dirty little secret, you scandalous troll!

Fortunately, the sun had already set. And, so far, I hadn't been noticed. And I needed to keep it that way.

To kill time, I pulled out my phone and began googling Rich Montgomery.

There were plenty of entries about that trick. Her bio, her shopping sprees, her party life, her family.

I read every last one of them, absorbing every torturous detail. The most recent accounts were of her and Justice together. They were calling him "JB, the Heart Throb Crooner."

Ugh.

I kept scrolling, then stopped at the entries on her pending birthday bash. Her publicist stated it would be the party of all parties. The most extravagant bash of the century. "All of Hollywood's royalty will be vying for a slice of the Pampered Princess's birthday cake."

I rolled my eyes.

I hope she chokes.

I glanced at the clock. It was almost ten o'clock. I couldn't believe I was still sitting out here, lurking in the shadows.

Waiting...

I picked up my night-vision binoculars again and zoomed in. I couldn't see a damn thing. I needed to see something. Anything.

I know who your mistress is. The married, man-stealing whore!

No, Daddy wasn't perfect. No one was. But he wasn't the problem. Rich's mother was. That ole, nasty, man-stealing *bish!*

Just like her daughter.

I stole a glance at myself in the rearview mirror.

This wig is hideous.

I straightened it on my head before reaching into my bag and pulling out a black ski mask.

I leaned over and grabbed the small can of red paint from off the passenger's side floor, then grabbed the ice pick and paintbrush.

Desperate times called for desperate measures.

Rich didn't want to be friends. Fine. She didn't have to be. And I'd be damned if I was going to beg her. No. Starting tonight, all of my energy was being diverted to something much more important than her raggedy ole friendship.

Destroying her man-stealing mother!

I was going to become Logan Montgomery's worst nightmare.

Okay, Rich. Let's see how fabulous *your life is when I'm done.*

I slid out of the car. Shut the door, then made my way across the dimly lit street. Dressed in all black, like an omen.

25

Heather

"Clutcheeeeeeeeeeeen' peaaaaaaaaaaarls!"

Oh my God!

Oh.

My.

God!

You felt that?

Was it an earthquake?

'Cause I swear I felt the ground shake, open up, and suck me in.

Or maybe . . . maybe . . . it's not that deep. Maybe my heart just took flight and jumped off the cliff.

Because now I can't breathe.

But wait.

Wait.

Relax

Count backward.

Five . . .

Four . . .

Three . . .

Get it together now.

Chill for a minute.

Inhale.

Exhale.

Repeat.

Slowly, I turned around.

Of all the party crashers...

Whyyyyyyyy was this thing here?

I knew Satan was ridin' my jock, but daaaaaamn kazam, I had no idea he was on it like this.

Queen Hoesque-Ratchet-Rich Montgomery was somehow standing in the doorway of my bedroom balcony, mouth *alllllllll* twisted.

And judging by the beam in her stretched-wide brown eyes and the greasy smile on her face, she'd just witnessed me and Nikki in a lip-lockin' escapade.

Dead.

Rich's chubby and bacon-greased lips glowed as they popped and slapped against each other. "Hold up. Wait a minute." She grinned, shamelessly, batting her fake lashes at least a thousand unnecessary times. "Is it a bird? Is it a plane? No, it's Heather with some sugar in her tank. Fix it, Black Jesus. 'Cause I spot some Mexican tea with a dash of rainbow in it." She placed one arm behind her back and did a holy dance. "Yaaaaaaaaaasssssssss, honey. Yaaaaaaaassssss!" She waved her hands to the heavens. "I am here for the sizzle-sizzle pride life. Hag-central, baby." She paused. "Don't get it twisted, though. All of this baked-bean-brown goodness is strictly stickly. Feel me? Boxer and brief zone. But I see you two kissin' fish swimmin' all up and through the lady pond."

I couldn't believe this.

Of all the times me and Nikki have kissed and kicked it.

The movies.

Walks on the beach.

Netflix and snacks.

Bowling.

Dinner.

Ice cream.

For the past month, just straight chillin' and managing to keep the dopest secret: in public we were BFFs, and in private we were boo'ed up.

But.

Now.

We were effed up.

Straight up on Blast Street.

'Cause the top hood-bugger horse-mouth ho of Hollywood High was all up in my cloak and dagger.

Think...

Think...

Think...

I can't be nasty to this creepette. So I'ma have to wing it. How am I supposed to do that, though? I can't stand this chick. But I better think of something quick before this overweight Kermit starts spilling tea everywhere.

Okay... okay... let me try this. "Hey, Rich!" I gave her a smile so fake it's a wonder my whole grill didn't crack. "Look at you, girl. Looking all cute and—"

"Bzzzzzzzzzzzzz! Bzzzzzzzzzzz! Annnnnnnnnnnt!" She screamed, sounding like a game show buzzer. "Clutching pearls! Wrong answer! Try again!" Rich stepped completely onto the balcony, shoving a hard hand up on her hip. She batted her lashes. "Why are you flirting with me? Calling me cute. What's next? You two gon' want a threesome? I'm all for love and light, but I don't want a wife." She looked over at Nikki. "And all this time I thought this lil fetus-lookin' thing wanted my man and she been lookin' at me. Sniffin' around my panties." Rich wagged her index finger. "Honey-bunny-sugah-plum, you will never get up in these size seven drawls, little girl. Neverrrrrrrrrrr." Rich shook her head and her words slightly slurred. "La-la-lost my good-good man 'cause I thought Waitress Fruit Loop wanted him."

I looked at Nikki and she looked at me. Obviously, we were thinking the same thing. This slore, Rich, was drunk.

I looked back over to Rich as tears filled her eyes.

Why is she crying?

"Lost my baby, Knox! Knoxxxxxxxxx!" She howled.

I walked over to her, and for the first time ever in my life, I wrapped my arms around this she-wolf and said, "Everything will be all right." I patted her broad back. "Don't cry. You're with Justice now."

"But I could've had 'em both." She sucked up snot, and her voice quivered. "It's seven days in a week, and I would've given Knox at least one and a half. Oh lawd! Fix it, Black Jesus! Fix it!" I did everything I could not to shove Rich away from me. But this bird reeked of beer. Queen Michelob.

"Umm, Rich," I said.

"Ya-ya-yeah?"

"Have you been drinking?"

She sucked up more snot and stepped out of our embrace. "Yaaaaaaaaaasssssss, honey! Yaaaaaaassssss!" She pulled out a six-pack of beer from her oversized Louis V tote and sang, "I been drankin'. I been drankin'." Then she snapped her fingers, dropped down, popped a twerk, and topped it off with the nae nae. "Now watch me whip..." She sang.

Me and Nikki just stood there and stared.

"Why is she here?" Nikki mumbled, while Rich did the stanky leg.

I shrugged. "I have no idea. She has never rolled up over here."

"Well, I'm getting ready to leave."

"Good idea." Rich snorted, now staring at us. "'Cause I need to talk to my fellow Pampered Princess. And no frogs allowed. So hop along."

"Rich," I snapped. "Don't speak to her like that."

"Awwwl, tain't that sweet. You're trying to defend lil Caitlin Jenner. Don't be fooled, Heather. Just 'cause she has a cute lil tennis dress on doesn't make her a lady. She's a nasty ole thing. Trust me. She was all up in my business with Knox. She's probably the reason we broke up."

"No, you and all the thugs you cheated on him with is why you two broke up," Nikki snapped. "You know what, Rich." Nikki paused. "I'ma let you get that and I'ma leave. Because if I keep standing here I'ma give you what Knox should've: one to the mouth."

"Wheeeeewwwww, I'm scared." Rich pretended to shiver. "I gotta admit, though, that was a cute lil read. Needs some tweekin', but you tried it. Now see ya." Rich waved her hand.

"She doesn't have to leave." I sucked my teeth. "Unlike you, she was invited here."

Nikki interjected, "Heather, look, I don't have time for this. I'll call you later." She stormed away, leaving the echo of a slamming front door behind her.

"Come on, Heather." Rich sauntered from the balcony into my room, flopping her bubble butt across my bed. She propped one pillow behind her back and another across her stomach. Then she kicked her red bottoms off and snatched one of the beers away from the six-pack. "We should talk," she said, opening the beer tab, then guzzling.

I stood in the middle of the floor, struggling to keep my anger at bay.

I couldn't believe this stankin' heifer. How does she just make herself at home? In my spot. She had no rhyme or reason to be here. She was just here. Chillin'. Perpetratin' like we were down. But knowing we would snatch each other's scalps off at any given moment.

I took a deep breath. I knew I needed to tolerate this chick, at least long enough to convince her that the kiss she'd witnessed was a pissy drunk illusion. The last thing I needed was this cow flappin' that gullet of hers.

I uncurled my lips and eased them into a smile... well, a crooked grin. "Umm, Rich," I looked her over, as she continued to guzzle. "Why are you here?"

She swished the beer around in her mouth, swallowed, then said, "Oh. That was rude. What I can't come see you?" She popped her fingers. "We *are* in the same crew, ma'am. You don't like me or something, Heather?"

Umm, no. I can't stand you. And if you were on life support, I would definitely unplug your machine to charge my phone. You make every hair follicle on my body stand up. And therefore you can't just run up over here 'cause you feel like it. I can't just roll up on you!

I pulled in a deep breath and pushed it out. "Rich, I never said I didn't like you. I just wanna know why you're here."

"To bond with you. You know, we could be like play cousins. Like God sisters." She raised her beer can in the air like she was making a toast. "I prayed to Black Jesus about you, and Black Jesus said, 'Go hither and see Heather.' " She gave a drunk chuckle. "So here I am."

Rich took a sip, patting the spot next to her on the bed. "Now let's bond." She said. " 'Cause last I heard from Spencer you were a junkie whore, laid up across your counselor's desk, ready for his bull's eye. Don't tell her I told you that, though. I don't need the drama. And, you know, Spencer is a shit-starter. And her only true friend is my brother, RJ." Rich rolled her eyes. "Spencer doesn't think I know, but I know—'cause my PI told me—that she snuck off and went over to England last weekend to get her British jezebel on with my brother. That slum slut."

Rich picked up her second beer and downed it. Then belched. Loudly. "And Spencer knows he's pimpin' every lil white girl he meets on those British cobblestone streets. Yet, off she went to be an Old World freak. Now back to you, Heather. Tell me. How long have you been a lesbo?" She handed me a beer.

I hesitated. I sooooo wanted to chop this heifer in her throat. "First of all, I'm not a lesbo."

Rich gulped and belched again. "Ewww, don't tell me you're bi? I can't witchu. You all confused. What you need is something tall and chocolate. So you can turn up properly. You need me to hook you up?"

"How did you get in here, Rich?"

"The garage was open. I walked in and looked around your house until I found you. And, wait, stop the press and hold the mess. Whyyyyyyy is your mother spread-eagled across her bed, in that same white gown and matted mink slippers? Every time I see this woman she is in the same gear. Like, who does that? Like, is she okay?" Rich took her index finger, pointed toward her temple, and twirled it around. "Or are the rumors true?"

I curled the corner of my top lip and tapped my foot. In

a minute, this trick was gon' get tossed out and into the street. "What rumors?"

"Clutching pearls! You didn't know everybody said Camille was a drunk cray-cray? Spencer was the main one calling her names."

Don't trip...yet. "First of all, I will handle Spencer. And second of all, I don't need you coming up in here, uninvited, talking about Camille. I suggest you fall all the way back. Because you're pissing me off." I stood up.

"Oule, touchy-touchy." She popped open another beer. "What, you need a hug? Relax girl. Sit back down. We're in Hollywood. Rumors are everywhere. And besides, if they ain't talkin', they ain't gawkin', and everybody needs some press. Feel me?"

"Yeah, you're right," I quipped back, reluctantly taking my seat. "Rumors are everywhere. Like the rumors about your daddy being a low-down ho, with a basketball team of bastards running around."

"Whaaaaaaaat?!" Rich spit out her beer, spritzing it all over my bed.

Oh hell no! This ho had to go. Not now but right now.

I looked over at Rich, and her eyes burned through me. Seems we had the same vision: us rolling around on the floor, arms swinging and hair flying.

I continued, "And what are you looking at me like that for? You need to be changing the linen on my bed!"

"Clutching pearls. Umm, Heather. You better catch yourself, girl. 'Cause you almost got yo' mouth tore out. Now, I understand you wanna turn up, but you bout to turn up the wrong way. I came over here to invite you to my party and to tell you to bring your reality-TV camera crew. 'Cause you need me to make your show a hit. I don't need you,

I'm already a star. So the last thing you should do is try and drag me or my daddy. And down low? You're the only one around here on the down low, bruh." She wiggled her neck and sucked her teeth. "See, this is why nobody likes you."

"I don't need you, yo' daddy, or your whack crew to like me." I stood up again. "I'm cool. And I'm not on the down low, I'm just not a ho." I grimaced. "You're the one over here desperate for free publicity at your dumb whack party! Screw you and that party! 'Cause what you need to do is stop running your mouth about Camille; go handle yo' daddy's scandal; and hope that his long-lost bastards stay in their place and don't show up on your doorstep."

Rich sucked her teeth. "Girl, bye. Me and my mama wish a ho and ho's brood would. Chile, cheese. Boo, please. One thing a side-chick's kid will never do is rock my daddy's girl spot."

He already has a daughter. Camille's voice filled my head.

I don't care what he has! I'm his daughter too.

I swear I should tell Rich! Get it off my chest. And wreck her night the way this has wrecked my life! I continued, "Yeah, well, when they come knocking we'll have to see about that."

"What? You know one of 'em?" Rich pressed. "Is that what you're so mad about? I tell you what, tell the trash to bring their azz. Tell 'em I said to come over. Please. I dare 'em. We eat breakfast together er' morning. My mother, my daddy's wife, makes sure of that. So tell 'em to ring the bell. Then let's see how quickly they get handed they birth certificate back! 'Cause if they were a real Montgomery, they'd be up in the château with me. But they're not." She rose off the bed. "And I don't know what you care for, but you need to mind your business and worry about Empress Wino in the other room."

Rich shoved her tote's strap up and over her shoulder. She continued, "I don't know what I was thinking coming over here to this trap house cottage. Any. Way! Got me all down in the ghetto-valley-hood!"

"Empress Wino?! Trick, you are straight out of order." I pushed her on the shoulder, causing her to stumble back and her tote to slide down her arm.

"Whaaaaaat?! Clutching pearls! I can't believe this. I can't help it if your mother is off the meat rack! You got me messed up!" She shoved me to the floor, and the next thing I knew we were wrapped up in a beer-smelling, hair-pulling, and slappin' brawl.

Her neck was in the crook of my arm. And she had a fist full of my hair, yanking it back. We tossed, turned, and rolled from one side of the room to the other. And with every slug that landed, my pictures fell off the wall, my books rocked off the bookshelf, and ish was everywhere. I was doing my all to tear this big beyotch up for the old and new. And no, she wasn't an easy feat, but I was getting some major blows in.

"Heaaaaatherrrrr Suzaaaaaaaaaanne!" Camille screamed rushing into my room and yanking us apart. "What is going on in here?!"

I huffed, completely out of breath, and peered over at Rich. Her hair looked electrified on top of her head. Her clothes were disheveled. Her makeup was smeared across her face. And all I could think about was how Camille breaking us up allowed Rich to hook me dead in the jaw and get the last hit. Now I needed to push Camille outta the way so I could toss Rich off the balcony. Otherwise, I was gon' punch Camille dead in her grill.

"What is going on here?!" Camille screamed, looking at me. And judging by the reflection in her eyes, I looked as if I'd been to World War III. Camille's head whipped over to Rich, "Little girl, I suggest you get the hell outta my house!"

"You don't have to put me out, Norma Marie, 'cause I'm leavin! And you better stay away from me, Heather, because I will come back over here. And I will spank yo' ass again!"

"I said out!" Camille screamed.

I spat, "Come over here if you want, Rich, and see what you get!" I tried to reach for her, but Camille snatched me back.

"That's enough!" Camille snapped.

"Let her go." Rich insisted. "Don't hold her back 'cause as soon as she steps this way, I'ma lay her to rest. Slam my elbow right in her nasty carpet mouth and murder her rainbow-lickin' skittles behind!"

"I said get out!" Camille yelled, snatching Rich by the shoulder, shoving her out of my bedroom, down the steps, and finally outside, where she slammed the door in her face.

Dusting her hands, Camille whipped around toward me. We were now in the living room. "Didn't I tell you to leave those Montgomerys alone? Didn't I?"

"She came over here! I didn't invite her!"

"Suuuuuurrrreeee you didn't, Heather." Camille walked over to the bar. "I don't know what it's going to take for you to learn." She stirred her scotch. "But you gon' learn. Got this home-wreckin' spawn up in my house, disrupting my nap, and causing me to be late for my evening cocktail. Are you crazy? Really, are you crazy?! And what does she mean, carpet mouth and rainbow licker! Do you need to tell me something, Heather Suzanne? 'Cause I gave birth to a daughter, not a man!"

"I don't know what she's talking about! And you need to be thanking me, considering I was taking up for you!"

"I don't need you taking up for me. Take up for yourself and save me the drama. You always have something going on, and that's why I can never have no menz company up in here. I'm lonely, Heather. Don't you think I need a gentleman caller? I need to be touched too." She downed the rest of her drink and immediately refreshed her glass. "I swear, you are not going to learn until Richard Montgomery spits in your face!" Camille shook her head, and as she stormed away, her kitten heels banged angrily into the floor, while the hem of her infamous white nightgown swirled behind her.

26

Spencer

I cringed the minute I heard "Ho" by Ludacris blaring from my phone.

Rich.

It was my new ringtone for her.

"Oh no, oh no, oh no, ohhhh nooooo!" I said, shaking my head at seeing her big face on my screen. "You's a *ho,* goshdiggitydanggit! And I am *not* in the mood to stamp your ho-card. Not tonight. Ole nasty lollipop licker."

I let the call roll into voice mail.

Rich was a dangerous kind of ho. She didn't dress like one. She didn't look like one. And she didn't *always* act like one.

But she'd brazenly throw herself at a boy at the drop of a dollar and offer up her bedroom treats without batting a lashed eye.

She wasn't a skank-ho.

She was a scandalous one.

And her *ho*-ism was a genetic trait.

Her daddy was a man-ho, sleeping with all those women

and creating all kinds of illegitimate babies along the way, just sprinkling his man milk in every woman's cookie bowl. Just nasty!

Mmmph.

And her mother—ole Miss Shoot 'Em Up, Bang-Bang (the retired gang banger, ex-con, ex-parolee) was a groupie ho, stalking locker rooms and camping out backstage of any-and-every concert show in all of her skimpy ho wear until she managed to snag her meal ticket out of the gutters of Watts.

Rich's father, Mr. Montgomery, forever known as M. C. Wickedness.

Oooh, their ho line ran deep!

So you see. Poor, poor Rich had no control over her destiny.

She was destined to be a *ho*. And it was all she aspired to be.

*Ho*ish.

Two seconds later, "You's a ho" was playing again.

No, no, no, noooo...

I quickly pressed IGNORE, sending her straight to my voice mail.

My phone chimed, alerting me I had a text.

ANSWER THE PHONE, TRICK!!!! U C ME CALLN U!!

Ignore.

"Get a clue, chickie! I'm over you!" I said aloud.

Ole nasty cooter!

I tossed my cell onto my bed. I was still a little hot and sour at Rich for wasting my precious time in the girls' lounge last week, knowing good and dang well I could have spent my time in study hall instead of using up all my good advice on her, only to learn that she was stuck on stupid about that thug daddy of hers.

Then to learn she'd slept with Corey.

COREY?!

He was the enemy!

So goshdang what if she didn't know that that boy was public enemy number one, two, *and* three. She still should have known better than to get tangled up in the sheets with him again.

She should have exercised better judgment.

But *nooooo!* That girl's thighs were like a set of glass doors, just sliding open for anything with a pulse and a pet rock.

Her hot pocket had more miles on it than—

Brrrring. Brrrrring. Brrrrrrring.

Oh no, oh no, *ohhhhh noooooo!*

Now she was ringing my home line. And I *knew* it was Rich because no one else had the number to the Batgirl line, except *her*.

I didn't answer.

Nope.

But in true stalker fashion, Rich kept coming—oops, heehee—I meant, calling and calling. Two times, three times, four times, then times that by three.

Ugh.

She could be obnoxiously annoying, like a bad rash that wouldn't go away no matter how many tubes of ointment you used.

I finally answered on the fifth ring. Not saying a word. I just clutched the phone and listened to the grizzly roar.

"Hello? Hello? Spencer? *Spennnnnncerrrrrr?* I know you're on the other end of the phone. I know *you* know it's *me* calling you, trick! Don't do me! Don't. Do. Me!"

Click.

Last I checked, she said our friendship was over and

she chose that junkie, Heather, over me, and now she wanted to call *moi?*

Oh, uh, no ma'am. I don't think so! I don't play leftovers to anyone.

Rich could kiss my sweet—

Brrrrring. Brrrrrrring.

She rang my line again.

This time I snatched it off the receiver. *"Whaaaaat?!"*

"Turn up! Turn up! Tuuuuuuurn uppppp! Boom-bop-drop-it-like it's-hot! Stop what you're doing. I gotta bottle and some tea on fleek...!"

"The number you've dialed has been disconnected," I said, imitating a computerized voice. "Please hang up and try your number again."

Click.

I slammed the phone back down onto the receiver.

But being hung up on didn't deter her. The ole pesky flea called my cell again.

"I saaaaaid, turn up! Turn uppppp!" she yelled the minute I picked up. "I got some tea to pour! Yes, *hunni, yassss!*"

"What tea, Rich? I told you I don't drink that mess. It stains your teeth. But since you keep pressing me to sip with you, I'll let you pour me a half a cup. And it better be the good juicy kind. Or I'm going to toss it back in your face. Now start pouring, girlie."

"Wellllll, get your cup out, honey! And let me let you sip on this right quick. Honey, I just left Heather's house, and she was prancing around in a pair of boxer shorts! Yassss, honey, yasssss! Heather is a rug chewer. Carpet Fresh all in her mouth! That girl is a fish kisser. She was bumper-to-bumper with—"

I rolled my eyes up in my head. Rich was an exhausting liar!

"Oh please, Rich. Heather is not prancing around wearing boxer shorts. That girl likes coochie-cutters, the yeast-building kind."

"Ohhhhmygooodness, *Spennnnncer!* You're so brain-dead. So stupid! So, so pink helmet special."

I blinked. "Um. Who is this again?"

"Spennnnnnncer! Spennnnnncerrrrr! Get it together. Who do you think it is? Who else would call you a dumbo to your face? Or—wait, in your ear on the phone?"

I pursed my lips. "I don't know. Tell me."

She sucked her teeth. "It's me, stupid. Rich. The only one who halfway likes you, girl. Don't act like you don't know me, *Spennnnncer!*"

"Umm, what did you say your name was again?"

"Whore, don't play stupid with me, although I know that's not easy for you not to do since it comes natural. You're naturally dumb, Spencer. But I forgive you. It's your mother's fault."

I bit into my bottom lip. Counted to sixteen. "Two... four... six... eight... ten... twelve... fourteen... sixteen... What do you want, Rich, huh? A country ham? A biscuit sopped in man gravy?"

"*Ewwww*! Clutching pearls! Tramp, don't do me! I like my man's gravy fresh out the can. Not slopped on some damn biscuit, girl. You know I'm on a low-carb diet!"

I shook my head. "Have you been drinking?"

Rich groaned. "Ohhhhhhmygod, *Speeeeeeencer!* What are you, my Breathalyzer now? My twelve-stepper? Get up off my tongue, girl. You are team too much right now. You stay doing the most! Yeah, I had me a little taste. So what? I'm a grown woman. And I know how to handle mine, hon."

I clucked my tongue several times, and wondered how many times she stood in the middle of her bedroom—slathered in sparkles and wrapped in a tutu, with a giant horn propped up on her head, spinning around the room thinking she was a magical unicorn.

Mmmph. Probably every day.

I yawned. "Uh-huh. Whatever you say, Rich. Whatever. You—"

"Wait, hold that thought," she said, rudely cutting me off. "I think that's my man calling in." She pauses, then says, "Oh, no. False alarm. It wasn't him."

"I swirled my eyeballs up and around in my head. "Which *him,* Rich?"

"Don't do me, *Spennnncerrrrr*! My real love, girl! Justice! Who else? You know I was searching for a real love, someone I could call my own. And I have him. Big, strong, strapping chocolate. That's the only man for me! Stop being so forgetful. You know me and my bae got that real love; don't hate!"

"Girlie, bye."

Click.

Oooh, that girl gives me a bad case of the cramps, I thought, eyeing my cell ring as Rich's theme song played. I knew Rich. She would keep this up *alllllll* gotdiggity-dang night unless I gave in.

I sighed. "Umm, yessssss, Rich. How may I direct your call?"

"Don't do me, *Spennnncerrrrr!* So, how's your house? Is it burned down to the ground, yet? Can I come over to assess the damages?"

"My house is just fine, chickie. And, *nooo,* you may not come over here to assess a dang thing. You're not invited, or welcomed, here. Go on back over to Beverly Hills and play friends with Heather. I'm..."

"Well, get over yourself, *Spennnncerrrrr!* It's too late! 'Cause I'm at the door."

I blinked. "What door?"

"This door, ditsy," she announced, swinging open the double doors to my suite. She held her phone in one hand and a leather bag in the other, while her purse dangled in the crook of her left arm. "And Heather and Knox are dating the same girl."

She sat the bag up on one of the marble tables.

I rolled my eyes at her. "Rich, bye. What girl are you talking about?"

She sighed, plopping down on my chaise, dropping her purse to the floor. She adjusted her earpiece, kicking her heels off.

"That hooker-ho that broke up my life. Tore up my love life! Stole my man from me. Nikki, honey, Nikki! Her and Heather are—"

I eyed her, shifting my phone from one ear to the other. "Trick, please. You broke up your own life. Who's more of a hooker-ho than you?"

Rich reached for one of her shoes and tossed it at me. But it missed, hitting a wall instead. "*Bish,* don't try me!"

I eased back on my bed, watching *her* watching *me* as we talked on the phone. "Girl, face it. You're the biggest whore in the world. You're transatlantic. Internationally known. And how dare you call here, calling *me* about Heather, like I give a damn about whose carpet she's been cleaning! Heather's a lot of things, but she is no carpet cleaner. That girl hasn't lifted a dustpan in her life. And it shows with all those nasty little dust bunnies all around her baseboards." I shot her a nasty look. "So don't come here with your lies, telling me nothing about that girl. Or I'm going to hang up and throw you out of my house. Now try me."

She threw her other shoe. But it flew over my head, smacking up against my armoire. "Tramp, lies! I had front-row tickets to the *Vagina Monologues* starring Heather and that man-stealing whore, Nikki!"

I slammed the phone down on her, then hopped off my bed, pointing a finger in her face. "Get out of my house, Rich. Now."

She ignored me, pressing a button on her phone. My house phone rang again.

I blinked.

Rich tilted her head. "Oh, so you're really not going to answer the phone, huh, Spennnncerrrr, huh?" She slapped my hand down. "You're just going to stand there watching the phone ring, knowing I'm sitting here calling you, huh, Spennnnncerrrrr? Fine, don't answer it."

"Get out, Rich."

She ignored me again. This time her theme song started playing on my cell.

"Ohmygod, Spencer! I used to love this song, girl!" She started bopping her head, throwing her hand up and singing along. When the call went into voice mail, she called back. "*Yasssss,* ho, *yassssss!* You did that!"

I giggled, then clapped my hands and shimmied my shoulders forward and back, singing the hook. Then I said, "You stay doing ho activities, gotdang it!"

"Yassss, yassss. I love me some good ho activities. Wait a minute! I know you're not trying to say I'm a *ho*, are you?"

I waved her on. "Girl, no. Ludacris is."

"Oh, okay," she said, getting up from the chaise, "'cause I was about to say..."

"I know, I know. Don't do you," I finished for her, giggling.

She gave a dismissive wave. "Girl, no. I was getting ready to say the grass ain't always greener on the other side. Hoing ain't easy."

I blinked.

Alrighty then…

"Annnnnyway"—she pulled out a bottle of Ace of Spades—"get your mind right, *Spennncer*. I bought us some bottles to turn up with."

She popped the cork, and I licked my lips. My mouth watered. I hadn't sipped on my favorite champagne in weeks.

"Oh, so we friends again?" I asked, staring at the sparkling elixir as the bubbles rose to the top of our glasses.

"Until the drinks are gone," Rich stated, handing me a flute.

I pursed my lips. "Then let's drink up, so you can get the hell out of my house."

We clinked our glasses.

27

Spencer

Forty-five minutes later, Rich and I were stretched out across my bed, guzzling down the second bottle of champagne. We were on our stomachs with our bare feet dangling in the air, passing the bottle back and forth.

I listened to Rich go on and on about Heather and that Nikki girl. I decided to keep my fluffy lips shut, and just take it all in.

The dirt.

The filth.

Ooh, it sounded simply too scandalous and too dang juicy to be true. But what if it wasn't gossip? What if Heather really was a carpet cleaner? What if Rich really did walk in on Heather combing through Nikki's rug with her tongue?

I couldn't stand Heather. But, but, oooh, but . . . I couldn't stand the thought of not knowing if Rich spewed lies from her hot, drunken mouth. Or if that laser surgery she'd had really had given her clearer vision, and she really did see what she claimed.

As if reading my juicy thoughts, Rich punched in the pass code to her phone, then slid it over to me. "Trick, you don't believe me," she said. "Then feast your eyes on tomorrow's headlines."

I snatched her phone up and slid a finger over the screen.

My jaw dropped open. Heather's tongue was tied up in Nikki's mouth.

Deargodsweetjeezus.

The truth did set me free.

I'd seen the light.

Heather Suzanne Cummings was the new Rainbow Brite.

"Seee, girrrrrlll," Rich slurred. "I told you Heather was a carpet cleaner, shampooing rugs with her spit and lips."

I shuddered, then eyed Rich as she grabbed the neck of the champagne bottle. She took it straight to the head. Gulped some down her short neck. Then belched. "When that liquor gets up in me, I'm a beast, girrrllll. These boys don't want it with me."

Oh, wow... how random was that?

See. Whore.

See. Rich.

I popped my lips. "Uh-huh. I know they don't." I reached for the bottle, then took two swigs of the bubbly. "But I'm so not interested in that. Rich, I'm going to ask you this four more times. And don't you lie to me, like you've been doing."

"Girrrrrrl," Rich garbled. "You know I don't lie. I've been baptized. Saved. And born again."

"Mmmmhmmm. Keep on lying, Rich. Now tell me the truth. Are you pregnant?"

"*Whaaaaaat?!* Clutching pearls! How dare you insult

me, ho? I practice safe sex, hon! Except for that one time when I slipped up and gave one of my one-night stands a little taste, two years ago. But that's been it. I use the withdrawal method. Ain't nobody shooting water guns up in me. No ma'am. I push, push, pull out! Don't do me. I gotta spring in my coochie! I pops 'em out!"

Ugh. Yes, yes, *yessss*. She was a nasty, low-down, dirty trollop. The only thing stopping her from being a good whore was the fact that she didn't have a price on it. She just gave it away. Always running a two-for-one sale.

Just nasty.

Mmmph.

She snatched the bottle from me, and took a sip, then wiped her mouth with the back of her hand. "So to answer your question: *No*, I'm not pregnant. God, Spencer. I can't believe you'd ask me some mess like that. Not after what I went through with Knox. Being up on that table in Arizona was too much for me. No, ma'am. I learned my lesson. I'm done with being some boy's dumping ground. Next..."

I craned my neck and let my gaze flutter over her wide hips, then around her pudgy waistline. I narrowed my eyes. "Okay, if you say so. Now tell me. Is that chocolate thug daddy stomping on you? Because I still remember when he put his hands on you and I had to go upside his watermelon with my nunchucks."

"And like I told you then, Spencer. He didn't hit me."

"Okay. He was choking you. Same difference. He *still* put his hands on you. So let me know, now, so I can run up on him and crack his skull open. Then gut his kidneys out."

"Lies! He was not! And choking and hitting are two different things. So stop dumb-thugging. It's so not cute."

Dumb-thugging?

"You know I'm against violence, whore!"

"Then what's that lump upside your head? Who put it there, Justice?"

"Nooo. I was beaten by a grown man."

I batted my eyes. "Whaat? Who was he? Tell me now," I said getting my hype on. Now I'll go upside her head, but no one else had better touch her. "Now who was it?"

Rich belched. Then said, "His name is Heather."

I blinked. "Heather?"

"Yes. Heather Suzanne Cummings and her wino mother, Camille, jumped me."

My mouth dropped. Dear God.

This girl was delusional.

Next thing I knew, I'd slapped Rich upside her face.

"Oww, bish! Why'd you hit?"

"Because you're drunk talking and you're lying. And you're taking up for some boy who's been beating on you! Heather and her mother did not lump you. That thug daddy did. So stop with your lies!"

Rich gave me an incredulous look, holding her face. "*No,* my man doesn't put his hands on me! He loves me. So don't ever accuse my man of putting his hands on me. He would never. I wish he would. Next."

Rich flipped over on her back, then shot up from the bed. "Oh no, oh no, hooker! Not tonight you won't! I warned you before, ho! Stay out of my business! You're not for me. You're against me. Then you wonder why I don't do you. All in my panties and my relationship like you're the next Iyanla Vanzant. Girl, bye! You can't fix my life! Fix your own! My life is fabulous!"

"Whaaat?"

She stomped over to the chaise and snatched up her handbag. "I didn't come here for that, tramp! I came over here to pour tea and turn up! Not be insulted by the likes of some *thot!*"

I blinked. Blinked again. Then had to talk myself out of running up and hopping on her, gouging her eyeballs out from the back. Oooh, she was lucky I'd changed my ways, or I would have snatched my lighter from off the dresser and singed her dang edges off. Ooh, I had a taste for a good dang fight. But I knew Rich was no real match for me. So I dismissed the idea. No matter how sweet the thought was.

"Umm, where are you going?"

She whirled around, eyes wide, glassy, and crazed. "Home, you ungrateful skank!"

"Rich, you've had too much to drink. I don't think you should be on the road. You can sleep outside in the gazebo on one of the lounge chairs."

"*Gazebo? Outside?* Trick, I'm not some homeless charity case! I don't do lounge chairs unless I'm riding cowgirl! I'm a grown woman! Kiss my—"

"And you're drunk," I said calmly.

"I am not! You see me stumbling? You see me tripping over my feet? No. I handles mine, boo-boo. So don't worry about my liquor intake. Worry about your own."

"Rich, really, you shouldn't be behind the wheel. You don't have to sleep outside. You can sleep in one of the maids' quarters."

"*Whaaat?* Clutching pearls! Oh, so now I'm the help! Oh no, Miss Celie. Not me. I'm out!"

She swung open the doors.

"Don't leave, Rich."

"Girl, bye! Now watch all this fabulousness shake out the door!"

I pursed my lips. Tilted my head.

Okay then... have it your way, booger-boo.

I grabbed my cell, then sauntered over toward the window and peered out. I waited until Rich got inside her Bugatti, revved the engine, then spun off, her wheels screeching as her rear end fishtailed around the circular driveway. She drove around in circles twice before zipping down the driveway.

A smile eased over my lips as the gates opened and she sped off.

I placed my call.

"Nine-one-one. What's your emergency?"

"There's a drunk on the road. And her name is Rich Montgomery..."

28

Rich

My life has gone straight to hell in a media frenzy handbasket. I was on every freakin' blog, gossip rag, and *E! News*, and for once I didn't wanna be.

I couldn't believe I was in jail. Jail! Picked up for underage drinking and drunk driving.

I looked at the processing officer as she handed me a clear plastic bag with my car keys and half of my jewels missing.

It took everything in me not to cuss her out. But I didn't. I played it cool 'cause all I wanted was to get outta there.

And yeah, I was drunk, but so what? The cops knew who I was. They could've drove me home instead of hatin' and locking me up. Straight up, that was effed up. But it's all good. I'ma let 'em live. Besides I had bigger things to deal with, like making up with my man.

"Rich," my attorney said, handing the processing officer the paperwork he'd signed, "your parents said they expect you home immediately."

I rolled my eyes so hard it was a wonder they didn't

pop out and fall to the floor. "Puhlease. After they left me here all night, they are the last set of people I need to see right now. I need to relax, chill, and get my mind together. Not be stressed out by the gangster rapper and his wife."

The attorney shrugged. "I'm going to have to call your parents."

"Call 'em." I tossed over my shoulder, as I stormed out of the building to the parking lot and into my car.

I hopped on the freeway and didn't stop until I reached Manhattan Beach and was knocking on Justice's door.

Justice opened the door and immediately handed me a twenty-dollar bill; then he snatched it back. "Oh, I thought you were my Chinese food. What? What you want?"

I bit the inside of my jaw. "I, umm, wanted to know if I could talk to you for a minute." I took a step toward his doorway and he completely blocked it. "I know you don't think you getting' up in here? You betta go 'head wit' all that."

I felt so stupid. Breathe. Chill. Relax and just say it. "Justice, just hear me out. I'm sorry. I am. I know I've been trippin' lately. But I miss you so much, and I know you miss me too." I paused, hoping he would say something... anything... but he didn't.

I continued, "I love you so much, and the last thing I want is to lose you. So I'm asking you to please find it in your heart to forgive me."

Silence.

Nothing. Not one word. "Justice, please say something!"

"A'ight. I'll say something. Are you finished?"

I blinked. Feeling my knees about to buckle, I pressed my hand into the wall. "Am I finished?"

"Yeah, you done?"

Before I could answer he said, "Good. Now beat it." Then he slammed the door in my face.

29

London

"Well, well, well..." I felt my stomach churn as her heels clicked toward me. "If it isn't London, the Laughing Cow. I knew I smelled dung wafting through the halls. It was you."

Hand on hip. I slammed my locker shut and faced her. "What do you want, Spencer?"

She met my eyes with barely a blink, before she tossed bouncy curls from her face, her hair coiffed to perfection, scanning the length of me. "Ooh, your feet look cute stuffed in those heels. I didn't know Louboutin made pointed-toe pumps *that* big." She shifted her large satchel stamped with the Louis Vuitton logo from one hand to the other. "What are they, size fourteens?"

I could feel eyes peering over in our direction, waiting with anticipation for something to kick off between us. I couldn't stand this girl. But I really wasn't in the mood for a morning brawl or to be splattered on the pages of some sleazy magazine. I had more important things on my mind, like juggling my classes while monitoring the whereabouts of my father, instead of getting reeled into the ditsy antics of Spencer.

She was despicable, and embarrassingly stupid. So I refused to waste one brain cell trying to decipher her kind of crazy. And I definitely wasn't about to argue with her.

No. Spencer wasn't worthy of a good fight or having me plastered in the headlines with the likes of her. Not today.

Besides, my therapist told me to pick and choose my battles. To not let any of these atrocious so-called Pampered Princesses lure me into their drama.

And I wasn't.

Out of my peripheral vision, I noticed several kids elbowing each other and pointing over at Spencer and me. Once again, this whore was trying to make a spectacle out of me, like I was some exotic animal on display at the local petting zoo. I could almost see it. A group of nosy hoes gossiping wildly in their chairs about what they'd seen in the hallway this morning. Even if it weren't much of anything, they'd make up something juicy just for the sake of having something messy to say.

I looked up at the elaborately carved ceiling, then glanced down the teakwood corridor before landing my gaze back on Spencer's annoyingly flawless face. "No. They're the right size to clomp a hole in your—"

"Oh no, oh no, ohhhhh noooooo, chickie," she hissed, stomping a Jimmy Choo heel into the gleaming floor. "If you can't take a compliment, then say so. But don't you ever threaten me, you ole whiskered Lorax. I will set it off on your face up in this mothersucker. I came over here loving and kind this morning."

"*Whaaat?*" I shrieked. "Are you *kidding me?* You call that *loving and kind?* Girl, bye. You're delusional."

I held my breath and walked off, leaving her standing in

the middle of the hall. I wanted so desperately to exhale, but my body was still tense and my stomach knotted.

I despised that trick! I was so over—

"See. Next time I'll just leap up on your wide back and claw your edges out," she said, startling me as she stalked up alongside of me, her footsteps falling in sync with my own.

I huffed. This girl was contaminating my space. "Spencer, do me a favor. Stay the hell away from me."

She giggled, twirling a lock of hair around her slender index finger. "Ooh, that's the team spirit, London."

I sighed, agitation coursing through every nerve ending in my body. I counted to twenty in my head. Steadied my breathing. I couldn't afford to be hauled off the school grounds with the paparazzi lurking around outside, waiting for their next scandalous headline. I had to keep it together.

I stopped in my tracks. Clenched my teeth. "What is it you want, Spencer?"

"Oh, London, stop playing coy with me," she said, lightly touching my arm as if we were long-lost pals. "You know I want to know how you're holding up..."

I frowned. "I'm holding up just fine. Why do you care?"

She smirked. "Oh, trust me. I really don't. But I don't want you doing anything stupid, either. The world knows how unstable you are, London. Now what kind of frenemy would I be if I didn't at least touch base with you, huh? It's no secret I can't stand you—"

"Well, the feeling's mutual," I snapped, cutting her off. "So how about you do us both a favor and go find a cliff to jump from."

She threw her head back and laughed, clutching my upper arm as if we'd just shared a delicious joke. "Heeheehee. Cute, London. But no thanks. I'll save the cliff-hanging for you."

I yanked my arm free. "Get your damn hands off me."

"Ooh, see. This is the feisty London I came to despise. Not that other girl you've been pretending to be. Anyway, I need to make sure you aren't considering jumping over any rainbows now that Rich finally knows what type of scheming, conniving slore you are. Too bad she doesn't believe you were whoring yourself out with that Brooklyn thug dog before she was. Rich is just stupid like that. But, oh well. How does it feel to be America's Most Unwanted?"

"Screw you, Spencer."

Her eyes widened. "Tramp, I don't go that way! Don't you ever come onto me like that! If you're trying to clean carpets, you had better call on Heather, booger-bear!"

I blinked. Opened my mouth to say something, but then stopped myself. It wasn't worth it.

Spencer snapped her fingers. "Oh, wait. I have a little treat for you."

I quickly stepped back in case it was a bomb or something corrosive she might have wanted to toss in my face. After the way she attacked me at my home with hair removal, I wasn't crazy enough to take any chances when it came to her.

She reached down into her satchel and pulled out an issue of *Teen Weekly*. She tossed it at me. "Page seven. Read and weep."

And, then, just like that...she was gone. Melting into the crowd of upperclassmen as they made their way to their respective homerooms. I knew I had less than three minutes to get to mine, but I couldn't resist. I needed to know what was on those pages. JEALOUS HOES THIRSTY FOR SOMEBODY ELSE'S MAN screamed the headline. The story read:

> Is it true what they say about a Clean Up Girl lurking around the love nest for another princess's manly treasures? A source close to Hollywood High's Pampered Princess Rich Montgomery says flop model London Phillips—and ex-friend to Rich—is desperately trying to sink her claws into Rich's fiancé for her own pleasures. After being dumped by her longtime beau Anderson Ford, the son of an oil tycoon, London seems to have become obsessed with the idea that Southern Cal's latest heartthrob, Justice Banks, was her man first. When asked if there was any truth to the rumor, Rich blatantly said, "Look at me, and look at her. You see all of this fabulousness? That whore is straitjacket crazy. She could never get my baby's loving. My man would never have that trick." And there you have it, dolls. We'll take that as a yes.

My knees knocked. I didn't realize I was standing in the middle of the hall, shaking, until Rich brushed past me—with a hint of an elbow jab—and slipped inside her homeroom just as the bell rang.

30

Spencer

"Now, c'mon, Cleola, I gotta get you out of here before them Mississippi boys come and get you . . ."

"Daddy, I'm not Cleola! I'm Spencer, your daughter! Now put that gun down right this instant!"

"I know who you are, pumpkin," he shot back, lowering the rifle. "My mind hasn't gone completely bye-bye, yet." He shot a look over at Kitty. "I'm talking about that fine, sexy gal right over there beside you."

I laughed. "Daddy, you're so silly. Hahaha. That's soo cute. That's not Cleola. That's Kitty. My mother. Your ex-wife."

He shook his head. "No, no. That gal right there"—he tossed a knowing glare over at Kitty—"is Cleola Mae from Leflore County, Mississippi. Wanted for murder. Aint' that right, Cleola?"

A horn blows in back of me. I flutter my lashes up into the rearview mirror, narrowing my eyes. The old geezer in back of me gives me the finger, cursing me. I throw my car into PARK, swing up the car door—and just so I make myself loud and clear—I reach for the one-mile bullhorn in the backseat and hop out of my car, jamming up traffic as I give him a piece of my mind, talking through the bullhorn.

I storm back over to my car, shutting the door tight, then shifting my car into gear and running through the red light. I had things to do. Places to be. And people to meet. Well, uh, um, one person, to be exact.

My Dick. Tracy, that is.

My PI.

Enough time had already been wasted playing footsies with the unknown. Trying to decipher all of Daddy's incoherent storytelling was slowly starting to shred my brain cells to pieces. Daddy had half his noodle missing. Most days, he couldn't remember the days of the week or where he was. Yet, somehow, all he could remember was some motherstinking *Cleola Mae!*

It was time to get real acquainted with the truth.

Who in the heck was this enigma from Le Flore County, Mississippi, that Daddy was so obsessed with?

Daddy was insistent that Kitty was her, Cleola, this mystery woman he'd felt compelled to hide from the po-po. *"You better hide, Cleola Mae. They coming for you, baby."*

But why would they be coming for her? This Cleola?

"Them boys down in Mississippi. It isn't safe, Cleola. You know I been keeping your secret... Did you hide the gun?"

What secret?

What gun?

It was no secret that Kitty was messy and hateful and ruthless. That she was an ole nasty cougar that stalked boy toys in schoolyards, then mauled at their most precious organs until she'd rendered them helpless and of no more use to her. Kitty was a user! She was a nasty hotbox. A dirty slosh bucket. A stank hot pocket. A gold-digging tramp who threw her Hello Kitty up in the lap of a desperate old man who was forty-two years older than her, then spawned him an heir to his fortunes. And when that wasn't enough for her, she rotated her hips and pumped her pelvis up and down the ladder of opportunity for her own riches.

Yes, she was calculating and cunning.

But was she deceitful enough to be involved with guns, and police, and murder? Was she scandalous enough to concoct a whole new identity?

I didn't know. However, what I did know was, I was going to peel back the truth covered in layers of lies. Somehow, Kitty was the rancid meat stuffed inside this clandestine box. And, betchabygollywow, I was going to dig up every rock, every stone, every dang inch of earthly soil and get to the bottom of this dang mystery. Then I was going to butter Kitty's biscuits real good and drag her through the mug-gahfuggin' gotdanggit gutter!

Yes, honey, yessss! I was going to singe Kitty's cat hairs and burn a hole in her liner the minute I uncovered the truth. My mouth watered with anticipation.

I could feel it clinging on the tip of my tongue.

So sweet and thick and ooey-gooey delicious.

I licked my lips.

The honeyed taste of something real juicy oozing out all over me.

I floored it, swerving in and out of traffic, tires kicking up dust and stones as I sped off the freeway toward salvation.

Seek and you shall find. Isn't that what the good book said?

Well, as of today, I was looking high and low, leaving nothing unturned.

My mission was to track down Cleola Mae.

And air out her filth for all to see.

31

Heather

WHAM!

Splash!

Smack!

Ahhhhhhhhhhhh!

"NOW EAT IT!"

I hopped outta bed, the shock of my eyes suddenly being on fire forced me to do a possessed dance. I couldn't believe it! My face was drowning! And my neck dripped in Camille's musty scotch!

My room hadn't been cleaned since me and Rich tore it up yesterday, and now I was stumbling over everything.

WHAM!

Splash!

Smack!

Ahhhhhhhhhhhh!

I hit the floor.

More scotch scorched my eyes.

"I swear to God!" I managed to spit out, "When I get up from here, I'ma bust you dead in the mouth, Camille!"

"I wish you would!" Camille's hand blazed the side of my face, forcing my neck to the left. And then suddenly the room was spent. And all I could see was dark, blurred clouds and monstrous waves.

Ahhhhhhhhhhh!

My arms thrashed everywhere. I jumped up and down, wringing my hands into my eyelids, desperately trying to rid my eyes of the liquid hell Camille had shot into them.

Ahhhhhhhhhhh!

Whap!

"I'ma kick yo' ass, Camille!" I promised her. Angry tears mixed in with the singeing scotch.

"And you will die up in here today!" She knocked me down to the bed and yanked my hair. She forced my neck back with one hand, then took her other hand and crammed a balled-up piece of paper into my face and twisted it.

"I should shove it down your freakin' throat! Now read it!" She yanked my hair again, forcing my eyes to bulge open.

I tried to wrestle my hair from her grip, but it only caused her to snatch it harder. "I see you didn't get enough of Rich whupping your behind, Heather Suzanne. Just know if you even think about attacking me today, you will die. You little trick." She pushed the paper deeper into my face. "I SAID READ IT!"

"I CAN'T!" I tried to wiggle free, to no avail.

"Okay, well, let me read it for you!" She managed to keep her grip firmly on my scalp with one hand while flinging the paper open with the other. " 'Guess who's on the down low?' says one blog! 'Girl power on another level!' says another. 'Teen star Heather Cummings caught making out with college cutie Nicole Ashford of San Diego State. Both pictured below."

WHAM!

Camille's hand slammed into my cheek. She tossed the paper at me and mushed me along the side of my head. "How dare you do this to me?! How dare you embarrass me like this?! First you wanna be a junkie, and now this!" She screamed. "Now this..."

I knew Camille continued to scream, but my heart thundered too loud for me to make out what she was saying.

My mind was scrambled. I couldn't believe this was happening! I was going to kill Rich. I was going to slaughter her today at her breakfast table.

Either the scotch had stopped stinging or I was too numb to feel it.

I opened the wrinkled paper Camille had tossed at me and saw that it was an e-mail from Kitty. FILMING RESTARTS TODAY. HEATHER BEING GAY IS TOO HOT OF A STORYLINE TO MISS. READ THE HEADLINES BELOW AND CLICK ON THE LINKS TO THE ARTICLES! THIS SHOW WILL BE A HIT! ONE CAMERA CREW WILL ARRIVE TO YOU AT ANY MOMENT AND THE OTHER CREW IS ON THEIR WAY TO SAN DIEGO.

Nikki!

My heart stopped.

I looked up, and there they were, the camera crew, all around the room. Zooming in on me.

Had they been here all along?

Was Camille tossing scotch in my face and ripping me from the bed scripted?

Was this a role Camille was playing?

I looked over at Camille, and I knew then that this was no act.

She was disgusted.

Enraged.

Disappointed.

Tired of me being too much and not enough all at the same time.

I looked back up at the camera crew and screamed, "Get that freakin' camera outta my damn face!" I jumped up and pushed one of the cameramen, then I moved on to shove Philippe, the producer. He smiled and said, "Yes, dahling! Bring it on! Bring it on! Push me again. I wanna see that rage, that anger. I know just the music to play over this when we edit it!"

"I SAID GET OUT!" I screamed, and just as I prepared to slap the ish outta him, my cell phone rang, and my chest caved in. I knew it was Nikki by the ringtone.

I ran over to the nightstand and snatched my phone off of it, and that's when I saw that Nikki had called me at least a thousand times.

"Who is that?!" Camille grabbed my phone. "Hello?" Camille snapped.

"Give me my phone!" I tried to grapple it away. I couldn't.

Camille screamed into the receiver. "You wretched bulldagger! Don't you dare call here or come back around here! You have ruined me! You have ruined meeeeeeeeeeee! And I will make sure you are torn apart!"

I reared my hand back and knocked Camille so hard in her head, it's a wonder she didn't drop dead on the spot. Instead she dropped the phone and stumbled to the floor.

I reached for the phone before Camille could regain her balance. "Nikki!"

Nikki yelled, and I could hear the tears clogging her throat. "I'm done, Heather! Reporters are all over campus! My family is calling me, demanding that I come home and explain what's going on! My friends are questioning me! Why would you do this to me?!"

"I didn't do anything!"

"Liar! You did! How else would the blogs and everybody know what we've been doing for the past month, when it was only the two of us! I'm finished with you!"

"Nikki, wait!"

Click.

The room was spinning again. And it had to be at least a hundred degrees in here. It had to be. And the floor was sliding from beneath my feet.

I couldn't breathe.

I couldn't think.

And I needed to think.

Think.

Think.

Think.

"I'm done, Heather! Reporters are all over campus! My family is calling me, demanding that I come home and explain what's going on! My friends are questioning me! Why would you do this to me?" Nikki's voice screamed in my head.

Tears slid down my cheeks and into the creases of my neck. My hands were clammy, and the bile in my stomach eased up my throat.

I closed my eyes.

I felt like bugs were crawling all over me.

It's starting.

I'm losing my mind . . . again . . .

I gotta get outta here.

I have to.

Otherwise, I'ma go crazy . . .

32

London

Stretched out across my chaise lounge, I scanned Rich's Instagram page, sneering at the most recent selfies she'd taken. This trick was obsessed with posting selfies on her page. There were over eleven thousand comments on one image of her bent at the waist in some type of multi-print Jersey-type dress, cupping her breasts in her hands. The caption read: COME N GET EM. The dress was *cute*. Slutty cute. It left very little to the imagination, showing off her smooth, brown thighs and an abundant amount of boob crack. It was sickening. But apparently the vast majority of her Instagram followers thought otherwise, judging from all the likes and favorable comments.

Bunch of obsessed Stans.

Of course there were a few haters. There were always haters. And I lived for them, especially when they were slinging hate on someone other than *me*.

I read the comments and giggled. One chick in particular really tried it when she posted: THIS THOT NEEDS TO COME 'N' GET A GROUPON CERTIFICATE FOR VAJAYJAY REJUVENATION.

"Hahaha! Whore!" I laughed out loud. "The whole world knows your coochie cavern has more visitors than a Motel Six. Tramp!"

I read another comment. Some chick with the screen name GreenEyedBandit posted: WEALTH & FAME DOESN'T AFFORD YOU CLASS! YOU'RE STILL TRASH!

"And you think you're so fabulous," I said aloud, giggling. "Trick, please."

Quickly tapping my screen, I decided to add my own dose of haterade up on her page. I posted: WHORES LIKE HER ARE WALKING CONDOM DUMPS!

"Now! Boom-bop-drop on that!" I shouted out loud.

I should write something about her whorish mother, I mused, as I prowled through the rest of her selfies.

Ugh.

I rolled my eyes up in my head, stumbling on a photo of Rich and Justice, with him standing in back of her, his arms wrapped around her waist, kissing her on the neck. She had a wide Crest-stripped smile on her face. The caption read: ME 'N' MY BAE. LOVE HIM MORE THAN LIFE.

"Yeah, and he's going to be the death of you too," I muttered to myself. "Enjoy it while it lasts, dumb *bish!*"

A knock on my door drew my attention away from Rich's Instagram page. "Yes?" I called out begrudgingly. I was so not in the mood for being distracted from my cyber-stalking, but oh well...

The door to my suite opened, and Daddy popped his head inside. "Hey, sweetheart. Can I come in?"

"Oh, hey, Daddy," I answered, sweetly. "Sure."

I sat up in my seat and eyed him as he walked across the threshold into my room, casually dressed in a thin V-neck sweater and a pair of jeans, with an expensive pair of loafers on his feet. His cologne warmed my room, and I breathed him in.

I always loved the way Daddy smelled.

He walked over and leaned in, kissing me on top of my head.

For the last week and a half, he'd been back and forth to his London office, so it was nice finally having him home again. "So, how's school going?" he asked, sitting across from me.

I shrugged. "Okay, I guess. I feel so out of place being back there."

Daddy nodded knowingly. "It'll take some time to get back into the flow of things, but you'll find your groove."

"I hope so. Mister Westwick is really working my nerves with his morning shakedowns."

He shook his head, and smiled. "He runs a tight ship."

"No. He runs an upscale prison camp."

Daddy chuckled. "Well, try to stay out of the headlines."

I groaned. "Ugh. Easier said than done. Everywhere I turn, seems like someone's lying in wait with a zoom lens, trying to catch me slipping..."

My mind drifted back to the days after my return from Milan. Bandaged and broken. Photographers and mysterious cars stayed camped outside the gates of our estate, desperate for a glimpse of the damaged girl, for any juicy morsel of news to turn into a headline. On those rare moments when I'd forcibly leave the confines of my tomb and leave the property, they followed my chauffeur-driven car around town relentlessly, peering out of car windows with their telephoto lenses, trying to turn my misery into a cash cow. London Phillips, daughter of famed model Jade Obi Phillips, clinging onto life by her fingertips.

I shuddered, dwelling on the memory a bit longer than

I should have before shifting in my seat and looking over at Daddy, finishing my thought. "Why couldn't you be a barber or a butcher or in some other nondescript profession?"

He laughed. "So you're telling me you'd rather not have that Phantom Drophead parked out front in the driveway? Or a closet the size of an apartment full of designer digs?"

My stomach quaked at the thought of a life of public transportation and bargain shopping at department stores.

What a travesty!

I shook my head, vigorously. "No, no. On second thought, I'd rather take my chances with the paparazzi."

More laughter. "Unh-huh. I thought so." He shifted in his seat. "So how are things with you and Rich? Have the two of you made amends yet?"

Why? So you can try to make her my new stepsister? Not! I shrugged. "Not hardly. I tried. But she hates me. And, at this point, I could really care less. I'm so over her, Daddy. I came to her like a woman..." Daddy gave me a look. "Well, a young lady, trying to apologize for everything that's happened between us, and all she did was lash out and give me attitude. I refuse to sign up for any of her disrespect."

He slowly shook his head. "I'm sure things between the two of you will work themselves out. Give it some time."

I grimaced. "I truly doubt it, so I won't be holding my breath on it. I'm so over her." Okay, it was a lie. I'd become obsessed with tearing down her happy kingdom. She thought her life was so picture-perfect. Ha! What a mockery. I couldn't wait to snatch the proverbial rug out from beneath her bejeweled feet.

"Have you spoken to Mother?" I asked, changing the

subject. I tilted my head and eyed him ever so carefully. I still couldn't believe he was a cheater, crawling around in the sheets with the enemy's mother.

And I couldn't believe my mother was willing to let a good man slip right through her manicured fingertips by being so damn obstinate, not fighting for her marriage *and* her man.

I was so angry with her for that, practically seething every time I thought about it.

My therapist had the audacity to tell me in my session this afternoon that I needed to let the two of them work things out in their own way, and on their own time. Oh, how lovely that would be—if my mother were doing something to fix things. But she wasn't. And the longer she stayed away, the more time she gave that thieving whore to pierce her way into Daddy's heart.

I wasn't about to sit back and let that happen. No. Not on my watch. And that's exactly why I'd hidden tiny GPS tracking devices inside all three of Daddy's vehicles to keep account of his every move when he was in L.A.

If my mother didn't want to fight for what was rightfully hers, then I sure as heck would. I was going to—

"Your mother sent me a text this morning," he said, slicing into my musings.

Oh.

I tucked a lock of hair behind my ear. "And? Did she say when she was coming home?" I was sure she hadn't.

"She said sometime next week." He didn't sound convinced. And he didn't seem to really care.

I frowned. "Is she going to be mad at me forever?" I asked, biting my bottom lip.

Daddy shook his head. "Jade isn't mad at you, sweetheart. She's just..."

"Avoiding me," I concluded for him, shifting in my seat.

It wasn't a question, but Daddy responded anyway. "Your mother isn't avoiding you, London. Why would you think that?"

I raised my brow. "Well, she's avoiding something." Or someone. You.

"Your mother has a lot going on right now with the modeling agency. We both do."

I gave him a yeah-right look. "Daddy, please don't make excuses for her. Or try to patronize me. There's something wrong here, and you know it. So if she isn't mad at *me,* and she isn't avoiding *me,* then what's really going on? Are the two of you getting a divorce?"

Daddy's forehead creased. "A divorce? Why would you ask that?"

I shook my head. "Daddy, please. I'm not a baby. I see how the two of you barely speak to one another on those rare occasions when you just happen to be home at the same time, except for when you absolutely have to."

He ran a hand over his face, then said, "Things between your mother and me have been a bit tense since..." He looked away, ashamed, perhaps embarrassed, about what I'd done.

I finished the sentence for him. "Since my suicide attempt."

"No, sweetheart," he said gently. "Long before then."

Oh.

I decided to confess to him. "I heard the two of you arguing down in your study before we flew back to Milan. It was over me, wasn't it?"

He nodded. "Partly," he offered. "But our problems go far beyond you, London. So don't ever feel like you're to blame."

I played dumb. Didn't want him to know that I knew what the real source of contention was for the two of them: My mother was a rigid prude. And he was out feeding his oats to that moose-faced Logan Montgomery.

Daddy ran a hand over the side of his handsome, smoothly shaven face, and sighed as he shifted uncomfortably in his seat. "Things are complicated right now between your mother and me, sweetheart. But don't ever think for one moment that either of us loves you any less. You are our number one priority."

I stared at him, tilting my head. I'm their number one priority? Really?

I felt like asking him—in between his law firm and shacking with his mistress and Mother's obsession with securing models for her stupid ole modeling agency—when, where, and how was I either of their top priority?

Instead, I settled on, "So the two of you *are* getting a divorce, then?"

I held my breath.

Daddy's cell phone rang. Reflexively, he reached for it where it lay beside him facedown. I eyed him suspiciously as he glanced at the screen, then sent the call to voice mail.

"I didn't say that."

I exhaled. "Daddy, you didn't have to. The writing is all over these pristine walls. I'm not blind, you know."

He sighed. "Sweetheart, it's complicated."

I gave him a confused look. "How so? Either you both want to be married or you don't. What's so complex about that? Is Mommy cheating on you?"

Daddy's face twitched. If I'd blinked, I might have missed it. "No, no. Of course not."

Uh-huh.

Of course she isn't.

You are.

I tilted my head. "How can you be so sure?"

He slumped his shoulders, shaking his head. "I'm not. But I know your mother. Well, at least I believe I do. She's never cheated before."

Mmm. I'm sure she never had a reason to. But Daddy, on the other hand... not a word. I pursed my lips. "Yeah, but there's a first time for everything, isn't there? And the fact that she's never here, always so quick to run off to Italy, makes me wonder..." My voice trailed off. I didn't really think she was cheating. She was too uptight and frigid. However, I never thought in a million years that Daddy would either. But he was. So I wouldn't be surprised if she were off getting her swerve on with some Italian stud muffin.

Daddy was quiet for a moment. Finally he said, "I don't want you to ever think ill of your mother..."

Umm. Too late. I already do.

"... she loves you."

Yeah, okay. What's love got to do with this conversation?

Daddy loved me, too. And look at him. Trolling around with the rich and ratchet.

Logan Montgomery.

Ugh.

I felt myself getting sick.

Daddy leaned forward and fixed his gaze on me. "Listen, sweetheart. I don't expect you to understand this right now. Maybe someday when you're married and have your own family you will. But sometimes a couple gets to a point in their relationship where they both want something more, something neither of them are capable of giving—or getting—from the other."

"So does that mean they should run off and get it—whatever *it* is—from somewhere else because they think the grass is greener on the other side?"

"No, of course not, sweetheart. It's not always about greener pastures. Sometimes it's more about couples growing apart."

I gave him a saddened look. "Like you and Mommy?" When he didn't respond, I continued, "Doctor Kickaloo said open communication was key to addressing problems in relationships."

Daddy smiled, warily. "Your therapist is right, sweetheart. For any relationship to work, there has to be communication. And a sincere commitment to want to work through things."

I swallowed. I wasn't sure if I really wanted Daddy to validate what I already knew, but I asked the question anyway. "Have you ever, um . . . cheated on *her?*"

I know, I know. I should have asked if he *was* cheating on her right now. Even though I already knew the truth. Still, in my heart, I simply wanted to give him some leeway.

For what, I'm not sure.

Daddy looked at me, his face difficult to read. A lawyer thing, I supposed.

Still, I wasn't sure if he was pondering an answer that wouldn't hurt, or if he was trying to conjure up a lie. Either way, I waited for a confession.

And then . . .

His stupid cell phone rang again.

33

Spencer

"Spencer?"

"Uh, yeah," I said, glancing at the screen, adjusting my earpiece. My screen flashed UNKNOWN CALLER. But the voice sounded like sweet dreams and snuggly teddy bears. I just wanted to cuddle up with whomever was on the other end of my phone line. "How may I direct your call?"

"I miss you."

I rapidly opened and closed my eyelids, my lashes flapping up and down. "Oh, yeah? What is it you miss, Mister Mystery Man?"

He chuckled. "Nah. I'm no mystery man, boo. But to answer your question: I miss your sweet lips, your warm mouth. I miss the way you used to make my toes curl. I miss them little tricks you used to do with your—"

"Wait one goshdiggitydang minute, you dirty phone perv! You, you nasty trick daddy! I'm not loosey-goosey with my tricks and treats. So when and where did I ever have these sweet juicy lips on you?"

He laughed.

My heart skipped three beats, then almost stopped and dropped me dead.

I knew that laugh. It was infectious. And it had been so long since I'd heard it.

I gripped the phone. Swallowed. "*RJ?*"

"Yeah. It's me, babe. What, it's been that long that you've forgotten my voice?"

Everything inside of me melted.

RJ.

RJ.

RJ.

Oh how I used to love him. Okay, okay. I still did. Deep down in every inch of my heart, I knew I always would. He'd always held the key to my treasures. Always. He was the only boy I ever truly loved. Or whom I felt always loved me back.

But why was he calling me now, and after all this dang time?

I got up from my love seat and started pacing the length of my room, my feet sinking deep into the plushness of my Persian rug, its silk fibers caressing my painted toes.

Oh, RJ . . .

Richard Gabriel Montgomery Jr.

Future heir to Grand Entertainment, his father's record label.

My first love.

My only love.

And the truth remained the same: No matter how many boys I dropped down and got my wobble on with, no matter how many I toyed with, RJ was the only boy I could ever really love.

My mind drifted back to Aspen. That one winter break when I'd spent the holidays with Rich and her family. And how RJ and I had lain sprawled out under the covers in front of an open fire, with our naked bodies pressed together like two crème-filled cookies. And how Rich walked in on us talking with our bodies. Ole jabba jaws couldn't wait to go back and blab to her parents what she'd seen. She'd ruined my love train before I could finish the ride.

I never fully forgave her for that.

I blamed Rich for ruining what could have been my almost perfect love story.

Almost.

I sighed. "Um, why are you calling me, RJ? What, you ran out of English snow bunnies to spear your man sword in? Have you gotten tired of emptying your ball bag into every British hoochie, willing to spawn a nation of little mixed babies? Don't think I don't know all about your bed bouncing, RJ. You, you manwhore! Rich has told me all about your daytime romps with the Queen's peasant girls."

"Rich is a liar," he calmly stated. "She's a hater. And you know it. She's always hated on me, even as a little girl."

Well, he had a point. It was true.

Still . . .

"And what about all them weeds you've been pulling up and smoking, huh, RJ? I heard you're a full-blown weed head these days. What are you over there smoking, anyway, dandelions? Wild violets? Clovers?"

He chuckled.

"I don't know what's so diggity-dang funny, you, you grass junkie! I'm not interested in having another junkie in my life. Heather was enough. Although she was crushing pills, and you're digging up weeds, still . . . a junkie's a junkie, no matter how you chop it up and smoke it."

He laughed uncontrollably. And that only pissed me off.

Just like an addict to take nothing serious! "Let me guess. Rich told you that crazy mess too."

I huffed. "Well, yes. Duh. How else would I know you were one match away from rehab?"

"Spencer, I've tried weed—not *weeds*—a few times. That's it. I got caught with a blunt and got arrested last summer, and my mom flew here and tried to choke the life out of me. You know how loose she can get when she's turned up." I giggled. Yeah, like her raggedy daughter. Those two were ratchet.

"I haven't touched anything since then," he continued. "Rich is terrible. She's a pathological liar. But that's still my sister. And I love her no matter how many times she tries to smear my name to my parents—well, my mom. She knows Pops isn't going for it."

I opened the French doors to my terrace and stepped out into the warm air. The sun shone on my bangles, and their diamonds danced in the light, almost blinding me.

I blinked.

Yeah, yeah, yabba-dabba-doo. I feigned a yawn. "So, why are you calling me?"

"I'm home for Rich's birthday party."

I rolled my eyes up in my head. Whoopty-dang-doo! RJ hadn't been home in over a year. It was to be a brief visit, from what I'd heard. Nevertheless, he was here. And he didn't even have the dang decency to phone me or to stop by to say *hello*. Nothing.

Screw him!

I clucked my tongue. "*And?*"

"And I wanna see you, Spencer."

"Uh-huh," I responded dryly. "Why?"

"I miss you." His voice dipped dangerously low. "You're all I ever think about, Spencer."

In my mind's eye, all I could see was RJ hovering over me...all I could feel is his hands cascading all over my body.

My body shook.

Stop it, Spencer!

Get your mind out the gutter. And out of this boy's boxers.

"I need to see you, baby."

I smirked. "Oh, so now I'm *baby?*"

"You've always been my baby, Spencer. Just because I'm across the globe, that hasn't changed what I feel for you, what I've always felt for you."

I swallowed. Ran my fingers through my curls. "And what's that, RJ?"

"Love," he whispered into the phone, causing my body to slowly heat. "Real love, baby." He sighed into the phone. "I can't wait until Rich's party. I need to see you now, Spencer."

Rich hated me with RJ. She always felt like I'd chosen him over our friendship when we were younger, which is why I got my creep-creep on with him two summers ago and kept it on the low-low.

The idea of her finding out that he and I were off creeping somewhere, again, would surely drive her batty.

A slow grin inched across my lips.

"I'll be there when you open your eyes in the morning," I finally said, wrapped up in the heated memory of how he used to claw the sheets and mutter my name every time I'd climb his pet rock, the way I had climbed the Swiss Alps.

Wild and reckless...

34

London

Usher was singing the hook to Wale's "Matrimony" when I finally decided to flip on the radio. I sat cocooned inside the tinted windows of my latest rental—a navy blue Honda Accord, on another stakeout.

I tracked Daddy's car here.

No, no. Actually, I tracked him back to the gated house, the same house I'd followed Rich's mother to a few weeks ago. It was clear. They both had access to the *same* house. Was it Daddy's secret man cave? Was it their little private love nest?

My mind raced with questions as I sat parked across the street, waiting, for him, for her. But thirty minutes later, the gate slid open and out came Daddy again. Alone.

If my mother didn't want to know what Daddy was up to, shame on her.

But I sure as hell did.

And tonight, his Bentley led me here.

In Malibu—*again.*

On the Pacific Coast Highway—*again*.

This time at Nobu.

Perched up on top of the waves.

One hour and ten minutes out of L.A.

I was seething. How dare he meet his concubine—his, his... tramp—at one of my favorite restaurants. I'd never step foot in that establishment again, knowing he'd had a clandestine meal with his whore there.

So what if Nobu had other locations?

It was the principle.

The memory of Daddy being here would always be stamped in my head. And no matter how much I loved the sushi and sashimi, knowing Daddy had been here playing footsie under the table with Rich's mother would leave a bad taste in my mouth. It would ruin my appetite, for sure. So there'd be no point in going. Ever.

My temples began to throb.

I took a deep breath.

Before I found myself in therapy and had my big-girl voice under control, I would have killed for a pack of those scrumptious lemon Oreo cookies. I swear. I would have eaten a whole sleeve right on the spot. Or would have sunk my teeth into a box of oatmeal cream pies. I'd be sitting, slouched down in this rental with my lips covered in cream-cheese frosting.

Eating my way into a sugar attack.

I cringed at the thought. I refused to give in to my binge cravings. Thanks to my therapy, I was putting my B.E.D. (Binge Eating Disorder) to B-E-D. But the stress of Daddy's affair was making it tempting to lick across a few powdered donuts.

Stop it, London!

Get a grip!

I shifted in my seat. Then glanced over at the restaurant.

Where the heck is this trick?

Maybe she's already inside.

Hmm. Maybe.

Luckily, I was in the perfect spot to observe the entrance to the swanky restaurant without being seen. I'd watched Daddy go in by himself, capturing his every move on camera. But I knew he wasn't dining way out here *alone*. And I knew he wasn't meeting some client here, like he'd claimed when he took the call, said a few cryptic words, ended the call, then told me he had to meet a new client. No. Client, my plump rump! My gut told me he'd planned to do some fine dining, then go off and roll around on some silk sheets somewhere nearby.

A Nikon AFS 800mm camera was in my lap, mounted with a super telephoto lens. It was a recent purchase guaranteed to snap vivid pictures at a great distance.

I sat in my rental, trying to imagine what it'd be like being a private investigator, being hired to spy on someone's cheating spouse. I was sure it was a dirty job. But someone had to get his or her hands muddy. Still, my heart ached for the one on the receiving end of his or her mate's betrayal.

Cheaters be damned!

Catching my reflection in the rearview mirror, I adjusted the front of my wig, then flipped its bangs from out of my face. Curly brown hair flopped over one eye. This was what my life had become.

Wearing wigs.

Crouched down low in rentals.

Spying on Daddy.

Stalking his mistress.

Wale changed to Meek Mill, who had all eyes on him.

And I had all eyes on Daddy.

And on that despicable Logan Montgomery.

With the disguise, I wasn't too concerned about Daddy spotting me. He'd never expect this from me. Besides, I was careful to stay at least two cars in back of him the whole time I tailed him.

My mother's voice echoed in my head. *"I know who your mistress is..."*

I shook her voice and reached for my cell, then called her. She answered on the fourth ring, breathlessly. "Hello?"

"Are you and Daddy getting a divorce?" I asked, point-blank.

"Excuse *me*?" she shrieked. "What did you ask me?"

I repeated the question. I could tell she was taken aback. But I didn't care.

"Where in the world did you get that notion, London?"

I sighed. "Well, are you?"

She let out a heavy breath. "Are you taking your medication, London? You sound a bit...how do I say...off."

My jaw clenched. "I'm not *off,* Mother. And I'm not hearing voices, if that's what you're insinuating. I'm the sanest I've ever been." Yeah. Now that she'd stopped counting my calories and micromanaging my carb intake.

"I've insinuated no such thing," she huffed.

I rolled my eyes. "Okay, Mother. Whatever you say. I didn't call to argue with you."

"Then why are you calling at this ungodly hour?" she asked, brusquely.

"When are you coming home?"

"I don't know," she stated, curtly. "Now, with the launch of my new fragrance in a couple of weeks, I'm not sure when I'll be there." I'd forgotten that her new fragrance,

Jade,—after two years of trying to perfect her signature scent—was finally making its way into high-end boutiques and retail stores across the globe.

I frowned. "That's not what Daddy said," I stated, feeling my anxiety kick up a notch. "He said you'd be home sometime next week." I reached for my bag and dug out my bottle of anti-anxiety medication. "Now you're saying in a couple of weeks."

"Well, things changed, London."

I popped two pills and swallowed. "As they always do when it comes to you, Mother. It's always about you, isn't it?" I reached for my bottled water.

"You had better watch your tone with me, young lady. Is this what that fancy, high-priced therapist is teaching you, London? To be disrespectful, huh?"

I took a deep breath and unscrewed the cap. "No," I snapped, eyeing the entrance to Nobu. "She's teaching me to be assertive. To stand up for myself and to speak my mind, something I was always too afraid to do. Now answer my question, Mother. Are you and Daddy divorcing?" I took a sip of water. Swallowed again.

She snorted. "London, stop this. Do you hear me? I have no intention of discussing this with you, London. Your father and I are fine."

I huffed. "Ohmigod, Mother. Please, *stop* with your lies. Don't think for one moment I don't know what's really going on." I would finally tell her what I'd overheard that night down in Daddy's study as I stood by the cracked door and listened. "I know Daddy's cheating on you. So, stop with the lies. You can stop pretending everything's so perfect in your world. I know the truth. You're not perfect. And neither is your marriage. There are cracks, Mother. And the longer you stay away, the wider they become."

"London," my mother snapped. "How dare—"

"No, Mother. How dare *you*? How *dare* you let Daddy's whore win?" I choked back a sob. "How dare you not fight for your marriage, for Daddy?!"

"London! I will not stand for your tone or for this line of questioning! I will not tolerate this level of disrespect. You had better mind your manners..."

"Or *what*, Mother? Are you going to threaten to snatch my trust fund? Turn your back on me the way you've turned your back on your marriage, on Daddy? Well, guess what? You turned your back on me the moment you chose going back to Milan over *me.*"

"Nonsense, London. I've done no such thing. You could have come too. But you wanted to stay there. You made your choice."

"And *you've* obviously made yours, Mother." I wiped tears from my face with my hands. "You should have never had me if you didn't want to be a mother!"

"London, you stop this nonsense, right this instant! I gave birth to you. Of course I wanted you."

"More lies, mother! *You* didn't birth me. Your *surrogate* did! Yes, I know all about it. I overheard that, too, Mommy dear. So don't lie."

I could hear her sucking in the air around her on the other end of the phone. "Okay, London. Yes. I paid for a surrogate. What else was I supposed to do? I was becoming one of the most sought-out models. Casting calls were in abundance. So, yes, London, I'm guilty as charged. That doesn't mean I didn't want you. You are still as much a part of me as if I'd carried you myself."

I snorted. "Ha! Yeah right. We both know you've always wanted your career more. You should have just given me up for adoption like you—"

I stopped midsentence and blinked. Shot up in my seat. There was Rich's mother. Adorned in her fine jewels and slutty wear.

"Look. I have to go. It's obvious you aren't interested in being a mother or fighting for your marriage or for Daddy. But no worries, Mother. I'm not losing Daddy to the likes of some other woman."

"And what is that supposed to mean?"

"It means just what I said," I responded, tersely.

"London, you stay out of this. Don't you dare—"

"You don't get to tell me what to do, Mother. Like it or not, I'm taking matters into my own hands."

"London, do not meddle in your father's and my affairs. I'll handle this my own way."

"Bye, Mother. It's too late." I hung up, then quickly grabbed my camera and zoomed in on Rich's mother. Through tear-blurred eyes, I snapped the perfect shot of her making her way toward the door.

If I were perfectly honest with myself, I'd say Rich's mother was pretty—okay, okay, breathtaking—if you went for the hood goddess type. Mmmph. Apparently, that's what Daddy wanted these days. Hood trash.

I was on the verge of a full-blown anxiety attack. I swear I felt it coming like a raging storm. I reached for my medication bottle and unscrewed the top, then popped another pill. For a fleeting second, I entertained the thought of taking the whole bottle but quickly decided against it. With my luck, I'd survive and end up a vegetable. No, thanks.

Still...

Between Daddy's trotting off every chance he got to be with Rich's mother, and my mother's nonchalance about it, I felt myself slowly becoming unglued. I quickly grabbed my cell and sent a text to my therapist. I needed a therapy session—*ASAP*—first thing in the morning.

I narrowed my gaze at the restaurant's entrance. They'd been inside for almost fifty-five minutes. How long did it take to suck down a sushi roll and a bottle of sake?

Geesh.

What in the world were they in there doing, for God's sakes?

I wish there was a way I could slip inside to see them front and center.

The glass doors of the restaurant finally opened—it was about damn time!—and Rich's mother stepped out first. Daddy held the door for her as she went through. She tossed her head back and laughed at something he'd said. Even from this angle, her diamond hoop earrings danced under the light, the stones glinting ever so bright.

She looked so carefree.

So, so damned happy!

My nose flared.

I didn't remember ever seeing my mother laugh so freely around Daddy. But here was Logan Montgomery just a heeheeheeing.

Easing my window down a bit, I poked the lens of my Nikon through the opening and took multiple shots in rapid succession of them together.

Oh sure. They were ever so careful not to hold hands or walk arm in arm. Still, they were comfortable enough together to *look* like a couple.

Oh God, oh God!

His hand went to the small of her back as they walked, the first sign of intimate contact. He whispered something in her ear, and she laughed again.

His hand went back to his side.

Through the long lens of my camera, I watched Rich's mother steal my father away from his family, from me. By the look on the two lovebirds' faces, they were seemingly enjoying each other's company. I fought the tears that were threatening to spill over.

My heart ached.

The truth was excruciating.

Not only was that, that wolf-dragon clearly ensnaring Daddy in her web of seduction with her sultry body and cunning ways, Logan Montgomery was also clawing her way into his heart.

"*Bitch,*" I hissed.

Oh, how I wished her a slow burn in hell.

35

Rich

"Heels, heartache, and headlines seem to follow famed socialite Rich Montgomery everywhere she goes. From public brawls with her fellow Pampered Princesses and boyfriend Justice Banks to being arrested and released on charges of alleged underage drinking and driving while intoxicated. Phone calls have been made to her reps; however, no statement has been released. More when we return from commercial break..."

"Turn it off!" I screamed at my stylist's assistant, as he stood in a freakin' trance watching *E! News* lie on me and rip me to shreds.

"What is wrong with you?!" I yelled, seconds from drop-kicking his scrawny behind dead in the throat. I looked down at my stylist, Stephanie, who was clearly frustrated with not being able to zip my dress and said, "He gotta go!"

Stephanie looked over at her assistant, and his guilty behind simply grabbed the remote and hit the POWER button. But he didn't leave; instead, he gave me a fake smile and an even phonier apology. Whatever. I had bigger things to worry about. Like how I was hot and cold at the same time and felt like I was about to throw up at any minute or, worse, pass out. Or like how my effin' birthday ball was happening at this very moment with paparazzi and guests packed into the ballroom, waiting on me.

But.

I was stuck in my dressing room stuffed into a too-small Stuart Weitzman gown.

To think I'd only tossed back a few drinks this week.

And I starved myself all week.

No carbs.

Only water.

But nothing worked.

And here I was with ten unexpected pounds hanging around.

Ugg!

My divaliciousness was supposed to be on fleek, not meek.

And usually I could slap on two pairs of Spanx and it would be "Boom, guess who stepped in the room."

But not tonight.

Tonight, not even my Spanx would fit me.

"Stephanie, Miss Rich." I sucked my teeth; obviously, this cavity creep was trying to make up with me. He continued, "May I suggest the gold-beaded Gucci gown. It's absolutely fabulous, and if I remember correctly, you haven't worn it yet, Miss Rich."

I snapped, "Umm, excuse you, rainbow love. But I was saving that dress for when me and my baby-boo JB got back together and he won his first Grammy. Thank you very much!"

"We'll make you another one by then," Stephanie said, sounding exhausted. "But that one is a little bigger in the waist than this one, and right about now, a little extra room is exactly what you need."

I rolled my eyes to the cathedral ceiling. I didn't even have the energy to fight. "Whatever." I snapped. "Get the dress."

A few minutes later, after I was dressed and all set to go, my mother's rude behind flung my door open and burst into my room. "Your guests are all here, and you have them waiting a little too long for you." She paused. "You changed your dress? Why?"

None of your freakin' business, lady. Now do me a favor and get out my face! "I just wanted to wear something different," I said with a fierce attitude.

Of course, Logan shot me a warning eye. Why? 'Cause she is mad petty and can't ever let anything go, and that's why after I said what I had to say, I gathered the hem of my swoop train and clicked my heels right past her.

The closer I got to the ballroom, the more I could hear the buzz of the crowd. Nerves filled my stomach and made me even more nauseous than I was before. I did all I could not to walk too fast. The last thing I needed was to stumble, especially when all my Richazoids expected me to sparkle. So a misstep wasn't an option.

Besides, I didn't need me falling on my face in the headlines. I needed the headlines to say, *Rich Montgomery's birthday party was everything!*

Therefore, no matter what I was feeling, I had to get my lil life together. Right now.

I stood behind the ballroom's French double doors, with my honey-colored and muscular escort at my side.

"Hear ye, hear ye!" My trumpeters began. "Welcome, family and friends, to Princess Rich's Birthday Ball!" The double doors opened, and my eyes drew in the beautiful royal court. From the gold and cream walls to the luscious red carpet. The gold chairs and round tables, draped in overflowing gold fabric and with large candelabras as the centerpieces. There were jesters and jugglers in every corner of the room. Balloons and streamers were everywhere. Sparkling lights hung above the DJ booth. And in the center of it all was a makeshift stage, where J. Cole awaited me.

"Rich Montgomery! We love you, baby!" J. Cole said, as the crowd went wild and the paparazzi went crazy. Cameras clicked, and the guests' phones were high in the air, recording every moment. I was on high.

J. Cole continued, "Everybody join me as I wish the hottest chick in the room a very happy seventeenth birthday!"

Er'body was hyped, and if I didn't feel so faint I would've whipped the nae nae. But I couldn't; all I could do was smile and grip my escorts' arms as they walked me onto the stage, where J. Cole gave me the biggest hug in the world. "Happy birthday." He lightly kissed me on my cheek as he whispered in my ear, handing me the mic.

I cleared my throat and did my best to keep my balance. "Thank you all so much for coming." I paused, as a cold chill ran through me. "And umm, I umm... appreciate everybody turning up for my birthday and—"

"Hold up, Rich." Heather popped up on stage outta nowhere, snatching the mic from my hand. She was dressed in a clear plastic catsuit with leopard nipple tassels and matching thong and seven-inch clear plastic platforms that lit up. Heather swung her twenty-four-inch Yaky drawstring ponytail as she said, "I'ma let you finish, but, umm, I need to say this, and it'll only take a minute. No Pampered Princess's birthday would be complete without a freestyle from me."

I knew I needed to snatch the mic back, but I also knew if I moved I was gon' pass out. So I stood still and watched Heather carry on, "Everybody, clap your hands! Clap! Clap! Clap! Ah, clap ya hands!" She waved her arms from side to side, and the crowd screamed, "Go, Heather!"

She rhymed:

Unicorns don't exist and butterflies wanna die.
It's all an illusion except the conclusion and the confusion.
"The Gucci Clique" whispered is she white, is she black, or is she Mexican behind my back.
Never ever caring how I felt about that.
Well, I can't take it anymore, and I gotta kick in the door.
Waving the .44.
All you heard was Heather don't hit me no more.
But I got take it to her chest, 'cause she started this mess.
And let her know her know before I go
That we share the same daddy.
Richard Montgomery...
Now take that, whore!

She threw the mic down.

And then the room started to spin.

All the air left my body.

And just before I collapsed and tumbled to the floor, the last person I saw was London carrying a gift, walking through the door.

DON'T MISS

Dear Yvette by Ni-Ni Simone

All sixteen-year-old Yvette Simmons wanted was to disappear. Problem is: she has too many demons for that. Yvette's life changed forever after a street fight ended in a second-degree murder charge. Forced to start all over again, she's sentenced to live far from anything or anyone she's ever known. She manages to keep her past hidden, until a local cutie, known as Brooklyn, steps in. Will he give her the year of her dreams, or will Yvette discover that nothing is as it seems?

Chasing Butterflies by Amir Abrams

At sixteen, gifted pianist and poet Nia Daniels has already known her share of heartache. But despite the pain of losing her mother and grandmother, she's managed to excel, thanks to her beloved father's love and support. Nia can't imagine what she'd do without him—until an illness suddenly takes him, and she has no choice. And Nia's in for one more shocking blow. The man who'd always been her rock, her constant, wasn't her biological dad. Orphaned and confused, Nia is desperate for answers. But what she finds will uproot her from the life she's always known...

Available wherever books are sold.

Turn the page for an excerpt from these exciting novels...

1

Y'all Ready for This . . .

Let's be clear. I'm not no snitch.

I ain't no chicken-head neither.

Yeah, I got high. A couple of times. Offa weed.

But e'rybody smoke weed.

Includin' my cousin, Isis, and my ex-homegirls, Cali and Munch, who been out here draggin' my name.

And maybe I popped a pill here and there. Or sometimes laced my weed wit' some coke.

But so what?

And ok . . . yeah, I hit the pipe. Once. Okay, twice. Maybe three times wit' my daughter's father, Flip. Mainly 'cause he was doin' it and I needed somethin' to clear my mind. And Flip was always chilled, so smokin' rocks wit' him seemed like a good idea. Plus, he swore it would take the edge off.

It didn't.

It made me feel sick. Twisted. Paranoid. Scared the cops was always lookin' for me.

So I stopped.

I had to. 'Cause I wasn't about to be nobody's junkie. Turnin' tricks. Or holdin' down no pimp. Now *that* woulda made me a chicken-head.

All I wanted was to get my buzz on.

There's a difference.

Anyway, that was then and this is now.

Now I got a daughter to take care of.

Somebody who loves and looks up to me.

There's only one problem though.

My rep is ruined and thanks to my old crew who turned on me, e'rybody lookin' at me like I'm some crack whore, wit' ashy lips, beggin' for money, and wildin' out in these streets.

Lies.

All lies.

I barely leave Douglas Gardens, better known as Da Bricks, the complex where I live, in apartment 484.

Twenty L-shaped, seven-story buildings that take up four blocks. All connected by a slab of cracked concrete—dubbed as "the courtyard." And a scared security guard, who stays tucked away in a locked, bulletproof booth that sits behind the black-iron entrance.

To the right of the gate is a basketball hoop. No net. Just a rim. To the left is a row of twenty rusted poles, where clotheslines used to be. It is always somebody movin' out and a squatter movin' in.

Old ladies stay preachin' out the windows one day and cussin' out anybody breathin' the next.

Winos stay complainin' about yesterday, e'ryday.

Ballers stay servin'.

Then there is me and my two-year-old baby girl, Kamari,

usually in the middle of the courtyard, chillin' on the park bench, and mindin' our bissness.

Sometimes I'm sippin' on a forty.

And sometimes I'm not.

Sometimes, I take a long and thoughtful pull offa loosie.

And sometimes I don't.

Depends on how I feel.

But still.

I'm not sellin' pipe dreams and droppin' dimes to pigs.

I'm too busy tryna decide my next move. Like how I'm gon' get a job. Raise up outta Newark, New Jersey, and finally live.

Yeah, I am only sixteen, five feet tall, and a hundred and ten pounds. Smaller than most girls my age, but I am grown. I ain't no punk. And I ain't gon' let nobody play me for one.

Family or no family.

Friend or no friend.

My rep is not a game.

That's why, when my ex, Flip, spotted me earlier this evenin', on the corner of Muhammad Ali and Irvin Turner Boulevard, comin' out the bodega, I couldn't believe it. The last time I'd seen Flip was a year ago, right before he got locked up over jailbait. Flip was thirty, and the broad was fourteen, same age I was when I got pregnant with Kamari. Only difference was the broad told on him when she had her baby. I didn't.

So anyway, about an hour ago, I'd looked Flip over in disgust, from his untamed high-top fade to his worn-out BKs. His six-foot frame was raggedy as ever, and his half-rotten mouth was loaded and leveling a buncha bull. "Heard you been out here snitchin'," he'd said.

"What?"

"You heard me." He returned my nasty look. "You used to be down. But now e'rybody say you buggin'. Guess I'ma have to watch my back fo' you drop a dime on me too."

He was tryna play me. I looked around and the block was buzzin'. The sun was fallin' and the night crawlers was makin' they way outside. People was e'rywhere. Some pouring out the bodega and some on the block just standin' around. I caught a few folks peepin' at me, like they'd heard what Flip had said and was tryna figure me out.

My grip tightened on Kamari's umbrella stroller. I needed to do somethin' to keep from stealin' on this mothersucker, so I snapped, "Word is bond..."

"A rat's word could never be bond."

My heart raced and my chest inched up from me breathin' heavy and being heated. I pointed into Flip's face. "You must be talkin' about them rattin' young cherries you bustin'. 'Cause from where I'm standin', you ain't nothin' to drop no dime on."

"Yeah, yeah. Whatever. Ain't nobody tryna hear all that. All I know is my mans told me that he messin' witcha fat homegirl."

I curled my upper lip. "Who? Munch?"

"Yeah, that's her name."

"And? So?"

"And she told him that you a rat. And the reason they got locked up was 'cause you ran to the cops shootin' off ya trap. Mad 'cause you broke."

Out of shock, I took a quick step back, then a quicker step forward. "What the... Excuse you?"

"Don't front. You know that Isis, that white girl, Cali, y'all used to hang with, and Munch all got busted for slangin' in school. And Munch said you was the one who told on 'em. And I believe it 'cause you stay in e'rybody's bidness."

"You need to..."

"No, what you need to do is learn how to shut up, carry yo' li'l azz in the house sometimes and keep my daughter out these streets."

I paused. I couldn't spaz on Flip 'cause I had Kamari wit' me, so I swallowed the urge to slide the blade from under my tongue and said, "Yo' daughter? Boy, please. I don't know why you worried about her being in these streets when that's all you do. Held up in some alleyway suckin' glass dicks. Or is you skin poppin' now? Yo' daughter? You better off bein' moondust than somebody's freakin' daddy. You shouldn't even wanna claim that title. Yo' daughter? Know what, let me just get away from you before I end up slicin' yo' throat for talkin' slick!"

"Whatever, Snitch. Bye."

Flip was still running his mouth and poppin' off when I walked away.

Once I got home to Da Bricks, I went straight to my room. My mind was spent and my stomach was in knots. I hated my hands was tied for the night, and it was nothin' I could do. Isis, Cali, and Munch had all moved out Da Bricks. Accordin' to Nana, Isis moved out of state with her mother, Queenie. She ain't know what happened to Cali.

But Munch.

I'd seen her from time to time, and I knew she lived somewhere around here. Plus, she still went to the same school. And one thing was for sure and two things was for certain, her lyin' behind caught the city bus to school, e'ryday.

At the same time.
E'ry mornin'.
I smiled.
Closed my eyes.
And waited.

1

The Umoja—pronounced *oo-MOE-jah*—(meaning unity) Poetry Lounge in L.A. swells with lively chatter and fiery energy. There are drums and congas and tambourines and hips swinging.

We've taken the twenty-five-minute drive from Long Beach—where I live—to be here tonight. It's a Thursday evening, and open mic night.

I'm at my table scrambling to finish my piece. It's a last-minute surprise for Daddy, who's sitting at the table with me.

And I'm anxious, really, really anxious.

This time.

As if it's my first time taking the stage.

My nerves are fluttering up around me.

Why?

Because I've decided at the very last moment—less than ten, no...eight minutes before open mic starts—to change my piece. And now I'm frantic.

Most of the people here are spoken word artists, like

myself, but much older; college-age and older, but an eclectic bunch nonetheless.

I'm one of the youngest.

An eleventh grader.

But I've earned the respect of the more seasoned poets. The poets with tattered notebooks filled with much more life experience and depth than I can possibly have at sixteen.

Still, I hold my own among them.

Being on stage is the only time I feel...

Liberated.

They embrace my innocence.

Embrace my openness about the world around me.

And allow me license to just be.

Me.

Free.

That's what I love most about poetry. The creative freedom. The freedom to weave words together. Colorful expression. A kaleidoscope of emotions, imagination, passion, hopes, and dreams. We are surrounded by similes and metaphors.

We listen.

We hear.

And tonight will be no different, no matter how anxious I am becoming. There's an uncontrollable energy that lifts me, and sweeps around the room. The feeling is indescribable. All I can tell you is I feel it slowly pulsing through my veins.

Like with all the other open mics, there are no judgments, no stones cast.

Well...not unless you are just unbelievably whacked, that is.

I am not.

Whacked, that is.

Well, okay...at least I don't think I am. So I know I should have no reason to be worried tonight.

But I am.

See. Tonight is special. I mean. It *has* to be special. It's Daddy's birthday. I brought him here for dinner. And then, I had this bright idea to surprise him with a poem. My dedication to him, my way of thanking him for being the most wonderfully incredible father a girl could ever ask for.

I am an only child. And Daddy is my only parent.

See. My mom was killed in a car accident when I was six. So for the last ten years, Daddy has been singlehandedly raising me on his own. Well, wait. Okay. He did have help caring for me the first five years after my mom's death. Nana. My maternal grandmother, she stepped in and helped Daddy provide some normalcy in my life.

But then...she died, too, from cancer.

I was eleven.

So you see, Daddy is all I have.

It's him, and me.

And, no, this isn't a sob story.

It's my reality.

My truth.

I've endured heartache and loss; more than I've ever hoped for. But I know love, too. Real love.

Daddy's love.

And, for me, there is no love higher than his. He has helped me to endure. Still, I can't lie. I lost pieces of me when my mom was killed. And even more pieces of me when my nana passed. But, over time, Daddy salvaged me. Helped put me back together. Loved me whole again. His unconditional love has been my soothing balm. It heals me. It protects me. It gives me promise.

That there's nothing I can't get through.

And I love him for that.

I know there are no coincidences. Everything that happens to us in our lifetime happens for a reason. And sometimes that reason is much bigger than us. We can't see it. We can't always understand it. Still, it happens because that's the order of destiny.

Daddy taught me that.

That we live, we love, we—

Daddy must sense my trepidation. He reaches for my hand and gently squeezes it. I look at him and smile. No words are needed. His touch is all I need. But he gives me more. He always does. "You've got this, sweetheart. This is your world."

I smile wider.

Instantly, I calm enough to focus and write a few more verses.

Maybe I should just speak from the soul.

Let words flow from my lips in synch to what I feel in my beating heart.

I quickly glance around the dimly lit room. Candles flicker on the tables.

Suddenly, I am feeling nervous again.

I try to calm myself, to no avail.

I try to—

"Peace and blessings, my beautiful people," I hear the emcee say. I look over toward the stage. She's a beautiful brown-skinned woman, the color of milk chocolate, wearing a fire-engine-red halter-jumpsuit that complements her curves and her complexion.

Her skin shimmers under the glow of the light.

She stands at the mic, confident.

Proud.

Graceful.

Her presence is electric.

"Peace and blessings," the crowd says in unison.

"Y'all ready to get lifted?"

The crowd raises their arms, fingers snap.

"I am Sheba, your host tonight. And trust me. Tonight you are in for a real treat. We have a lineup of some of the west coast's finest spoken word artists slated to take the stage and stimulate your mental. So sit back, relax, and enjoy the prose. First up to take the stage is Nia..."

I am taken by surprise when the emcee introduces me.

Oh no.

That can't be—

I think I am hearing things, but then she announces my name again.

Nia Daniels.

I hoped to be somewhere in the middle. Not first.

Never first.

Daddy must sense my hesitation. "Go do your thing, Butterfly," he says beaming. I smile back nervously, then lean over and kiss him on the cheek. Daddy has been calling me *Butterfly* since I was three years old. He says it was because I would get excited every time I saw one in our yard, and that I reminded him of one because I was light on my feet and always flitting about as a child, never settling on one thing for any length of time before moving onto something else, like a butterfly.

I push up from my chair, grab my book, and head toward the front of the lounge. I slowly take to the stage, the glare from the lights blinding me.

I blink. Blink again.

My nerves are getting the best of me.

I am literally trembling.

My piece isn't finished.

I'm never unprepared.

Never.

But tonight...tonight I'm feeling mentally disheveled.

I stand at the microphone, head bowed, hands clasped, trying to collect myself, trying to gather up my anxiety.

I clear my throat.

Take a deep breath.

"Hi, everyone. Tonight I'm sharing a piece I've written for the most special person in my life. My rock. My anchor. My world. My one constant. Since birth, he's been everything to me." I glance over at Daddy. He leans in, his attention fixed on me. "And, tonight, I want to share with all of you a piece of who he is, who he has been, to me." I glance over at Daddy again. "Daddy, this one's for you."

He smiles.

I look out into the crowd. "Y'all please bear with me. I didn't get a chance to finish it, so I..."

Someone says, "Take your time, little sister."

"That's all right," someone else says. "We got you."

I smile.

Glance over at Daddy one more time. Then grab the mic, and close my eyes.

Mother
Father
Protector
Provider
Best friend
Wrapped into
one
beautiful gift.
You are...
Pancakes

smothered
in warm maple syrup,
eggs scrambled hard,
grits with lots of cheese.
You are . . .
Sugar cookies
and
ice cream cones,
lemon pound cake
and
painted toes . . .
tree houses
jump rope
hopscotch
hide 'n' seek
and Barbie dolls.
You are . . .
Easy-Bake Ovens
crayons
and
Play-Doh;
Rollerblades
carousels
and
no-hand
roller coaster rides.
You are . . .
Saturday morning
cartoons
and
hot fudge sundaes.
Sandcastles
and seashells;
rushing waterfalls
and Venice Beach.
You are . . .

Gershwin piano keys
Bach French Suite
No. 1
in D-minor;
toothy grins
crooked parts
lopsided ponytails
and
colored barrettes;
that's what you are to me.
Bedtime prayers
and
nursery rhymes;
candy-coated rainbows
sweet dreams
and lullabies;
shiny trinkets
and glass slippers.
Pixie dust
and
scraped knees
drenched
in kisses;
gentle
warming
so full of love;
that's what you are.
Tea parties
And dress up.
My inspiration
My hero
No
No
My super hero
Always there
to save the day...

sunshine in the rain.
The gentle breeze
beneath my
fluttering wings . . .
Morning hugs
and tummy tickles;
vanilla skies
and butterfly kisses . . .
That's what you are.
Mother
Father
Protector
Provider
Best friend
wrapped into
one
beautiful gift
That's what you are.

"And I'm the luckiest girl in the world," I say, so full of joy. "Happy birthday, Daddy. I love you."

The room erupts with applause. Then everyone joins me in singing "Happy Birthday" to the world's greatest dad.

With my heart full and my soul fed, I step away from the mic and glance over at Daddy. The look on his face says it all.

He is so very touched.

And I am loved.